The
Maricopa Trail

The Maricopa Trail

NOEL LOOMIS

Sagebrush
Large Print Westerns

Library of Congress Cataloging-in-Publication Data

Loomis, Noel
   The Maricopa Trail / Noel Loomis.
      p.   cm.
   ISBN 1-57490-363-2 (lg. print : hardcover)
   1. Large type books. I. Title

PS3523.O554 M37 2001
813'.54—dc21   2001032062

Cataloging in Publication Data is available from
the British Library and the National Library of Australia.

Sagebrush Large Print Westerns are published in the United
States and Canada by Thomas T. Beeler, Publisher, PO Box 659,
Hampton Falls, New Hampshire 03844-0659. ISBN 1-57490-363-2

Published in the United Kingdom, Eire, and the Republic of
South Africa by Isis Publishing Ltd, 7 Centremead, Osney
Mead, Oxford OX2 0ES England. ISBN 0-7531-6449-3

Published in Australia and New Zealand by Bolinda Publishing
Pty Ltd, 17 Mohr Street, Tullamarine, Victoria, Australia, 3043
ISBN 1-74030-306-7

Manufactured by Sheridan Books in Chelsea, Michigan.

The Maricopa Trail

This book is dedicated to
RANDY LEE LILJENBERG
beyond any question the most precious grandchild
born into this family during 1955

PREFACE

THE BASIS OF THIS STORY IS THE AFFAIR AT THE SITE of what later became Fort Yuma, when about five hundred Yuma Indians, outraged past all patience by the tyrannies of the scalp-hunter John Glanton, killed him and ten others.

The actual sequence of events at the time of the massacre is somewhat complicated, and those complications are not followed here. John Glanton, of course, is mentioned in a great many source books of the Southwest.

General Patterson built the ferry as related, and turned it over to the Yumas, who hired a man named Callahan to operate it. The Glanton men destroyed the ferry and tossed Callahan into the river, and Glanton's edict that the Indians could not cross the river except on his ferry seems to have been the final straw that precipitated the massacre. It is a matter of record that a Dr. Lincoln or Langdon (from Missouri or Louisiana or Tennessee) also perished that day with his pet dogs.

The man who actually escaped from military jail at San Diego was named Brown, and apparently he never was tried for any of his activities, but ended up as a deputy law officer in Los Angeles.

J. P. Brodie and Major Heintzelman are characters from early California history; so are Cabello en Pelo, Macedon, and Pascal, the Yuma chiefs.

Warner's rancho, Alamo Mocho, Cooke's Wells, the Tinajas Altas, Quitobaquito, Casa Grande, Sacatón, the Colorado, Gila, Salt, and Santa Cruz Rivers will of course be recognized by those versed in Western

1

history; many of these geographical features have retained their earlier names to this day.

Three men down by the river escaped from the massacre, and their precarious adventures make quite a chase. Unfortunately there does not seem to have been much else in their lives that would qualify them as protagonists.

As suggested in the story, a somewhat abortive expedition was sent out from the coast to punish the Yumas for the massacre, and after various desultory engagements in which an unsatisfactory number of Indians were killed, this force retreated into the stockade, from whence they sallied on occasion to destroy the Yumas' crops. It just wasn't fittin' in those days—nor is it yet in many places—for an Indian to touch a white man, no matter who the white man was or how much he mistreated the Indians.

A brief story of the ferry episode appears in a little book entitled *Feud on the Colorado*, by Arthur Woodward. Curiously enough, the word "feud" in the title does not have any relation to the ferry affair. (Writers know that it is a privilege of editors to retitle books; that usually is provided for in the contract between publisher and writer, but as yet there has appeared no accepted provision that the title must bear some relationship to the contents of the book.)

Some of the earlier sources are the *Pacific Surveys*, now seldom available in complete form except in large libraries, and difficult to use even when found; Bartlett's *Personal Narrative*; Lieut. Emory's *Reconnaissance*; and Major Emory's (the same man) *Report on the United States and Mexican Boundary Survey*. Other fragmentary references occur in many places, but Woodward seems to have uncovered some interesting new documentary evidence on the massacre.

At any rate, this was only one small incident in the multiphased operation known as "going West."

Place names have given some difficulty in the story. The site of Glanton's camp, which became Fort Yuma a short time later, had no name at the time of this story. It is perhaps well to recapitulate the route of emigrants from the United States via this southern route to California. Usually they left either Independence, Missouri, or Fort Smith, Arkansas, and went to Santa Fe. From Santa Fe they followed the Del Norte (Rio Grande) south, and near the southern New Mexico border they cut across country west to the Gila River, and followed it east across Arizona until it flowed into the Colorado (known more specifically as the Colorado of the West). It was there, at the junction of the Gila and the Colorado, that the ferry was established. Some crossings were made farther north, where Bill Williams River (now called Williams River) flowed into the Colorado, but these were mostly government parties. It rather seems that the emigrants preferred the southern trail along the thirty-second parallel—probably because the dry stretches were shorter.

I have not found sufficient evidence to indicate that the route along the Gila River was widely know as the Maricopa Trail, but I have given it that designation for fictional purposes. Otherwise I believe the story is substantially historical.

NOEL LOOMIS

Minneapolis, Minn.
April 3, 1956

3

CHAPTER ONE

OLD SAN DIEGO WAS, IN THE YEAR 1850, A TINY, ancient Spanish settlement of brown mud bricks and thick walls. There were still the mist-topped mountains to the east, the ten-mile strip of coastal grass on which the town itself was built, and the thundering Pacific on the west. Like all Spanish towns, San Diego had an air of immutability.

Tiny columns of fragrant cedar smoke rose here and there from an adobe hut. Black-eyed women appeared briefly, glanced at the United States soldier in his green jacket and pants, pacing slowly before the adobe jail, and then disappeared in a flash of brown-skinned movement, their red or yellow skirts swirling. Black-eyed children bobbed up from unexpected places, stared for a moment, and disappeared. Chickens clucked, for it was late afternoon, and occasionally a dog barked or a pig grunted.

Sometimes the cool wind from the ocean paused for a moment and the sun would be pleasantly warm, and just at that time the purple masses of bougainvillea would cease their restless moving, the great red or orange or yellow blooms of hibiscus would quit nodding, and the warm, sweet perfume of Easter lilies would for a moment lie gently in the dusty, crooked streets.

Then the breeze would come again, and the long red *ristras* of last year's chile peppers, hanging from the ends of the rafters outside the brown houses, would swing and rustle, and little swirls of dust would form in the timeless, ungrassed patios of the *pobres* and move toward the hills east of the village, there to settle again

4

among the herds of the *ricos*, who lived in exactly the same kind of houses except that they were bigger.

Northeast of the town were the olive groves and the fig orchards of the mission, and the hills were dotted with horses and cattle.

Very little had changed, Joshua Pickens saw, since the United States had taken over in California—nor would it, if the Spaniards had their way. The *norteamericanos* had built a Newtown closer to the ocean, with cheap frame buildings made of native lumber brought down from San Francisco as ballast by streamers on the way to Panama for more overloads of gold-hunters. Over in Newtown was the ring of hammers and the scrape of saws, but in Oldtown all was quiet and serene. The Spaniards did not like the U.S. occupation, but they wouldn't let even that interfere with their morning chocolate or their afternoon siestas or their evening shindigs— *bailes*, if you were a *rico; fandangos*, if you were a peon.

Joshua knew the Spaniards fairly well, having been raised in the brush country along the Rio Grande, and he knew something of California, having been one of the first to come looking for gold.

He reached the end of his post, turned, and paced the thirty steps to the other end. His green jacket was too short at the cuffs, and it was wrong anyway, for green was the color of riflemen, whereas he had joined as an infantryman—but uniforms were scarce, having to come all the way around the Horn. His pants were green too, and the brass buttons of his coat were marked with a capital R.

He was not a man to care about the color of his uniform as long as he was clothed and fed. He was tall and slender almost to the point of narrowness, but everything about him gave the impression of strength. It was not a showy display of power, and had been deceiving on occasion, but those who took time to observe the smoothness of his movements knew, without being told or shown, that his reflexes were very fast and his movements swift and deadly.

He reached the end of his thirty paces and turned, not militarily but smoothly, and started back for the hundredth time, his .60-caliber musket on his shoulder.

His gray eyes caught a movement at the corner of the brown adobe, and he said in a pleasant voice that carried without being raised, "Juana?"

She came slowly from the corner of the house, the sun at her left, shining on the glossy black hair that showed from under her flowered rebozo, warming her olive-brown skin. Her eyes were as black as her hair, and she wore a yellow cotton skirt and a loose white waist. She was barelegged and barefooted, but her blouse, low-necked and loosefitting, was immaculately laundered and virginal white.

She moved slowly toward him, her eyes watching his, her brown hands bearing a heavy *olla* and a bundle wrapped in white linen.

He nodded toward the barred door of the brown wall before which he had been pacing. "Go ahead," he said.

She went to the door and set the *olla* on the ground; it seemed heavy, and he walked closer and saw the inevitable stew with frijoles and chile. She pushed this under the bars without a word, and then untied the bundle to reveal a stack of paper-thin tortillas, which she also pushed under the bars.

"White!" said Joshua. "It's suppertime."

There was no sound from inside, for there was little to

6

make a sound. The floor was of dirt, and the bed was a bearskin.

Then a shuffling came from the dark interior, and White appeared behind the long bars that formed the door. He was a man with a concave face and a sharp chin, and he hadn't shaved for several days. His whiskers were brown, and his shirt, unbuttoned at the front and not tucked into his pants, showed a chest with patches of brown hair, like a buffalo losing its wool in May. He stared at Juana, and suddenly reached between the bars and caught her forearm in big, hairy fingers.

She tried to pull away. Her lips parted but her white teeth stayed together, and she made no sound. There was only, for a few seconds, the scuffle of moccasins on dirt.

Joshua said sharply, "Turn loose, White."

White paid no attention, but pulled the girl toward the bars. Her struggle became frantic. Then Joshua stepped up. He whipped a long knife from his waist, and coldly but with considerable strength brought the back of the blade down on the ridge of muscle that showed on White's forearm.

The man grunted. His fingers opened. Juana darted away. White rubbed his arm while Joshua slid the knife back in its sheath.

White said with suppressed antagonism, "Why are you puttin' in for her? She's nothin' but a greaser."

Joshua's wide black eyebrows raised. "I like Juana," he said.

White kicked the olla, and the frijoles and goat meat splatted over the dusty street.

Joshua turned away. "You'll be hungry before morning."

7

"I won't eat that greaser grub," White said vehemently.

Joshua put his musket back on his shoulder and paced to the end of his post, turned, and started back. White stopped him as he passed the door. "Where'd you come from, soldier?"

Joshua paused. White sounded somewhat more agreeable. "Austin, Texas," said Joshua.

"How'd you get out here?"

Joshua looked west to the gray haze that marked the ocean's horizon. "Like everybody else," he said, "I came to hunt gold."

"No luck?"

Joshua shrugged. "Not enough."

"Where'd you prospect?"

"Feather River, mostly." He dropped the musket butt to the ground. "There was gold there, but by the time I found it, there wasn't enough water to work it."

"Why didn't you stay on a little longer?"

"I stayed my limit. I borrowed six hundred dollars from the banker in Austin to make the trip. It took over half of that to get to San Francisco. The rest went for outfit and supplies. The supplies ate me up—eggs at two dollars a dozen, pork a hundred dollars a barrel, pies five dollars apiece, flour a dollar a pound. No man could live without finding nuggets every day."

"So you joined the Army?"

Joshua looked at him. "Not exactly. I went to San Francisco to get work, but I was shanghaied down on California Street, and woke up on a ship bound for Australia. She put in here at San Diego, and I broke out of the cabin where I was locked and got ashore. I saw the soldiers and I knew I'd be safe in an Army uniform—and I'd have a chance to feed up and get my breath and decide what to do next."

"So you been in the Army how long?"

"Six days."

"What are you goin' to do next?"

Joshua was thoughtful. "Hard tellin'. The first thing is to make some money to pay back the six hundred I borrowed."

"You sure won't do that in the Army."

"No—but being in the Army will give me a chance to look around while I figure out how to get back to the diggings."

White said, watching him, "There's a lot more to be made out of the emigrants coming to hunt the stuff."

Joshua looked at him curiously. "For instance?"

"You ever wondered how the overland emigrants get across big rivers like the Colorado?"

"Never gave it any thought," Joshua admitted.

"You can ford—and risk losing your stuff. Or you can ferry—if there's a ferry handy."

"You know where there's a ferry on the Colorado?"

"Yes—where the Gila runs into the Colorado. That's the best place, for the emigrants from the East head first for Santa Fe. They strike south from Santa Fe and then cut over to the Gila and follow it down through the Pima villages and the Maricopas—they're friendly Indians—and on down to the Colorado. That way they can be sure of water most of the way."

"Some go north, through the Great Salt Lake country."

"Too much desert," said White. "More are comin' by the Gila every day."

"Well, that's neither here nor there. It doesn't help me pay back my loan."

9

"It might," said White. "I know the man who owns the ferry at the mouth of the Gila."

"Name of what?"

"Glanton. John Glanton."

"Sounds familiar," Joshua said, thinking.

"He's a new man out here. Come from back East."

Joshua thought White said this rather glibly, but it wasn't important and he gave it no further consideration.

Joshua looked at the cluster of frame buildings with the U.S. flag flying over them, at the orderly row of military wall tents. "One thing about the Army," he said. "You eat regular."

"Eating won't pay back that six hundred bucks."

"No." Joshua studied him. "You driving at something?"

"I want out of here," White said quickly, "and I'll pay six hundred to get out."

Joshua shook his head. "You're an Army prisoner. I—"

"Nobody takes the California army seriously. They wouldn't pay any attention."

Joshua raised his eyebrows. "You don't know Major Heintzelman."

"Sure I know him." White was emphatic. "He's only a captain, brevetted major—out here killing off Indians to make a name for himself so he'll wind up a colonel on the retired list."

Joshua shook his head. "There's mighty few officers in the Army would kill Indians just to get a promotion."

"Anyhow," said White, "I'm only in here for taking a blanket."

"Then you'll be out soon."

10

"The Major doesn't like me," said White. "He threatened to keep me here for weeks."

Joshua idly read the inscription on the lock plate of his musket: "Springfield 1842."

"Listen!" White's voice was a whisper. "I was sent here to get supplies for Glanton. If I don't get back I'll lose out with him. That ferry is making thousands of dollars a month, and I can't afford to lose out." He thrust his hand through the bars and spread his fingers.

Joshua stared at the heavy roll of gold double eagles in the open palm.

"I'll give you that six hundred dollars to walk around the corner for a minute," said White, watching him intently.

Joshua frowned. He moistened his lips. "I couldn't."

"Why not?" White demanded. "You know yourself the Army loses a tenth of its men every month by desertion—and what do they do about it? What *can* they do about it?" He added, "I deserted the Navy myself less than six months ago—and what are they doing about it? Nothing!"

Joshua shook his head. "That's not—"

"It would pay your debt, and you could start all over. How else will you ever make six hundred bucks?"

Joshua considered it in spite of himself. It was true that the Army was a haphazard institution; men almost seemed to come and go at will. But . . .

White said fiercely, "What could you do if I broke out in front of you? Your musket isn't loaded, anyway."

Joshua said coolly, "I could knock your brains out with it."

White hesitated. "Just walk around the corner for a minute," he said. "Here. Take the gold."

Joshua looked at it. If the man was imprisoned for

11

stealing a blanket, what was that? A dollar or two. He could well afford to pay the price of it. His eyes raised to study White's. The sun had now dropped into the haze on the Pacific horizon, and the earth was covered with a soft light that seemed to penetrate the jail room and illuminate White's features. He was a hard man to figure. His face told nothing, and his eyes were unreadable.

"One minute," pleaded White. "Give me one minute's start."

Joshua held the musket with his right hand around the lock.

"If they were worried about me," said White, "they would of had you load it."

That made sense.

"Six hundred will pay your debt back home," said White.

Joshua said uncertainly, "I have no key for the lock."

White snorted. "I've had that lock open a dozen times with a piece of brass wire." He held out his hand. "Do you want the six hundred or don't you? I'm going to get away anyway. You might as well take it."

Joshua looked at the dully gleaming gold. Six hundred dollars to get him started even with the world again. He'd have a chance to get back to the gold fields. He'd heard all about the business opportunities in connection with emigrants, but he wasn't interested in those. He'd been in the icy water of the Feather and the Yuba, and he'd carried gravel to the sluice box and he'd panned what was caught on the cleats, and he'd seen flakes of gold on his forefinger, and it was a thing that got into a man's blood. He wanted—he *had* to get back to the diggin's and look for that mother lode. When he hit it, he'd be rich overnight. He looked up at White.

12

Then deliberately but quickly he took the money and walked on to the corner of the adobe. He turned the corner and walked another fifty paces. Then he did his own version of about-face and walked back.

When he reached the door, it was open. He pushed it shut and snapped the heavy brass lock. Then he resumed walking the post with his empty musket. He went on to the corner, feeling the gold heavy and comforting inside his shirt. He turned, went past the jail door again. Behind him he heard a very small sound, as of a moccasin on hardpacked dirt. He turned. White had his arm raised and a cudgel in his hand. Joshua stared at him. "Why are you still around here?" he demanded.

White's concave face was hard to understand. He seemed very sure of himself. "You didn't think I'd let you keep the money, did you?"

Joshua looked at the lock. It was open again. White had hid in there to knock him on the head from behind. He jerked his head angrily at White. "It was bad enough that you bribed me, and worse that I accepted, but now—" His voice was rough with incredulity. "Trying to get the money back, are you?" He snorted. "Get back inside."

Something exploded on top of his head. He didn't see or hear it and had no presentiment of its coming. He tried to stand up but couldn't. His knees buckled, and dimly he heard White say to somebody behind him, "You got here just in time. He was starting to make trouble."

White was tearing open Joshua's shirt before he hit the ground. Then blackness flooded his brain.

He came to slowly, shaking his head, pushing up from the ground with his arms. Finally he got on his feet, picked up his musket, brushed off his clothes, and went to the jail door. White was gone, of course, but he made sure. Apparently White had had a confederate around the corner. He felt in his shirt. White had taken the money.

Joshua began to boil. He tried to figure out what to do. It looked to him as if he owed White something and the Army a lot. Also, White owed him six hundred dollars for value received. Joshua's anger mounted with every trip he made past the locked cell door.

Three soldiers came up from the tents. The leader, Bill Callahan, was dressed in green rifleman's clothes; he was corporal of the guard. The other two, the next corporal and the next guard, were in the gray-blue uniforms of the infantry.

Joshua met them.

"How are things?" asked Corporal Callahan.

"All's well," said Joshua Pickens.

"Juana got here with his supper, I see."

"Yes."

"I like that little Mex," Callahan said. "I think I'll marry her when I get out of the army."

"Marry a greaser?" asked Joshua, puzzled; his aching head was throbbing now.

"What's the matter with a greaser?"

"Well, I—"

Callahan nodded. "Sure, you're like most of 'em. You think a Mexican girl is something you buy for four bits and then toss away. But did you ever stop to think, Pickens, that a Mexican girl is like any other girl?"

"Meaning what?"

"Meaning you can't buy Juana. You might force her, but you can't buy her. And just like I said, I'm going to marry her someday."

Joshua changed his rifle to the other shoulder. "Have you asked her?"

"Yeah." Callahan said ruefully, "She turned me down. She said U.S. soldiers are *muy malos*—but I'll show her different."

Corporal Denver walked to the door of the jail. He put his face close to the bars for a moment, then swung around excitedly. "The prisoner is gone!" he said.

Callahan frowned and looked at Pickens, then strode to the door. "White's gone?" he asked.

Denver jerked at the lock. It was closed. "Sure." He looked at the tortillas and the empty *olla*. "Not very long ago, either, by the looks of those."

Callahan put a hand on Pickens' shoulder and spun him to face the door. "How?" he asked.

Pickens shook his throbbing head. "If I catch White I'll take it out of his hide."

Callahan's eyes narrowed. He said to Joshua, "You'll be court-martialed."

"Over a man who stole a blanket?" asked Pickens.

"Stole a blanket, hell!" said Callahan. "White wanted a Mexican girl who was living with a soldier, so he killed the soldier—cut his throat from ear to ear. The girl told it all to Major Heintzelman. White was being held on a federal charge of murder!"

CHAPTER TWO

PICKENS STARED AT HIM.

"I'm arresting you," Callahan said in a hard voice, "for disobeying orders."

Pickens drew a breath that hurt. "You—haven't

15

looked inside," he said cautiously. "You're not even sure he's gone."

"I've got the key," said the new corporal. He used it, and the brass lock sprang open. He pulled back the door and stepped inside. His own man followed him.

Pickens watched Callahan. The Corporal had a pistol in his holster, and the pistol probably was loaded. Callahan started for the open door. Pickens swung the back of his arm against the side of Callahan's head, and snatched the pistol with his other hand. The musket fell into the dust. Pickens sprang to the jail door and swung it shut, slipping the padlock into place and closing it in the same motion.

Denver swore at him.

"Shut up!" Pickens said in a low voice. "I've got a pistol."

Denver subsided into a mutter. Pickens backed away from the door. It would soon be dark. He looked at Callahan, sitting up and shaking his head. He was sorry about Callahan, but he couldn't help it.

"Callahan!" he said loudly, trying to make the Corporal hear through his daze. "I've been a damn' fool, but I'm going after the prisoner. You hear me, Callahan? I'm going to bring him back."

Denver said from the cell, "The Army will get him, Pickens! You stay here and do your job."

Joshua stared at him. "I'd be rotting in jail for ten years whether the Army catches him or not," he said in a low voice.

Denver tried to cajole him. "I'll ask them to take it easy on you."

Joshua paid no attention to him. No corporal's recommendation would have any influence with a court-martial. Besides, that dirty skunk White was loose out

16

there somewhere. He must have been crazy for a minute or two when he took that money!

He glanced at Callahan, who was starting to get to his knees. "I let him get away," he said, "and it's up to me to get him back if it takes the rest of my life."

He ran around the side of the adobe and headed for a grove of fig trees that marked a small Mexican saloon where Juana's father, fat-bellied Ignacio, sold American beer and Mexican *pulque*.

Pickens scrutinized the area around the saloon. A bay horse was tied to the wheel of a *carreta*, switching flies with its tail. Two oxen, probably from the *carreta*, lay comfortably on what had been the shady side of the adobe, and a burro nipped at the bougainvillea vine that covered the side wall.

The bay hadn't been there very long, for his coat was darkened with sweat around the stirrup leathers. Pickens slowed down to a walk and approached the bay. It was a Spaniard's horse, he saw by the silver-laden bridle and the long, showy tapaderos over the stirrups, and a moment later by the fancy brand on the left hip; no *norteamericano* who knew the value of a horse would disfigure it with such a brand. He put a foot into the stirrup, swung his leg over the cantle, and held onto the saucer-sized saddlehorn, over which hung a rawhide *lazo*, while he swung the bay in a tight circle and headed north at a trot. He looked back. Nobody was following him. Faintly he heard voices at the jail, but by the time they got a pursuit organized, he would he well into the hills on the way to the ferry that crossed the Yuma for it seemed likely that White would go that way.

Joshua pushed the bay at a steady trot for two hours before he stopped to let it rest and graze in a small open meadow behind a line of olive trees. From then on he rested the horse about ten minutes to the hour, and sometime after midnight he stopped in a small valley adjacent to a vineyard. He stalked out the bay with the *lazo*, took the saddle and bridle up to the vineyard. He hung the bridle on a trellis and laid the saddle on its side within the vines, where it would not be readily seen. He spread the horse blanket under the vines, lay down on it, and went to sleep.

He was awakened by the sound of loping horses. He swung to a sitting posture, one hand on the butt of the percussion pistol. Looking through the dense green foliage of the vines, he saw three men go by on horses that had the "US" brand stamped on them. It was early morning, and after they had disappeared, leaving a drifting line of dust to mark their passage, he took the bridle, threw the blanket over one shoulder, picked up the saddle by the horn, and went to the bay. He saddled up and rode across the meadow away from the road.

He went over a hill and sighted a band of sheep, just beginning to spread out for the day's grazing. He backtracked until he was out of sight under the top of the hill, and then followed the contour of the hill for a couple of miles before he ventured to cross the ridge again. The sun was not visible because of the mountains, although the foothills were well lighted and he could see several miles in any direction.

A Spanish *ranchería* lay below him—a cluster of adobe buildings, some large and others small, with some corrals made by adobe fencing, and a cluster of cottonwoods obviously grown up around a spring that watered the vineyard. A well-dressed ranchero came out of the largest adobe and mounted a beautiful chestnut stallion held by a servant. The servant mounted a brown mule, and they rode off up the valley at a stately walk.

Joshua considered. The ranchero was out to make his daily inspection of the estate before the sun got high. It was an opportunity.

Joshua cut far around the corrals to intersect the Spaniard's course. He was waiting by a large willow tree when the rancher drew abreast, resplendent and haughty in his great-brimmed sombrero, made of plaited grass covered with oiled silk, heavy and homely; a jacket of embroidered blue cloth; *calzones* or pantaloons made of black velvet, the legs ornamented on the outer seams with silver buttons, and the lower ends slit to reveal insertions of green cloth; the sash at his waist was also green, with both ends hanging. Joshua walked the bay into the Spaniard's path and held the pistol across the bay's withers.

The Spaniard drew up slowly, his black eyes taking in Joshua's uniform. "*Qué quiere decir esto, señor?*" he asked. "What is the meaning of this?"

"Señor," said Joshua, "I am reluctant to do this, but I have no choice."

"You want money? I have no money."

"No," said Joshua. "I want your clothes."

The Spaniard stiffened. "There are clothes at the ranch."

Joshua nodded. "Yes—and other persons are there." His hand that held the pistol moved restlessly. "I want your clothes—now."

He knew it was an affront to the Spaniard's pride, to be stripped at the point of a pistol before his servant, but he couldn't help it.

The Spaniard lifted his head still higher. "I will send my servant back to the house for clothes."

Joshua glanced at the servant. "No, he stays here. He would give the alarm if he returned to the house."

"*Don Jorge, puedo—*"

"*Silencio!*" snapped Joshua. "Don Jorge, are you going to do what I want?"

The Spaniard studied his gray-blue eyes. "Yes," he said finally. "I will—but I will never forgive you for this."

"I don't expect you to," said Joshua. He motioned with his head. "You can go into the bushes and toss out the clothes."

"I will not wear your soldier's uniform," the Spaniard said haughtily.

"It isn't necessary," Joshua said. "After I am gone, if you want to stand there in your skin, you can send your *mozo* back for more clothes. But now—"

The Spaniard took a deep breath. His chest swelled and his eyes flashed fire, but he dismounted. He looked at the bay, but Joshua had been careful to keep the brand turned away from the Spaniard. Don Jorge went into the thicket.

"You!" Joshua said to the servant. "Ride your mule into the bushes so you'll be out of sight from the house."

The servant said hastily, "*Sí, señor!*"

Joshua dismounted and stripped hastily. He wore no underclothes, and it was a little cool in the shade, but he tossed the green rifleman's clothes and the leather cap and the "bootees" that by regulations extended four inches above the ankle into a small heap, and got into the Spaniard's clothes. They were big enough but, like his Army clothes, too short in the legs and sleeves. But he was satisfied as he looked down at himself. With his dark skin and his black hair, he could pass for a Spaniard anywhere.

He put his pistol in his belt and mounted the bay, still

careful to keep the brand hidden. He saw the servant sitting the mule and ordered him to get down. He whacked the mule with his flat hand, and the mule jumped and broke out of the brush and ran out onto the open hillside. Joshua slapped the chestnut and watched it follow the mule.

"Now," he said to Don Jorge, "when I am out of sight you may send your man for help—not before."

The Spaniard's voice was filled with suppressed rage. "I will have you skinned for this, *soldado*."

"Will you?" asked Joshua. "You don't like the U.S. government anyway—and Major Heintzelman knows that." (He was stabbing in the dark.) "What good will it do you to complain?"

"There must be some justice in the United States government," said the Spaniard.

Joshua glanced at him and felt a little bit sorry; as a matter of fact, he would have been willing to take the servant's clothing, but he didn't know how clean it would be. "*Muchas gracias*," he said, "and don't be in a hurry to get back to the house."

But now a new complication appeared. As he started to ride through the brush, he glanced toward the ranch house and saw a rider mounting a horse. Obviously the rider was a Spanish woman, for she was mounting on the off side. Joshua considered for a moment. Somebody had observed the unusual proceedings on the hillside—the halting of Don Jorge on his tour of inspection, the appearance of a third rider, and then the disappearance of the first two—and now there was to be an investigation. If he were to flee, the rider from the ranch would come at a gallop, and he would soon be pursued. With his thought in mind, he turned the bay and rode toward the ranch house.

She was about twenty, tall enough, not plump as

many Spanish girls were, but well filled out and solid-looking. He knew she was an aristocrat, for any peasant girl of her age would have been married and the mother of three or four children, and too fat by U.S. standard. He knew it too by the length and richness of the mantilla that covered her black hair and her shoulders, and by the way she held her head and the proud way in which she rode.

He cantered the bay to meet her, and noted the way her dark eyes took him in, and the way they scrutinized the horse. He swept off the sombrero and bowed. "Señorita," he said, "may I be of service?"

He saw puzzlement in her eyes as she recognized his clothes, and the beginning of a crease across her forehead. "*Perdóneme*," she said in lovely Spanish. "I am looking for my uncle, Don Jorge."

He liked the way her full red lips moved, and the whiteness of her teeth against the olive skin. "He went out to make his tour this morning," he said in excellent Spanish, "but he met with a slight—accident."

Her eyes widened. "He is hurt?"

"No, señorita, he is in perfect health. He has had an embarrassing accident." He shrugged. "It is one of those things men understand—and all he requires is a clean outfit of clothing. Shall we ride back to the house?"

She turned with him. She wasn't satisfied, but there wasn't much she could do.

"This is your home, señorita?"

"No," she said, riding at his left. "My home is in Hermosillo, in Sonora."

He was relieved. "You do not know me, then?"

"No."

He liked the musical lilt of her voice. "I am José Péquen," he said, and added calmly, "a neighbor."

22

"You know my uncle, then?"

"Rather well, señorita." He remembered Don Jorge naked in the bushes. "Quite well, I would say." He glanced at her. "And your name, señorita?"

"I am called Natalia Brodie."

"Brodie?"

"My father is Irish. He is *administrador* of the cotton factory in Hermosillo. My mother was a Valdez on her father's side, a Cortiña on her mother's side. And her grandmother was an Andrade y Mendoza de Carillo. And my father's mother—"

"You," he said, smiling, "are Natalia."

She looked up at him. She blushed, and he knew she had been talking to cover her self-consciousness. Now her lips remained parted for an instant, and he would have liked very much to kiss her at that moment, but that would have been unthinkable. Besides, he did have to escape if he was to catch the man White, and he could not afford to go around stirring up trouble.

"Of course Don Jorge is your uncle—your mother's brother," he said, guessing.

"*Sí, señor.*"

"How long do you intend to visit here before you return to Sonora?"

"My father has said we are to start back tomorrow." She sounded glum. "We would like to stay here all summer, for it gets hot at Hermosillo."

He said casually, "It must be easy to get passage on the ships nowadays."

"We don't go by ship. We go overland."

"Across the Colorado?"

"Yes."

He looked up at the hills. "I'd think you'd get lost up there."

23

"Oh, no. The road is easy to find, there have been so many emigrants."

"Do you go straight east?"

"No. Northeast to Warner's rancho, then southeast across the desert to the ferry."

"I see." He was careful not to show the satisfaction he felt. He had heard much of Warner's rancho, up near the coastal divide, and this was all the information he needed to find the ferry. This was a good morning's work.

"I am sorry you are to leave so soon, señorita. I would like to see you again." He glanced at her and saw the confusion in her eyes. "I am not married, señorita."

"Oh!" She seemed relieved.

"Now, then." He stopped the bay and turned it toward her. "I must go on into town. You had best go to the house for a change of clothes for Don Jorge. And don't worry, señorita. He is quite well and in no danger whatever."

He watched her ride off. The cluster of adobes was only two hundred yards away, and a servant ran out on foot to meet her. She turned, and he waved and then swung the bay into the brush. He got through the brush and went downhill. Out of sight of the ranch buildings, he put the bay into a hard gallop, veering to the left. Fifteen minutes later, from an opening in the brush, he saw someone on horseback start for the place where Don Jorge was hidden, while the servant who had accompanied Don Jorge was walking downhill to meet the rider.

Joshua was amused but he didn't smile. He rode the bay down a small valley and over another hill and into a pasture where a dozen horses grazed.

This was a good chance to trade horses and get rid of

the bay, which was not only tired, but much too well known by now. He rode into the band of grazing horses, knowing better than to approach them on foot. He went alongside a sorrel and gripped it by the mane. It had saddle marks. He slid off the bay, looping the lasso over the sorrel's neck to hold it. Then he changed bridle and saddle and mounted the sorrel. He now had a different costume and a different horse. One more trade and he would be free for awhile; it would take them several days to unravel it.

He thought of White, putting many miles behind him as he traveled toward the Colorado, and he remembered White's lie and his theft of the six hundred dollars, and his determination to find the man began to take on an aspect of grimness. More than anything else he wanted to take White back to San Diego to stand trial.

He stopped at the top of the next hill. He was two miles from the ranch by that time, but he could see a trail of dust leading from the ranch in the opposite direction. Don Jorge's servant had gone after the detachment that was hunting Joshua Pickens. He thought about it for a moment, his eyes taking in the hills, the narrow plain along the coast, and the sea beyond. Then he turned the sorrel toward the settlement of San Diego.

CHAPTER THREE

HE LOOKED ENOUGH LIKE A SPANIARD—ALLOWING for a little foreign blood—to get by, but he wasn't riding like a Spaniard. He must remember, when he approached anybody, to sit back in the great boxlike saddle as if he were lord of the universe.

The sounds of the morning came out now: horses' hoofs pounding as they chased one another in the meadow, birds singing as though they were trying out voices on a new song in a new world, the regular whacking sound of a wooden paddle as some early-rising *lavandera* beat her clothes over a rock.

Joshua spotted a single small adobe far below, and followed a narrow lane of grass between two fields of grapevines to reach it.

The woman was down by the creek, beating clothes with a paddle. He paused at the hut, then walked the sorrel to the creek.

"Señora." He remembered to keep his hat on, as Don Jorge would do.

She looked up, half afraid. She was in her early twenties, a good-looking woman, but already beginning to spread out in the hips.

"You need have no fear of me, señora. I merely wish to purchase some clothing for my *mozo*, who has met with an unfortunate accident."

Within a few minutes he had another outfit. He rode off with it, and stopped at the first clump of brush to change. It was a shame to leave the ranchero's clothes to the elements, but he had no choice. He wadded them up, stuffed them into the hat, and pushed the whole thing into a badger hole under the roots of a pepper tree.

Farther along he heard the sound of hands clapping cornmeal dough into the form of tortillas, and came to a small brown adobe covered with purple and white flowers. He stopped there and bought a meal for five cents. A little later he traded horses again. While he was doing this the Army detachment galloped by on the way into San Diego, and he could hardly refrain from a wry smile. It would take the Army weeks to trace his

26

movements, provided he did not suffer some bad luck such as recognition by chance. He wasn't worried about the horses; eventually they would be restored to their proper owners by the brands.

Late in the afternoon he rode back into San Diego. He had to have more serviceable clothes for what he was about to do, and so he went around the tents and avoided the adobe jail, and stopped in front of a frame building with a sign that said: "General Store."

He bought wool pants, a red woolen shirt, miner's boots, and a black hat, and asked for a place to put them on.

The proprietor showed him a packing box. "You ain't no Mex," he observed.

"No." Joshua grinned. "I lost my money in a poker game, and this was all I could get to wear into town."

"You could have traded the horse."

Joshua noted that the man had sharp eyes. Aloud he said, "And walked half a mile?"

The proprietor smiled.

Joshua changed clothes and left the old ones, including the huge straw hat with its conical top. "Now, mister," he said, paying his bill, "which way to the gold fields?"

The storekeeper looked up with interest. "I thought you'd lost your money in a card game."

Joshua did not change his level stare, though he thought to himself the man was far too nosy. "So I did," he said, "but it must be plain to you that I raised a stake, or else I wouldn't have money to pay for the clothes. Now," he said, "the important thing is to win back what I lost as fast as possible—so which way?"

The proprietor's eyes were speculating, but finally he said, "Follow out the end of this street and keep to the

27

north and a little west until you get to the Pueblo. The Americans call it Los Angeles. You can ask from there."

Joshua left well satisfied. He had made the storekeeper believe he was headed north, and if a man who had bought miner's clothes and left on a sorrel horse should be connected with Private Pickens, the Army would look for him in the gold fields, if anywhere—though there were so many desertions, as White had said, they couldn't spend much time looking. Meanwhile, Joshua would have a chance to hunt up White and bring him back.

He thought about it as he left town, carefully holding the sorrel to a walk. He could have gone to the Major and reported what had happened and let the Army go after White, but he knew he would get several years in prison and lose out on the gold boom. Besides, he thought he had a better chance to catch White than did the usual run of Army men. He'd had considerable experience in the open, and he'd do it his way. He'd find White and bring him back, and he would decide later how to deliver him to the Army. It didn't matter, just so his plans to return to Sacramento were not interfered with.

He left the road as soon as he was out of sight of the settlement, and turned east. He rode up smooth green valleys, and that night camped in the high hills, from which he could see the ocean only a few miles away.

The old mission of San Diego de Acala, built seven years before the Revolutionary War but now in ruins, was surrounded by a few thatched huts. The grapevines were still in orderly rows, and probably tended by the peons for their fruit, which, dried, made excellent raisins, or, fermented, made very good wine.

The fig trees on the grounds of the mission were loaded with bright blossoms, and a black-haired Mexican girl worked leisurely at a cistern. An open roof over the well was covered with vines and red and white flowers, and the screeching of the ungreased windlass rose in the still air—slowly, it seemed, and almost leisurely. So thoroughly peaceful was the appearance of the country below, and so unhurried the girl's movements, that even the high-pitched grating sound seemed hardly obtrusive.

He went on up past the mission, walking the sorrel, for it was a considerable climb to the top of the hills, and he saw no signs of pursuit. Over on the Valdez place there was considerable activity, and he judged the vaqueros were rounding up horses and mules for the trip back to Sonora. Two Pittsburgh wagons and a number of Mexican *carretas* were in the yard. The heat of the day was past now, and children ran after chickens, dogs ran after the children, and pigs tried to get out of the way, with an occasional squeal coming through the cackles and yaps, all softly muted by distance.

He sat for a moment while the sorrel scooped up mouthfuls of bunch grass and broke them off with a crisp, crunchy sound. He supposed Natalia Brodie would go back to Hermosillo with the train, and somehow it made him momentarily sad, for she had beauty, grace, good manners, and a subtle way of making a man think she was interested in him.

He pulled up the sorrel's head and turned northwest.

That night he reached the tiny settlement of San Pasqual, and there he bought corn and dried beef and learned that White, with two companions, was ahead of him.

He slept in the open that night, not wanting to trust

29

himself to the *chinches* and assorted bedroom livestock that sometimes came out of the walls of an adobe hut at night.

At Warner's rancho he got more supplies, and John Warner mapped his course to the junction of the Gila and the Colorado. Warner said there had been two or three ferries there at various times, and all of them had made money from the emigrants. Twelve thousand persons had crossed at the Gila in 1849, said Warner. "And this year they expect forty thousand. The Maricopa Trail is a regular highroad. They come in bunches, usually. If they've got any sense—which not all of them have—they travel in trains big enough to keep off the Apaches. Sometimes they come through here as fast as they can get across the desert." He looked at Joshua. "I could make a fortune here if I had some young fellow like you that I could depend on to bring me supplies."

But Joshua shook his head. "Don't look at me. I've got a job to do at the Gila, and then I'm going north."

"You ever been in the gold fields?" asked Warner.

"Yes."

"Get any gold?"

Joshua said defensively, "No."

"Ever know anybody who did?"

"No," Joshua admitted.

Warner shook his head. "Then you're a fool to go back and work yourself day and night, and maybe get killed in a fight for something that never existed."

But Joshua's chest swelled. "It may be hard to find and it may be hard to bring home," he said, "but it gets into your blood. You've got to go back, because you might be the one to pick a nugget as big as your fist out of the water someday."

He discovered that the wells were all right as far as Carrizo Creek, but the creek itself sank into the sand within a few miles, and a lot of digging had to be done for water at New River and Alamo Mocho and Cooke's Wells. The others could not be depended on.

He left Warner's about midnight. Near Vallecito the trail went through a gorge of solid rock, too narrow for a wagon, and later the mountainside was strewn with great blocks of granite. At Vallecito were springs and an adobe house, and he took half a bushel of barley from the stores in the house, which had a musty smell of long disuse.

If White had left Warner's six hours ahead of him, he should reach Carrizo Springs about noon. That was good mileage—fifty miles in eighteen hours—and White probably would leave Carrizo Springs in late afternoon, travel all night across the desert, stay at a water hole the next day, and finish the trip the second night. The trip from Carrizo Springs to the Gila was ninety miles, and much depended on whether they were able to find water in between. With plenty of water, the horses could be pushed hard.

The way it looked to him, White and his companions were already pushing their animals, for droppings were few. He found one place where they had stopped to dig for water, but he judged, from the lack of horses' tracks around the edges of the hole, that they had not found it. Obviously they were not feeding the animals, for a horse or mule required more water when it was fed.

The day was sultry and oppressive, and the sorrel began to heave. Joshua stopped to give it a breather, but after that he drove it without letup, for he had to catch White at Carrizo Springs. There would be only three men at the creek, and those were odds he could cope with. Past the creek that fed the springs, if Warner was right, Joshua had no chance to catch White until they reached the Colorado—and at the Colorado there would be Glanton and a dozen others to side White. So the thing had to be settled at Carrizo Springs.

From the tracks, White and the two other men were riding three horses and leading a pack mule, for the mule's smaller hoofprints overlapped the tracks of the horses.

The sorrel was feeling the heat, for Joshua could sense the faltering in its stride. He considered stopping to dig for water, but decided against it. It was imperative that he catch the three men before they left Carrizo Springs. He himself felt like a piece of old leather. He stopped long enough to wet his shirt sleeve from his canteen and hold it over the sorrel's nose to cool off its lungs. Then he poured three fourths of the water into his hat and let the sorrel drink. He finished what was in the canteen, recorked it, and hung it on the horn. He let the sorrel munch a few handfuls of straw-colored grass, then mounted and rode east and a little south.

The sorrel regained its stride. Joshua felt dry all the way down to his stomach. The sides of his throat seemed to stick together. The sun burned into his arms and shoulders, but he stopped only to cut off a switch of screwbean mesquite to keep the sorrel going. The presence of mesquite meant water, but it didn't indicate how deep he would have to dig for it, for sometimes mesquite would send its roots down fifty feet to get water.

They pulled out of an *arroyada*, and Joshua pounded the sorrel to get it to the top of the ridge. The way was a well-defined wagon road, but the only fresh tracks were headed east. He had, he thought, another hour to go, and he forced the sorrel into a trot; there would be time for resting after he took White into custody. The sorrel tossed its head and tried to throw the bit, but Joshua kept applying the stick. Then suddenly the sorrel stopped in its tracks and began to tremble.

Joshua jumped off. He looked at the sorrel's rolling eyes and jerked out his knife. If he could draw a quart or so of blood, the horse might recover.

He opened a vein in the sorrel's belly. The animal was standing with its legs spraddled to keep from going down. He watched the blood spurt out. It was very thin and appeared to have melted tallow floating in it. Joshua started to plug the wound with his, finger, when abruptly the sorrel shivered violently and began to go down.

He knew the horse was done, and he held his hand over its nose to keep it from making a sound that would reveal his presence. It rolled over on its side. Its legs went rigid, then limp, and Joshua got up slowly. He took the canteen from the saddlehorn and hung it over his shoulder. He put the knife back in its sheath, settled the pistol in the waistband of his pants, and went on down the trail. It was almost noon. He could not be very far . . .

The usual camping place at Carrizo Springs was scattered with the bones and skulls of animals and a few rib cases still held together by dried hide, and over the place hung the rancid smell of sun-dried carcasses. The springs were surrounded with mesquite bushes, and Joshua kept under cover of these to go around the camping place.

Warner had said the creek would flow for half a mile or as much as three miles before it sank into the sand, and White's tracks indicated he had gone past the regular camping place at the springs; therefore Joshua probably would find them camped at the place where the water sank into the sand. He kept to the mesquite bushes, traveling as fast as he dared. Caution was essential, and he was not sure of the miners' boots he had bought. He stopped at a clump of willow trees, and heard voices ahead. That was good; they did not know they were being followed.

He came upon them as they were watering their horses. The heat was torturing as he watched from the side of an ocotillo—a cactus with many tall, slender stems that grew up from a common root.

He looked at the sun. It was later than he had thought. He must have walked for three or four hours. He watched as one of the men brought the mule up to the spring. He heard the bubbling of water and the noisy sucking of the mule, and White said, "Prewett, you better do something for that mule's back. You lay on a pack saddle like a stinkin' greaser."

"I done everything I can," said Prewett. "Maybe Carr knows something."

Carr was lighting a cigarette at a tiny fire. He was a tall, very thin man, with cold, flat eyes. "It takes a muleman to rig a pack saddle—and I ain't no muleman."

"Have I got to do it myself?" asked White.

"He ain't hurt," said Prewett. "I seen them greasers down in Chihuahua run mules till their shoulder blades was stickin' out."

White went up to the spring with a canteen, and got on one knee to fill it. "John Glanton won't like it when he sees that. Mules are worth three hundred dollars."

"Glanton is makin' that much every day," said Prewett.

"You can tell him," Carr suggested, "that you was too busy runnin' from the Army to be bothered with a mule."

"We shoulda got some pads," said Prewett.

Joshua looked at his pistol. There was a cap on the nipple, but the pistol could hardly be anything but a threat, for he had only one shot. The .54-caliber slug was, just the same, a threat of death, and a man could go a long way on a threat like that. Joshua took his knife in his left hand, the pistol in his right, and stepped from behind the ocotillo. "Put up your hands," he ordered them. "The Army has still got something to say."

CHAPTER FOUR

CARR LOOKED UP; A BURNING TWIG WAS STILL IN HIS fingers, and he seemed to freeze. Prewett, holding the stake rope on the mule's halter, twisted to stare at him, open-mouthed. White, still on one knee, was holding the canteen under the water, and the sound of the air bubbling out of it was loud for a moment in the silence that followed Joshua's sudden appearance. Then White turned slowly, his sharp eyes seeking out Joshua. His knees straightened as he rose, the canteen in one hand, its canvas cover dripping water.

"Come out into the open," Joshua ordered, "and turn your back to me."

White moved slowly.

"You bribed me to let you go," said Joshua, "but you hit me on the head and took the money back. That's robbery."

"Well, now, I'll—"

Joshua interrupted him. "But that isn't the worst. You

said you were in jail for stealing a blanket. That wasn't so. You were held for murder."

White said slowly, "So you're here to take me back."

"That's the way it sizes up."

"You ain't wearin' no uniform."

"That isn't necessary," said Joshua harshly. "I've got this." He motioned with the pistol.

White was still facing him. "How much more do you want?"

"I didn't come for money. I came for you. Turn around and back up slow."

White turned. Just then Prewett ducked behind the mule, and the burning twig dropped from Carr's long fingers.

Joshua couldn't do anything about Prewett, for he had only one shot. He closed in fast to get behind White.

But White did not stop turning when his back was toward Joshua. He made another quarter turn and threw the canteen at Joshua's face.

Joshua brought up his knife hand to knock down the canteen, but the opening was toward him, and his face was drenched with water. White jumped at him. Joshua held his fire. When White launched himself, Joshua moved, and White went into the sand.

A shot came from Carr, and Joshua grunted as the bullet took him in the back. The bullet made him flinch, and, before he could recover, White was up.

Joshua closed in with the knife, but White shot at his left hand. The bullet went through the palm, and Joshua's fingers lost their grip. The knife dropped as he fired his pistol with his right hand.

It hit White too low to be close to the heart, but White's eyes closed for an instant. Joshua snatched at White's pistol, a revolver, but at that instant Carr

36

clubbed him from behind with something heavy. He lost his balance and swayed for a moment; then Carr hit him again, and it was like running full speed into a mountain.

White said, "Don't kill the fool. He's U.S. Army."

Carr said, "How about you?"

"It hurts," said White, "but it isn't serious."

Joshua tried to get up, but Carr pushed him down, and Joshua's mouth filled with sand.

"What'll we do with him?" asked Carr.

"Beat the hell out of him," said White, "and leave him here."

The club exploded at the back of Joshua's head again. He sprawled for a moment, gathering strength. Then he leaped up. Prewett was in front of him. Prewett swung the end of the stake rope across his face. Joshua tried to grapple with him, but Carr hit him from behind. Joshua wheeled, and Prewett, using the rope like a whip, wrapped the knotted end around Joshua's neck and jerked.

Joshua went down, and he saw White's boots swinging at him. The rope raked his face, and he turned over. The club descended on his shoulders, and he knew it spattered blood. White jumped with both feet in the small of his back.

He rolled to his side and looked at White. "I come to take you," he said. "You better kill me if you don't want to go back."

The rope took off skin clear across his mouth, but still he managed to fix his eyes on White, and still he talked. "You killed a U.S. soldier," he said, "and you'll stand trial for that. If I don't take you back, somebody else will. But as long as I'm alive, White, I'll be—"

Carr kicked him under the left eye.

Joshua finished: "—after you," barely able to talk, because his lips had no feeling.

Prewett swung the knotted end of the rope and caught him behind the ear, and he fell flat and limp, not trying to get up again, even under the hail of boots and the numbing blows of the club and the burning rasp of the rope. He lay flat, his mouth full of sand, until he lost consciousness . . .

He came to, aching all over. His left hand throbbed. He looked at it, and saw ants crawling over the wound. He raised his head out of the sand, and a coyote darted behind a mesquite bush. Flies buzzed up from his head and started to settle back down. He shook his head and looked at the sun. He'd been there a couple of hours, probably. He saw two buzzards circling over him.

Well, he wasn't carrion yet. He got to his feet, swaying. There was a numb area in his back, but it wasn't a lung shot, and probably nothing more than an inconvenience.

He realized that he was terribly thirsty. The fight itself had dried up his tissues, and then he had lain in the hot sun for a long time. He got down to the creek and lay on his stomach and put his face in the water. His face burned in a hundred places, but he drank—very slowly at first, freely after a while.

He had both hands in the water. The ants floated away from his left hand. Then the water touched bare flesh inside of the wound and burned like fire. He closed his eyes for a moment, then took his hand out of the water.

His left eye was closed and he couldn't open it. There was a huge knot behind his ear. By careful exploration with his right hand he discovered that his entire face was a mass of blood and bruises, and he sat down at the edge of the water and began to wash it with his one good hand, slowly, cautiously. He wanted to be clean but he wasn't in a hurry.

When he had done the best he could, he tore a strip from his shirttail and bandaged his left hand.

His canteen was still hanging from his shoulder, and automatically he filled it and put the cork in tightly. Then he examined the camping place. The three men were gone, of course, and he found their tracks leading southeast. A while later he made them out, four black specks against the desert, far below. He considered. He had no horse and no rifle or pistol. The only way he could travel was by walking, and he wasn't sure yet what the bullet in his back would do to his legs. He looked again at the four black specks in the sand bed of the Carrizo. For the time being he would have to let them go.

The next thing was food. He remembered the knife he had dropped, and went to the spot of the fight and found it and put it in his waistband. He walked back up the trail, laboring heavily. At the place of the skulls and bones he found a discarded brass kettle, but no cached food. Then he remembered the barley he had left on the sorrel. He made sure the canteen was full, and then began to work his way on up the trail.

It was slow going. He moved a hundred yards at a time and then rested. He must have lost some blood, but the numbness was not yet spreading in his back. Maybe it wouldn't.

He reached the sorrel's carcass at sunset, and scared off four coyotes and a dozen buzzards. The barley sack was unhurt, and he took it, working slowly, laboriously. Then he turned the sorrel over and cut a large piece of meat from the ham that the scavengers hadn't got to.

39

That effort made his left hand throb with pain and left him exhausted, and he sat down to rest until it was twilight. Then he got up and started back to Carrizo Springs.

It was slow going. He had to be careful not to lose the way, and sometimes he got down on his knees to feel the sand with his hands for prints. The night seemed to be filled with scurrying rats, a shuffling bear that passed within a few feet, and skulking coyotes that seemed to be following him and waiting.

But Joshua kept on. His hand bled, not profusely but continually. The bullet in his back had turned to a dull, steady ache, but his legs still had feeling. He rested frequently, but he kept moving, and finally, long after midnight, he reached the place of bones and skulls and sank down in the sand to sleep . . .

The sun was over the desert when he woke up. He was dizzy when he got to his feet, but he stood there until his head cleared. His face and body ached and burned everywhere, but he tried his legs and found that the bullet in his back had not caused paralysis.

He studied the desert below, but could see no sign of human beings. Undoubtedly White and his men had traveled all night and would be halfway to the junction of the Colorado and the Gila by now. He looked for some of the thousands of emigrants who came down the Maricopa Trail, but saw none, and realized it could very well be several days before the next train would come.

But what he really wanted was to go east. He wasn't worried about living; he had barley and a brass kettle, and he could live quite a while next to the spring. What he needed was a horse to go after White.

He started down to the water, but he was dizzy again, and this time he couldn't seem to clear his head by shaking it. He swayed for a moment and then went slowly to his knees and crawled through the sand to the water.

He put his face in the water, and the burning of the raw places brought him to for a moment. He drank, and then sat under a screwbean brush where there was scanty shade. He realized his hat was gone, but he didn't see it anywhere. It must be down at the scene of the fight. He ought to get busy and boil some barley, but he didn't feel good, and that could wait. He looked at the sun and judged where the screwbean would throw its shadow for the next several hours, and moved so that he would be in it. He sank in the sand and lay on his back. If an emigrant train didn't come from the Colorado, perhaps a train of Sonorans returning from the gold fields would come from over the mountains. He remembered to put his arm over his eyes to protect them from the buzzards before he passed out . . .

Then it was late afternoon, and the sun had moved until he was no longer sheltered by the screwbean's scanty leaves. He felt desiccated, and the heat seemed to be inside of him more than outside. He felt his face, and he had a raging fever. He went down to the creek and took his time about drinking. He thought of boiling the barley, but realized for the first time that he had no matches. It wasn't important anyway, for he didn't feel hungry.

He scanned the desert for sight of an emigrant train, but saw nothing but scattered creosote bushes and small cactus of various kinds. He drank again and went back to the screwbean bush. The rancid odor from the dried-up carcasses did not bother him any more. Nothing, really, seemed to bother him. He wondered if emigrants would cross the desert the next day . . .

It was morning and he started automatically to go for

water, but found he could not walk. He remembered the barley and thought he'd better get it if he expected to go after White, but now he could not recall where he had left it.

Two ash-throated flycatchers set up a chattering noise in a mesquite brush ten feet away, and the noise hurt his head, and he tried to throw his knife at them, but it fell into the sand halfway to the mark. His head seemed to be on fire, and he began to face the fact that he was sick. He tried to think what he could do, but everything he thought of took medicine or food or transportation, and he saw no relief except to wait for help. Eventually somebody would be along, and he would stay alive until then. He drank the last of the water in his canteen; tomorrow, when he felt better, he would go down to the creek and refill it . . .

It was midafternoon the next time, and vaguely he realized that he had been out for almost twenty-four hours. The sun was fiery, and he looked at his shrunken fingers and realized he must have water. He lay on one side and tried the canteen; it was empty. He looked up and saw the buzzards circling over him; ten, eleven, twelve, thirteen, he counted. He tried to swear at them, to tell them he wasn't going to die, that they were wasting their time—but his throat was so dry he could make only a few croaking sounds.

He couldn't get to his knees, so he crawled on his stomach. The sun beat down on the back of his head and neck. A coyote watched him from the mesquite, and did not move even when he waved his arm at it. The scavengers were closing in.

He would fool them anyway, for he knew that it was just a matter of time until an emigrant train would come across the desert.

Eventually, crawling on his belly in the sand like a snake, he reached the edge of the stream and laboriously worked his way headfirst to the water. It seemed a long way, and finally he realized he was in the stream bed and it was nothing but sand. The spring must have temporarily dried up.

CHAPTER FIVE

THE NEXT TIME HE OPENED HIS EYES IT WAS TWILIGHT, and, instead of the buzzing insect life, he imagined he heard a rich Irish brogue and the chatter of excited Spaniards. This, then, was getting close to the end. Perhaps the buzzards knew what they were doing in their tireless circling.

He was still lying in the white sand of the stream bed, and the Irish brogue was close to his ears as he was picked up and carried out of the stream bed and through the area of half-dried carcasses. He opened his eyes and saw the buzzards, wheeling and circling, and felt a certain elation at cheating them.

"Where are you taking him, Father?" asked a girl's voice that seemed to be vaguely familiar.

"We've got to get him to the other spring," said the man who was carrying him.

He was laid down on a buffalo robe, and the girl's voice seemed full of anguish as it came from somewhere above him: "*Pobrecito!*"

Dimly he saw the bullet head of the man who carried him—a grizzled, redheaded man.

Somebody picked up his left arm, and pains shot from his hand clear to his shoulder. "It's all right," said the man. "There's no gangrene."

43

A cloth wet with brandy was held over his mouth and nose. He inhaled, and it seemed to revive him and to counteract the leathery dryness of his throat. Then a vision floated into his field of vision—a vision of olive skin with fascinating dark hollows, of white teeth, red lips, and liquid black eyes; and gradually, as his field of vision enlarged, he saw a girl with a snowy-white shirtwaist and a black *mantilla*, and slender, smooth brown arms with strong and competent fingers. The cloth wet with brandy came again, and presently she held his head on her lap and poured a few drops of brandy on his leathery tongue. He begged for more, but she said, "No, no," in a sort of crooning voice, and he was amazed that she could touch his face and head with her fingers without hurting him.

Her father was stomping back and forth, taking care of the disposition of the vehicle—two Pittsburgh wagons and a dozen or so *carretas*, with oxen, mules, and horses. Two Pittsburghs . . . He frowned.

"*Qué hay, pobrecito?*" she asked softly.

He tried to speak, but made only croaking noises, and pointed to his throat. She nodded and gave him a few more drops of brandy, and presently he sat up painfully, though he would have been quite content to leave his head in her lap forever. She let him have a sip of the brandy, and when he grasped the tin cup and tried to take more, she held him back, and he was astonished at her strength. He ached all over, and could use only one hand, for his left arm throbbed throughout its length. But eventually she let him drink, and he got the dust out of his throat and washed the sand out from around his gums.

The man began to clean the dried blood from his left hand with a soft wet cloth.

Joshua looked at the man and said, "I want to borrow a horse."

"What for?"

"I've got business on the Colorado—at the Gila crossing."

"Then you'd best stick with us. We're headed that way."

He nodded, relieved. Then he asked, "What day is it?"

The girl answered. "It's Wednesday—the day you would have died if we had not arrived."

"Is your name Natalia?" he asked.

Her eyes widened. "But—*seguro*. How do you know?"

He watched her eyes. "Haven't you ever seen me before?"

"No—I think not."

"Do you remember the morning Don Jorge, your uncle, was robbed of his clothes?"

Her eyes widened. "*Usted no es—*"

"I'm the one," he said, and smiled the best he could.

He enjoyed her confusion, because it made the color rise in her checks and left her more beautiful than ever.

The man stopped in his cleansing of the wound in Joshua's left hand. "Look here, lad, do you mean to say it was you who left Don Jorge naked in the brush that morning?"

Joshua nodded. "It was necessary. The Army was hunting me—and I was hunting a man named White."

A twinkle came in the man's eyes. "I myself thought it a rare joke, but I don't think Jorge's sense of humor will ever be equal to the occasion."

Joshua sank back with his head in Natalia's lap, to keep her from leaving. "I hope you forgive me,

45

Natalia, for I'm going to marry you," he said.

She looked at him, puzzled.

"That's not a thing to joke about, lad," said the man.

"I'm not joking," said Joshua.

"You've still a touch of the sun, maybe."

"No," said Joshua. "You're her father, aren't you?"

"Sure."

"Do I have your permission to ask her?"

Brodie frowned. "Well, now, that's something I can't answer until I know you better."

"All right." Joshua sat up. "You'll know me better." He turned around to look at Natalia. "You aren't married?"

She didn't answer, but got to her feet, and he thought she looked frightened.

"Lie back," said Brodie, "and take it easy. You're a terrible-looking thing right now, lad. You don't weigh over a hundred pounds, and what's there is skin and bones, but I've no doubt you'll fatten up if you get food and water, and maybe you won't look so much like a scarecrow.

"You think I look bad?" asked Joshua.

"To tell you the truth, you look so bad that it beats the hell out of me how you could think of marrying any girl or have the gall to think any girl would have you."

Joshua nodded slowly. "I suppose you're right—but I liked Natalia the first time I saw her."

"Very well." Brodie smeared his hand with bear oil and called for a clean wrapping. "When we reach the Colorado, we'll see if you are still of the same mind." He said, "I think we'd best leave that bullet in your back. It doesn't seem to be harming you, and I'm no doctor anyway."

They sat at the fire that evening, with the pine wood

making fragrant spirals in the mountain air, and Joshua broiled mutton before the fire and ate it with his hands, piece after piece, until midnight.

"You look better," said Brodie at last. "D'you want to go on with us tomorrow?"

Joshua nodded as he stripped the last piece of meat from a rib with his teeth.

"You've made a good recovery in the last few hours. You looked so bad in the stream we thought you were dead. The thing that puzzled us was the buzzards weren't tearing you apart."

He slept under a wagon that night. When he awoke at dawn he was hungry again.

With Brodie were about thirty Mexicans, some with their wives. They killed another sheep and ate it for breakfast, and Joshua picked out the fattest parts along the backbone. He seemed to crave fat more than meat. He had pains all over, but they had begun to lessen.

They moved on before daylight, down the dry bed of Carrizo Creek. Natalia rode a horse sidesaddle, on the off side, and Brodie and Joshua, with Brodie's foreman, Pedro, and half a dozen other Mexicans, rode mules. Others drove, while the Mexican women rode burros. They rode bareback and astraddle, managing to seem rather modest even though their brown legs were quite evident; they sat on the burros' hips, not in the middle of the animal.

They rested and fed the animals about midafternoon. "We hope to find water at the Big Lagoon," said Brodie. "If not, we'll be in bad shape to cross the desert."

In midafternoon they pulled up a long hill, and at the top of it Joshua reined in beside Natalia to wait for the wagons.

47

She turned to him suddenly. "It frightens me," she said. "It always frightens me."

"You've crossed it before?" he asked curiously.

"Yes—years ago, when Mother was alive."

"Your mother is dead?"

"*Sí*" She crossed herself. "It was the *vómito*—the yellow fever. She was on a trip to Vera Cruz with my father."

"Your mother was Spanish. Were they happy?"

"She and Father were very happy, I think."

"He looks like a man who would take good care of you."

"He has always done so—but the desert always frightens me. I have seen so many conquered by the sands and the sun—and lack of water."

He looked east, over a vast tableland of desolate, dead-brown waste, bleak and sterile, with a few tall, dead-looking ocotillos, dull-green creosote bushes, and dust-covered cactus low on the ground. There had been, in the hills, clumps of mescal and occasional bristling yuccas, whose narrow leaves ended in sharp spines that slipped into flesh easily but were hard to pull out. Where the wagons made the turn to leave the stream bed there was a small tree with bright-blue flowers, but he saw nothing as gay as that on the desert below them.

"What of your own family?" Natalia asked.

Joshua looked down at his brown hands, but his eyes did not see his long fingers. "I don't know much about them."

"Tell me—Joshua."

He stared at his hands without seeing them. "My father came out from Virginia in 1825," he said finally, "and took a claim in DeWitt's colony, near Gonzales."

"Is that in Texas?" she asked.

He glanced up quickly and then back at his hands. "Yes—east of Béxar. Then my mother went to join him, and they were married." He paused. "The Comanches hit them four months later. My father was killed and scalped, my mother taken captive."

"Oh!" she said, and added softly, "I am very sorry."

"I was born in a Comanche camp on the Staked Plains." Unexpectedly he felt strange, as if he had suddenly been brought face to face with a showdown that he had been avoiding—for he never had told anyone about his life before. But now he felt impelled to talk, and although it was hard to break a lifetime of silence, he was going to do it, for Natalia was listening. "My mother died. I never saw her. I was sold back to the whites three years later. I was raised by an uncle, and I found out he was the only kin I had."

"He wasn't good to you?" she asked perceptively.

"He raised me," Joshua said. "He saw that I was fed and clothed, and I'm grateful to him, for I was not his responsibility. Then he bound me as apprentice to a wagon-maker. It was a good turn, even though it was hard work, for a year later the Comanches came back and got his hair too."

"Then you were alone?"

He glanced at her. "It's a big world and there are many in it. I served in the Texas Rangers when I was sixteen; I traded with the Comanches out of Fort Smith; I served as scout for the Army; I was in the Mexican War; and then I came West in the gold rush."

He looked up. Her eyes were shining. "You have an exciting life!"

"No more than many others. No more than your father." He looked down the hill, where Brodie was helping the Mexicans hitch two extra yokes of oxen to a wagon. "How does he feel about you?"

She glanced at him sharply. "I think, since Mother is gone, he worries too much about me. I don't think that's good for him."

"He probably wants you to be happy."

"I don't think he can be happy *for* me."

Joshua remembered Brodie's reaction when Joshua had announced his intention of marrying Natalia, and Joshua began to see some of the problems he might encounter. Here was a well-to-do man who had married into a good Spanish family with ancestral lines that probably went back to the courts of ancient Castile, a widowed father with an only daughter—while he, the suitor, had no substance, no background; he was, in fact, a fugitive from the Army. Joshua wondered, now, that Brodie had not left him back at the springs.

But he had not been talking deliriously when he had announced his intention to many Natalia; he had meant every word of it. Her image had been in the back of his mind since he had seen her that morning on the Valdez ranch.

They were having trouble below, and he turned the mule, but Natalia's hand stopped him. "No, save your strength. We still have the desert ahead of us."

He touched her hand briefly and rode the mule down the hill. He was accustomed to doing his part. But the trouble was straightened out before he got there; one of the oxen had got on the wrong side of the chain, but Brodie hit one leg at a time behind the knee joint with his own knee, and pulled the chain under the ox's legs. Then Pedro cracked the long bullwhip, and the oxbows creaked and the chain snapped as the oxen moved forward, and finally the wagon itself began its slow journey uphill.

Back on top of the hill, Joshua saw faintly the outlines of mountains at a great distance to the northeast. South of them was Signal Mountain, a lone peak that Natalia said they used as a landmark. The road stretched away across the desert to the southeast, toward the far-famed Gila. This was not a desert of sand dunes, but rather of gravel, sand, and almost sterile soil that would not support anything but ocotillo, creosote bush, and cactus in very sparse growth.

Four miles down the slope they reached the Big Lagoon, a lake of slimy, brackish water that smelled of dead things. The water was warm, and unpleasant to the taste; the shore was muddy, like gelatin, and they had trouble watering the animals, but Brodie insisted.

He saw that the animals were given a feed of corn, and they all gathered around a fire of mesquite roots and ate a meal of mutton, chile, frijoles, skillet bread, and coffee.

"Drink all you can and fill the canteens," Brodie warned. "We're going on this evening. We'll travel all night and rest tomorrow during the heat; then tomorrow afternoon we'll pull out again and try to make the Colorado by daybreak."

"That sounds like a hard trip," said Joshua.

Pedro shook his head solemnly. *"Es malo—el desierto,"* he said.

"It isn't too bad," said Brodie, "if you're sure of water at all the wells—but some of them may be dry."

"In that case—"

"That's why we travel at night—to reach the river as soon as possible." Brodie went on. "How do you feel? Think you can make it?"

"I'm sore all over," said Joshua. "My hand is tender and I've still got a numb spot in my back. But I'll make it."

51

He got up slowly, using his right arm to steady himself, and studied the horizon to the southwest. It was sixty-three miles to the crossing at the Gila, and White presumably was there, probably with friends. There might be fifteen or twenty of them, and Joshua would have to lay better plans than he had laid at Carrizo Creek. He must have been afflicted with the simples anyway to think that he, armed with one bullet and a knife, could overcome three men. He wondered where White had picked up Carr and Prewett; if they were part of the crew at the Gila, or if they had been chance acquaintances. Whatever they were, they had been ready and willing to mutilate him.

He heard a step on the gravel behind him. Brodie's voice said, "I want to talk to you, Pickens."

Joshua turned. "It's your floor," he said.

Brodie squatted, his big hat shading his face, and pulled out a Querétaro cigar about three inches long. "Smoke?"

"No, thanks,"

Brodie broke a match off of a block and struck it on his trousers. He got the cigar going, and blew out a few puffs. "This man White you're after—is he the White who broke out of the Army jail?"

"Yes."

"You have any idea what you're headin' into?"

"They gave me a sample back yonder."

"Yeah." Brodie nodded vigorously. "But only a sample. These are bad hombres. You know who Glanton is?"

"The name sounds familiar, but I can't place him."

"Glanton is an ex-scalp-hunter. He was down at Chihuahua about 1838 hunting Apaches at a hundred dollar's a scalp—fifty for a squaw scalp—and he took

52

to killing friendly Indians and even Mexicans before the government got onto him."

"He sounds bad," Joshua admitted.

"He *is* bad. There's eight thousand dollars on his head. He's outlawed from Chihuahua and from Texas."

"I take it you're warning me."

"Yes—in a way. Also talking things over with you."

"Why?"

"I've got an interest in that ferry," Brodie said. "This Dr. Lincoln came out from Shreveport. I had met him there buying machinery for my factory, and I made him an offer to put up the money to build a ferry. He was to operate it and we were to divide half and half. I got one payment from him. Then Glanton and his men, run out of Chihuahua, sloped and followed the Maricopa Trail along the Gila until they hit the Colorado. They saw Lincoln had a good thing and they declared themselves in on it. I haven't had any money since then, so you see I have an interest in Glanton myself. Also, I wanted you to know the caliber of man you are up against."

"White is one of his men, then?"

"White went to San Diego to bank some money for him."

Joshua considered this. It made his problem a little harder.

"Nor is that the worst," Brodie said, rolling the cigar in his mouth.

"What's the worst?"

"Glanton deliberately lays for the Sonorans coming back from the mines. He not only extorts money from them for ferriage, but there are those who say he robs and kills them and throws their bodies into the river."

"Can't anybody catch him at it?"

"He has anywhere up to twenty men, all desperate

53

and armed to the teeth. No ordinary force of Mexicans can oppose him."

"How do you expect to get by him this time?"

"We're not going to cross at the ferry," said Brodie. "I have Natalia with me and I don't want a fight. We're going farther down. The Indians have boats and canoes down there, and we can float the wagons and swim the animals. I thought you should know this before we go any farther."

Joshua slowly flexed his left hand. He had been working the stiffness out of it. "All right," he said. "I'll go with you. You saved my life, and I'll help you across the river. After that—we'll see."

Brodie blew smoke in his face and Joshua looked up. He was astonished at the intensity of the blue eyes in the weather-beaten face. Brodie jerked his cigar over his shoulder.

Joshua stared. A horseman was coming down the trail less than half a mile away. At the same time, Joshua heard an exclamation from Pedro, and saw the Mexicans move together around the fire. Natalia looked out from one of the wagons. Pedro leaned over and picked up a rifle that was lying against the rear axle of a wagon.

But Brodie's hand was on Joshua's shoulder, and the power of his stubby fingers forced Joshua to face him. "I want you to know one thing, mister," said Brodie, "before we go a foot farther. Regardless of what happens at the Gila or any other time, no gold-field tramp is going to marry Natalia!"

Joshua stared at him. Brodie meant it. Joshua said slowly, "You might wait to see what happens."

"No matter what happens," Brodie said fiercely, "no matter—the likes of you won't marry my daughter.

54

She's all I've got left, and she's going to marry in her class. I would have told you this earlier, but I wasn't sure you knew what you were saying up there at the springs. But I've been watching you, Pickens, and now I'm warning you."

Joshua frowned. "I—"

Brodie got up. "We better go meet the newcomer," he said, and there was steel in his voice.

CHAPTER SIX

JOSHUA FOLLOWED BRODIE SLOWLY, THROWN INTO sudden turmoil by Brodie's edict. His first concern was over his own actions toward Natalia in the last couple of days. He had not touched her except to help her on and off her horse, but perhaps his feelings had been apparent to her father in his voice or his eyes, though he hardly thought so. Of course he had brashly announced his intention, but that had been under considerable strain, and although he had meant it, he had hoped that Natalia and her father would forget it so that he might later ask her hand with more graciousness. To that end he had been careful not to moon over her.

But Natalia herself? Had she been as reserved? The thought struck him with some force, and now he recalled her eyes on him from her horse, across the fire, at various odd times when it had almost startled him to find her observing him. It had been most pleasant and had created a glow that had grown so naturally and gently that he had responded to it without noticing it.

But Brodie had noticed. He had seen it and had not liked it, and he had spoken his mind; and for the first time Joshua realized how much the girl had come to mean to him in those few hours, because her father's outspoken opposition had saddened rather than angered him, and he had an unexpected feeling of loss at Brodie's warning.

Taking him unaware like that, Brodie had not left him much argument. Joshua pulled his hat down harder as he followed the older man across the gravel flat. Strange that he, who had been on his own for fifteen years and who never had been more than temporarily interested in any female, should suddenly feel that Natalia was the one he had to have. He'd heard about this but he'd never expected to feel it. He had thought love of this kind was a thing that happened to wet-eared young boys, not to men who had every reason to consider themselves grown up. But it had happened and there was no arguing with it. Now there was only one thing to do. He would find out for sure if Natalia felt the same way about him, and if so he would try to figure out how to win Brodie's friendship.

Brodie's crunching steps in the gravel came to a stop, and Joshua looked up. There was something familiar about the man on the horse, and Joshua tried to put his mind to it.

"Hello," said Brodie.

"Hello, mister. Mind if I get down?"

Brodie was studying him. "Sure. Get down. You from the Army?"

Joshua stared at the green pants and jacket—a rifleman's uniform. For a moment Joshua wished he had stayed back out of sight, but he knew automatically that it would not have helped, because this man in the Army uniform would be around for several hours, maybe longer.

"Josh!" said the newcomer.

56

"Bill! Bill Callahan!"

They shook hands, and Joshua introduced him to Brodie. Then he waited for the blow to fall, wondering what to do when Callahan tried to arrest him.

"I been ridin' hard to overtake you," Callahan told Brodie. "I almost caught you at Warner's, but my horse threw a shoe and I had to walk in."

Brodie looked at him and then at Joshua. "Why were you in such a rush to overtake us?" he asked.

Callahan hesitated.

Joshua said, "He knows what happened at San Diego."

Callahan rubbed the sweat from his horse's withers with his flat hand. "After White got away, Major Heintzelman raised the devil. He threw me in the guardhouse, saying that he felt sure I had something to do with it. I tried to tell him different, but he said it couldn't have been done without my knowledge. Also he claimed somebody told him that White had six hundred dollars in gold to buy his way out of jail."

Brodie looked narrow-eyed at Joshua.

"I told him I didn't know anything about it, and I didn't figure you as a deserter. So I talked him into letting me go after White. I figured he'd head back for the ferry, and I picked up his trail at Warner's." He looked curiously at Joshua. "You look like you had a run-in with a herd of buffalo."

"I found White."

Callahan seemed relieved. "I thought it must be something like that."

"White is at the Gila by now," said Brodie.

"I don't know too much about the desert," said Callahan. "That's why I was trying to catch you. Anyway, I understand you might meet Indians

57

anywhere from now on, and I figured we could help each other."

"You're welcome to come with us," said Brodie. "I see you're armed."

Callahan looked with satisfaction at the rifle in his saddle boot. "That's no Army single-shot, either. That's a Remington that shoots ten times with one loading."

"That might be useful," said Brodie. He lit a cigar. "You better water up and have a pot of frijoles. We're moving out in a little while."

"Glad to."

Joshua went with him to the muddy edge of the lake. "So you're after White," he said.

"That's my mission—but I admit I was a little surprised to run into you out here."

"Why?"

Callahan was removing the bridle. "I figured you'd head back to the gold fields. You was always talkin' about it."

"I owe White a visit," Joshua said.

Callahan kept a hand on the horse's rump as it took a step in the gluey mud. "You was free," he said. "They would never go lookin' for a common private."

"Anyhow," said Joshua, "we're both here, and we came for the same purpose. It ought to make it a little easier—two against twenty."

"Twenty!" The horse pulled back, and Callahan got a handful of mane. "I didn't know."

"They're twenty of the worst men in the West—scalp hunters."

Callahan whistled through sun-chapped lips. "It isn't goin' to be easy" he said.

"I never figured it was."

Callahan put the bit in the horse's mouth, and Joshua

58

liked the way he settled it in place without hitting the animal's teeth. "Listen, Josh, I been in the Army sixteen years, and I figured to stay out my old age."

"How about Juana?"

"Juana?" Callahan looked at him. "You sure remember the girl, don't you? Well, I figured I'd marry her when my term is up, just before I join up again. I might be a sergeant by that time, and I could have her on the post with me."

"In sixteen years," Joshua noted, "you haven't made sergeant?"

Callahan fastened the throat latch. "In sixteen years I been sergeant exactly sixteen times. I been busted so much they make out my papers back to private every time they promote me."

"Why do you get busted?"

"Mainly for not giving a damn. On the papers it says fighting, or drinking too much, or keeping a woman all night in the barracks." He winked. "Them things are hard for the Major to understand."

"So if you make sergeant, and marry Juana, what will happen if you get busted again?"

"I won't—not with Juana waitin' home for me."

Joshua broke a twig off a screwbean bush and studied it. "Does Juana make that much difference to you, Bill?"

"You can bet your life she does." He led the horse away from the mud and tied the bridle reins to a screwbean. "You bein' a young feller yet, you don't know how it is when a man gets ready to settle down." He untied the saddle straps from a tow sack and poured out a quart of shelled corn into his hat. He threw the sack over his shoulder and let the horse eat out of his hat. "But what I can't figure—I been in the Army sixteen years, and it's natural I wouldn't want to be a deserter, but you been in only a week. You could just as well—"

"Callahan," said Joshua, "I got personal reasons for wanting to take White back to San Diego."

Callahan nodded vaguely. "All right. You want us to do it together?"

Joshua grinned. "I said before, it would cut down the odds."

CHAPTER SEVEN

IT WAS TWENTY-SIX MILES TO ALAMO MOCHO OVER almost barren desert. The sun went down and gave some needed relief, for the animals suffered in the heat of the desert floor. They kept moving, men riding grimly, women silent, the wagons creaking, and the axles of the *carretas* screeching in the night. By daylight they reached the end of a sort of terrace. Thirty feet below them the desert started again, flat and barren. They camped on the edge. Below them, around a well, were bleached bones of cattle and horses—some only partly decomposed, others dried out and held together by iron-hard, tightly stretched hide. They stood on the edge of the cliff and looked out over the desolate scene. A broken wagon wheel had been thrown into a mesquite bush. A number of dead cottonwoods, now bleached gray by the sun, stood around the well. The surface of the desert seemed to be of clay, with a thin layer of dry sand, which the wind moved into ridges with a constant, mournful, rustling sound.

Callahan and Pedro organized the men to take the animals down to the well, and Joshua found a trail down the cliff. The well itself had been dug at the foot of the cliff to a depth of eighteen or twenty feet. Somebody had sunk a wagon box to keep the upper edges from caving in, and various nonmatching boards had been used beneath that. There was no bucket, and Joshua looked up at the wagons, thinking that it was going to be a considerable job to pull up water for all the animals.

He was astonished to see Natalia standing there watching him. "We'll need a bucket," he said, "and rope—and another bucket for the animals to drink out of."

She nodded, and disappeared with her characteristic quick movements. For a moment he listened to the rustle of the sand over the hard clay, and it seemed indescribably mournful. Then Natalia appeared with a bucket in each hand and a coil of rope over one shoulder. He met her and took them. "*Gracias,*" he said.

"*De nada.*"

He tied one end of the rope to the handle of the brass bucket and began to lower it into the well.

"I haven't seen you since yesterday afternoon," she said in a conversational voice.

He glanced at her. She was standing almost close enough for their elbows to touch, and this time her warmth and vitality seemed to radiate to him and create a glow under his skin. He took a deep breath and looked back into the darkness of the well. The sun was rising behind them, and presently the bottom of the well would be clearly visible. He said in a low voice, "Natalia, I meant what I said back there about wanting to marry you. I wasn't out of my head."

"I didn't think you were," she said.

He looked at her. The clear black eyes looked into his, and suddenly it was a moment of truth. He was a man and she was a woman, and she was ready to come to him when he asked her, and questions and answers were superfluous.

He crushed her against him and kissed her lips, and she was not passive. He heard the bucket hit the water below, but vaguely, and did not care. Her arms were around him. Then he heard Bill Callahan's parade-ground voice: "Look out below!"

He knew Callahan had seen them, and he released her immediately. Her lips were parted, and she seemed about to faint. He steadied her. "Natalia," he said, "I want you to know I am going to have you."

She nodded slowly.

"Your father doesn't want me for a son-in-law," he told her, "but I'll convince him. You'll see—and don't forget."

"I will not forget," she said. "I will wait until you convince my father. It will not be easy."

He grinned. "It may take a little longer, but wait." He dropped into the space formed by the wagon box, and then climbed down the sides of the well to get the rope. A small green lizard darted up the side, giving him a momentary start. He tried the water and found it warm and somewhat brackish, but there was plenty of it. He took the end of the rope and climbed up. For a moment Natalia was silhouetted against the cloudless morning sky as she watched; then Callahan's square, stocky shoulders appeared. "I can't water mules down there," he said.

"Don't be in a hurry. We've got all day." Joshua's voice echoed and re-echoed in the well.

He got to the top and pulled up the first bucket. Callahan handed it to Pedro.

"You're a deep one, Josh," Callahan said. "Here I'm telling you about women, and you already know."

"It was pretty sudden," said Joshua. "I wasn't too sure myself."

Callahan shook his head as he handed the empty bucket back to Joshua. "You don't need to wonder—after a kiss like that."

Joshua lowered the bucket until it hit the water, then gave it some slack so it would tip over.

"Only thing strikes me," said Callahan, "why did you have to pick on old Brodie's daughter? He's a big man in Sonora. How do you figure to break through the society rules and all? Them Spanish families don't change their ways in a million years."

"Natalia is willing," said Joshua.

"So I noticed," Callahan said dryly. "But I'll wager, Old Man Brodie would have at you with pistols at twenty paces if he knew that—or he'd horsewhip you."

Joshua pulled up the bucket. "So he gave me to understand."

"If you had any sense, you'd of fallen for a girl like Juana. Her pa will be proud to have me for a son-in-law because he'll figure he can live on me in a few years more."

"I like Juana," said Joshua, "and I think she'd make a good wife even if her whole family lives off you—but she isn't the one I saw first."

Callahan handed the bucket back. "Do it your own way, but mind what I said: Old Brodie is a tough nut to crack."

"I'll find a way."

Callahan grunted. "After watchin' you snatch a few seconds to improve your opportunities in the middle of the desert, I'm bound to say I think you can do it if *anybody* can—but I'm not sure anybody can."

"I'll find a way," Joshua repeated.

They got the animals watered, ate beans and mutton and drank coffee, and then disposed themselves in and under the wagons and carts to take advantage of the shade. Pedro stretched a piece of canvas between the wagons and crowded as many animals as possible under it. Then they settled down to a much-needed siesta.

Joshua was awake before noon. He rolled to a sitting position and pulled on his boots. He caught up a couple of mules and took them down to the well and began to pull up water . . .

They traveled along the edge of the upper terrace until about sundown. They reached the Mesquite Wells, and the dead bushes against a twilight sky looked like a dried-up swamp. There was no water there, but they rested the animals for an hour. They went on to Cooke's Wells, arriving a little after midnight, and found the well not dry but very low. The water was filled with fine clay in suspension, and the stock might have liked it, but there wasn't enough. Brodie nodded when they told him. "It's something you have to figure on when you cross the desert. You never can count on any of these wells. We'd best give the animals a breather and go on to the Colorado."

"How far is it?" asked Joshua.

"Fifteen miles as the crow flies." Brodie looked at him. There was no moon, but it was easy to make out a man's movements in the brilliant starlight. "It'll be five or six miles farther the way we're going." He paused. "Are you and Callahan going our way?"

"I am," Joshua said promptly.

"Me too," said Callahan, "if I can help."

"We may need lots of help at the Colorado," Brodie said grimly. "The Glanton band will be after us as soon as they hear we're coming."

64

"Maybe they won't know," said Callahan.

"They'll know," Brodie said, "as soon as daylight comes. They keep a man up on Pilot Knob—you'll see it in a little while—to watch for the dust that means travelers."

Joshua felt the handle of his knife just inside the top edge of his boot. Brodie saw the motion, and stared at him for an instant. Then he went to one of the wagons and came back with a six-shooter and a revolving rifle. "We have our own arsenal," he said, handing the weapons to Joshua. "In case you need them."

Joshua started to speak, then changed his mind and nodded instead. He examined the weapons, tried the cylinders.

"Here's ammunition," said Brodie. "You better load up."

Joshua bit off the end of a paper cartridge and poured the powder into a hole in the cylinder. He opened the other end of the cartridge and took out the round ball. Using a piece of the oiled paper as a patch, he pushed the ball in tight with the loading lever. He repeated this operation for all ten holes in the rifle cylinder. Then he loaded the six-shooter in the same fashion, and finally Brodie gave him a box of caps. In the meantime, all the men had been checking their arms and loading or reloading.

As the sun came up they saw Pilot Knob, standing up two or three hundred feet from the desert floor, and made out the green line of trees that marked the Colorado and its overflow area on each side—a comparatively narrow strip of land.

Joshua rode up alongside Brodie. "When do you look for trouble?"

"They'd have the best luck by catching us while

65

we're crossing," Brodie said a little anxiously. "I think it's good strategy to throw as many men as possible on the far side to act as guards."

"What if they come down this side?"

"They won't come this way, for then we'd only have to cross the river to get away."

Joshua nodded. Brodie knew his business. Joshua looked back at the little train. It seemed pitifully small to meet a force of desperate men like Glanton's. He looked at Callahan, and found him eying Pilot Knob, which seemed to be near the river. He looked farther back and saw Natalia. He caught her eye for a moment and then turned ahead.

They dropped down off the desert into the bottomland about two miles from the river. It was a different world. The bottomland was green with willow and cottonwood; the ground was laced with a network of *acequias* that the Yuma Indians used to irrigate small fields of corn, melons, and pumpkins.

Indians hurried out on burros to meet them, and tried to sell them food, especially runt ears of corn, which Brodie called maize. These Indians were dark brown, with glossy skin. They were well built, and the men wore breechcloths, the women short dark skirts only. The men's hair was braided in long rolls, the women's shorter, and cut straight across above the eyes; some of the women's faces were tattooed.

They gathered around Brodie with their ears of maize and their dried strips of pumpkin, shouting and holding out whatever poor item of food they could grab up from a donkey. To all of them Brodie shook his big head. He strode through them to stand on the bank of the Colorado, looking out over its red waters, his big black hat shading his eyes from the sun. He

66

looked upstream. As yet there were no dust spirals to indicate mounted men on the move. He turned back to the Yumas. "*Quil-hoh*," he said, holding up five fingers. "Canoe." He took cigars from his pocket. He pointed at the river and said "*Quil-hoh*" and held up five fingers again.

The Indians brightened and began to talk animatedly with one another. Their language was guttural and harsh and unpleasant to the ear. They came to an agreement, and one of them went up to Brodie. He tapped his chest. "I Macedon," he said, "chief. You want boat?"

Brodie looked at him levelly. "I know you're Macedon. I want boats—in hurry. Five boats."

"Five boats, five cans tobacco."

Brodie shook his head. "Five boats, two cans tobacco."

Macedon stared at him. He was a good-looking Indian, probably forty years old, intelligent. He turned to the others and they conferred while Brodie watched to the northeast.

"Can't you hurry them?" asked Joshua.

"It doesn't do any good," Brodie told him. "They've got a certain amount of rigmarole to go through. They'll take the offer, though, especially since there's been no wagon train through here for a week or more."

Callahan was watching upriver. "I hope it doesn't take them a week to decide."

Joshua studied the river. The surface was twenty feet below the overflow land.

"It'll come up in June or July," said Brodie, "and fill the channel and overflow this valley too—sometimes runs out on the desert."

"Then how do the Yumas raise a crop?"

"As soon as the water goes down, they come in and

start planting here, and they can raise as many crops as they want till next year."

An Indian broke away from the group and ran down a path to the water. Macedon, the chief, returned to Brodie and said gravely, "We take two tobaccos."

"All right." Brodie turned to Joshua and Callahan. His eyes were sharp, his voice gravelly: "Pickens, you and Callahan go across first. I'll send eight men with rifles to back you up. I'll keep Pedro to help with the wagons and stock." He looked suddenly at Joshua. "You scared?"

"Not yet," said Joshua.

"If I see dust, I'll try to arrange it so you'll have more men with you, but don't count on it. Eventually we'll have to use Pedro and his men to get the stuff across."

"I think we can hold them off," said Joshua, "but you'd better keep the women until the last."

Brodie nodded. "We'll get the wagons over first."

"How are you going to get them down to the water?"

"There's a little Indian town around the bend—Algodones, they call it—and for another couple of cigars I can get help. There's a slope there, and we can roll the wagons into the water. We'll empty the water kegs and use them for floats, and take the contents over in canoes."

"You got a couple of mules you can use to pull the wagons across?" asked Callahan.

"Yeah." Brodie chewed on a cigar. He looked up and saw the Yuma chief watching, and gave him one too. The chief grunted gravely and put the cigar in his mouth. Brodie held the match while the chief puffed. Brodie looked up at Joshua. "It's your responsibility on the other side," he said.

Joshua reassured him. "I'll do everything possible."

They used three canoes to take the ten men across. At the same time they were loading the other two canoes out of the wagons. The river was very wide, and it took some time to reach the other side. The ten men got out, and the Indians went back with the canoes. Callahan looked north. "We been spotted," he said.

It was getting toward noon, and the dust rising in the distance was only a thin haze against the brassy sky. Callahan had good eyes.

CHAPTER EIGHT

"How long have we got?" he asked Callahan.

"Couple of hours, my guess."

Joshua looked back across the river. "We can be almost across by that time."

"That would make it easier," Callahan said thoughtfully.

The goods were unloaded, and Joshua saw that they were piled in a flat place. One of the wagons came dripping out of the water, and Callahan put the Mexican guards to work loading it. Some of the Mexicans on the far side rode their animals across and led others by halter ropes. Some of the Yumas swam across and led animals.

"The old man is moving things," Callahan observed.

Joshua nodded. Now below the tower of dust he could see dark specks that were men on horseback.

The last *carreta* was launched into the current, tied behind a canoe. The weight of the cart pulled the canoe a little off course, but they landed a quarter of a mile below, and Brodie had an ox there to meet them.

"It's a good thing the river's no wider than it is," said

Callahan. "The rawhide that holds them carts together would stretch out and let the carts fall apart."

"They ought to use bolts," said Joshua.

"Bolts in Sonora?" Callahan snorted. "They'd cost more than the cart is worth."

Joshua took hold of a cart at one corner and shook it. "The rawhide *has* stretched out. This thing will fall apart in five minutes."

"With a load, yes," said Callahan. "But let that boiling sun keep on working, and the lashings will be tight as a drumhead again by the time we pull out."

Brodie came up, leading the ox that pulled the car. He shaded his eyes to look back across the river. The canoes were setting out with the women in them. Natalia was in the first one. Joshua looked northeast. The riders were less than a mile away. Joshua took the box of caps out of his shirt and saw that all the nipples of both revolver and rifle were capped. Callahan pulled the trigger of his Colt rifle back to half-cock and revolved the cylinder, being sure that it was loaded. Then he too capped the nipples and turned to face the riders.

Joshua looked around him. Brodie, looking as immovable and uncompromising as the Rock of Gibraltar, had in his arms a rifle like the one he had given Joshua, and two six-shooters in his belt. Callahan stood out in front in his green rifleman's uniform, Joshua to his left and a step back, Brodie to his right. Behind them were ranged eighteen or twenty Mexicans, black eyes sharp, their brown faces impassive beneath the great-crowned straw hats. They were armed with muzzle-loading flintlocks, and these were all freshly primed. None of the Yuma Indians was anywhere in sight.

The women, including Natalia, landed and gathered beside one of the wagons, watching the horsemen apprehensively. Pedro was supervising four Mexicans to finish loading and hitching up the teams.

Joshua could count the riders now—eight of them, all on good mules, all with six-shooters in belts or holsters, all with rifles held now over their left arms. Brodie took one step forward, and Callahan and Joshua moved with him.

The leader was the beady-eyed White. He pulled his horse up within twenty feet of Brodie, and his men pulled up silently behind him, spread out to each side. "Mister," said White, "maybe you ain't heard. We got a ferry up the river. Saves all this fooling around with the Indians."

Brodie answered in a hard voice, "I heard."

"You sound familiar," White said, and studied Brodie. "You was up here once before."

"I've been through here," said Brodie, "and I've used your ferry—and I paid through the nose."

A man behind White said, "That's Brodie from Sonora."

White looked harder, and his eyes narrowed. "Sure it is. He's the one complained about our charges and said he was half owner of the ferry. You'd think a man would patronize his own business, wouldn't you?"

Brodie kept still, holding his temper in check.

"And these here whites. You didn't have no escort like this when you come through before."

Brodie still didn't answer.

White looked insolently at Callahan. "You in the Army clothes. Ain't you the corporal at San Diego?"

Callahan didn't move.

White continued to take his time. His beady eyes

71

fixed on Joshua. "You look like you been beat up, mister."

"Hell!" Carr's sudden word was explosive. "That's the feller we left back at Carrizo."

White nodded slowly. "It sure is. I'd of thought the buzzards would of got him by this time."

Brodie stepped forward. "You want something, mister?"

Joshua brought his rifle into firing position, with the butt under his arm, and pulled the trigger back with the second joint of his thumb. He heard triggers clicking all around him.

White looked them over and decided on his play: He backed down. "I just come to find out why a man would rather swim the river than ferry it."

"You found out," said Brodie.

White straightened in his saddle. "Them two Army men—what are they here for?"

"They work for me," said Brodie.

White studied them, still insolently. Finally he nodded and wheeled his mule. He passed his men and spurred the mule into a lope. The men fell in after him.

When they were out of rifle range, Brodie turned around and lifted his hat and wiped the sweat from his forehead. "You two stood right firm," he said.

"Did you expect anything else?" asked Joshua.

"A man never knows for sure."

"You know now?"

Brodie suddenly smiled. "Sure."

"We'll just stand here for a little while until them coyotes get out of sight," said Joshua. "You go ahead and get your train started."

Brodie bawled; "Pedro! *Andele!*"

Pedro began to give orders in Spanish, and all those

back at the wagons and carts began to move around busily. The Mexicans who had been armed with rifles slowly dropped their weapons.

"Some of those hombres wanted to fight," Callahan observed. He glanced back, watching the Mexicans lining out the vehicles now. "Where do you and me stand now? White has seen us and he knows we're after him."

"It doesn't make it easy," said Joshua, "unless we can figure out a story."

"What kind of a story?"

"I don't know yet." He glanced at the fiery sun and then north toward Pilot Knob. "But we'd better be at it." Now that the outlaws had left, the Yuma Indians reappeared from hiding places in the willows and mesquite bushes and down under the bank. Brodie paid Macedon the tobacco agreed on, and the chief smiled and said gravely, "*Gracias, Captián.*"

Brodie nodded brusquely and turned to Callahan and Joshua. He looked at the column of dust, growing fainter in the northeast, and frowned. "I got an uneasy feeling about them," he said. "They know who I am, and they might try to get rid of me to be sure I won't come back to claim my share of the ferry money."

"We'll stay here with the Yumas and see they don't come after you," said Joshua.

"I got a better idea," said Brodie. "You two come with us across the desert to Sonoita. It's Apache country between here and there."

"It's Apache on the other side, too, isn't it?" asked Joshua.

Brodie studied him with unreadable eyes. "I know the people on the other side. I can get plenty of men to guard the train. But it's between here and there I'm

73

worried. This stretch of desert is within striking distance of Glanton's men."

"How could they leave the ferry that long?"

"Half a dozen of them, headed by White, might go, if they can make a deal with one of the Apache chiefs."

"Why Apaches?" asked Joshua. "I thought Glanton was hunting Apache scalps out of Chihuahua."

"There are a lot of different Apache tribes," said Brodie. "And any of them would make a deal with any white to get another white's scalp."

"Then you think there's a chance White will join up with some Apaches and attack you between here and Sonoita?" asked Joshua.

Brodie looked hard at him. "So strong that I'm willing to offer you that rifle and pistol and the mule you're riding to go that far with us."

Joshua nodded. "All right with me."

Brodie turned to Callahan. "The same deal with you?"

"All right with me."

"You're hired. Let's move out. Be sure your canteens are full. It's forty-five miles to the Tinajas Altas. That's the first water."

"Maybe we ought to wait till afternoon," said Callahan. This sun is pretty hot."

"It's inviting trouble to stay here. We've got to get out of sight as soon as possible. We'll rest toward evening and reach Tinajas Altas by daylight tomorrow."

Callahan shrugged. "You're running it."

Pedro and Brodie led out to the southwest, Brodie watching for a sign of Apaches. Callahan and Joshua brought up the rear, and Natalia dropped back for a moment on her horse. "You are very brave men," she said, looking at Joshua.

"We're gettin' paid for it," said Callahan.

Joshua thought it remarkable that she could retain her freshness and vitality in the heat and under the sun. "It's not hard to be brave when I'm watching out for you," he said.

She blushed very prettily, and rode up toward her father.

A moment later Callahan said, "You made a good appearance with the girl and you made a good show with Brodie—but what do you do next?"

"Something will turn up," Joshua said, watching her ride away.

The sand was heavy and white and so fine that the wagon wheels sank into it almost a foot, and made the going very slow. Brodie shifted teams and put all the oxen on one wagon and all the mules on the other. He had twelve oxen in one team, ten mules in the other. Most of the men were walking. The wagons were not overloaded, but the fine sand provided a heavy drag.

By midafternoon they were through the fine sand and into a portion of the desert with a firmer base; the sand was coarser, and the wheels did not sink so deep. But the mules were beginning to balk.

"And when a damn' mule quits," said Brodie, "he quits for good."

They stopped under the burning sky to let the animals rest. Brodie opened water kegs and gave every animal a cupful of water. "People can wait," he growled. "There'll be water at Tinajas Altas—but we won't get there if the stock plays out."

North of them was a mountain ridge, the Sierra de la Gila, Brodie said. "The Maricopas live northeast of that, along the Gila."

"You're not afraid of the Maricopas or Pimas?" asked Joshua.

"Never had trouble with either of them. It's only the Apaches in here you got to worry about."

Before dark they saw a mountain ahead of them in the distance. "That's the Tinajas Altas," Brodie said. "There's eight springs, one above the other, and there's always water in some of them. You see any sign of the Glanton outfit?"

"Not so far," said Joshua. "Do you think there's any danger now?"

Brodie nodded. "There's danger clear to Sonoita. They can follow up the Gila and cut across the desert ahead of us. Horseback, they can get there a lot sooner than we can."

They stopped again at midnight to rest the stock and give them one more drink, and again Brodie would not allow the humans to have water.

"He's a tough old cuss, ain't he?" said Callahan.

Joshua shrugged in the starlight. "You don't get the best of these deserts and the Apaches by being easy."

The sun was not in sight but it was light as full day when they pulled up to the base of the mountain. The mountain itself was barren, but at its fringes grew some fire bushes and a few green-barked acacias.

Joshua's mouth was leathery. He climbed with Brodie up to the first water hole, and found it empty. The second and third were likewise dry. Brodie began to look worried. The fourth, fifth, and sixth were damp, but did not contain water. The seventh was dry. Brodie took off his hat. "It'll have to be the top one," he said. "There's always water in it, but it's hard to hand it down. It'll take quite a while."

"Don't worry," said Joshua. "Send up Pedro and a

few men with buckets. Callahan and I will see that it gets down."

Joshua found the spring, sank his face into the cool water, and took a little in his mouth. By the time Pedro came up, he had swallowed a little.

Callahan clambered up beside him. "Thought I'd wet my whistle and take a look out over the desert for dust clouds," he said.

Joshua handed down the first bucket of water. "Would you look for it from behind?"

"What d'you mean?"

"They had plenty of time to head us off. Would you look for them to come across the desert in plain sight?"

"You mean if they're after us, they're already ahead of us?"

"Yes—or right here in the mountains."

Callahan stared at him. "You find sign?"

Joshua watched Pedro's back. "This is the only water hole within sixteen miles, according to Brodie—but when we came up here we didn't scare away a coyote or a bird or even a lizard."

Callahan turned white. "My God!" he said. "And I left my rifle at the wagon."

Pedro turned back with an empty bucket, and Joshua sank it in the water. "You'd better get it," Joshua said in a conversational tone, "and come back up here."

For himself he made sure that all caps were in place on his two firearms, and kept a sharp watch until Callahan scrambled back up the rocks. "Take a spot up there by the big cactus," Joshua said, "and sing out if you see anything."

"If they're here," said Callahan, "they should have jumped us before we reached the water."

Joshua agreed. "They should have, but it's hard to

77

tell. They might have sent a couple of Indians ahead to scout."

"You sure it wasn't whites at the water hole?"

Joshua nodded. "Nothing but an Apache could water without leaving any sign at all that I could read." He took an empty bucket. "It may be nothing," he said. "It might be a few Indians scared away by us." He shrugged. "Whatever it is, you can bet Apache eyes are watching us now."

Callahan nodded slowly. "I'll walk up that way." He looked at Joshua thoughtfully. "You been in Indian country before," he said.

Joshua, handing a bucket of water to Pedro, nodded. "You might say I have—in the Nations and on west to Comanche country."

"You never told me that."

Joshua took an empty bucket handed up from Pedro. "What was the need? This isn't Indian Territory."

Callahan went on and stood beside a mescal bush with his rifle held across his left forearm. Joshua saw that his own rifle was within arm's reach. He continued to hand down water, but it worried him that nothing happened. There were Indians somewhere in the mountains. Why weren't they attacking? Could it be that the Indians were just a few—a hunting party—or could it be that White was still trying to make a deal with them, perhaps smoking a pipe and going through the necessary protocol of a conference?

There seemed to be no immediate answer. Perhaps it was something he hadn't even thought of.

He looked out over the desert to the north. The white surface of the sand and gravel reflected the sun almost like a mirror; there was hardly a blade of grass anywhere, and only a scattered, sickly growth of cactus.

Nowhere did he see birds, not even a buzzard. To the north and east were low mountains, now hardly more than purple shadows in the glaring heat of the sun, and back toward the northwest were the tracks of their wagons and stock, a lonely trail into nowhere, and already fading out, for the wind had come up strong during the morning, and even now was filling in the indentations made by wheels and feet. In a few hours there would be no sign of their passage.

He was startled by Natalia's soft voice: "Joshua, is there plenty of water for everyone?"

He saw her tin cup, and knew she had come up the path merely to speak to him. He looked at her and wished he could take her in his arms, but instead he said, "I'll be happy to get water for you." He took the cup, reached far out under an overhanging rock shelf, dipped up cool water that had not been disturbed, and watched her drink. She emptied the cup and handed it back to him. "My father has told you that I may not marry you?"

Joshua leaned over to refill the cup. He could see her reflection in the water, and he hesitated to dip the cup into the surface, for it would destroy the image. "He told me that," he said, and filled the cup with as little disturbance of the water as possible.

She took the cup and held it in both hands while she looked into his eyes. "He has not asked me how I feel about it."

He was still on one knee. "I can understand that. You're his daughter—his only daughter—and he wants what is best for you."

Her voice was low and sweet, and her words indicated that she was self-possessed. "He did not ask me what I want."

He stood up. "It is not Spanish custom to ask the daughter whom she wants to marry."

"I am only half Spanish," she reminded him. "Besides, in a Spanish family the mother has much to say. In our family there is no mother."

Pedro handed up an empty bucket, and Joshua took it. "Pay attention to your father and do what he says." He grinned. "But don't be surprised to see me pop up in Hermosillo."

Her hand touched his shoulder as he knelt to fill the bucket. "I am not surprised at anything you do, Joshua."

He stood up. "You're ahead of me. There are plenty of times I can't figure out myself."

She went back down the steep trail. He watched Pedro give her a hand. She jumped lightly from one rock to another, and finally, as she reached the ground, she turned and waved briefly. He raised one hand with a bucket in it, and then knelt to fill it. At that moment a small round pebble rolled across the rocky surface and into the water.

CHAPTER NINE

HE LOOKED UP INSTANTLY. CALLAHAN WAS PEERING up the mountain but holding one hand behind him, fluttering his fingers.

Joshua seized his rifle and watched the horizon.

Pedro's voice came from below. "The water, señor?"

Joshua handed him the bucket without taking his eyes from the rocks above. "How much more do you need?"

"Not much, señor. The animals have been watered, and half of the kegs are filled."

"How far is it to the next water?"

"It is six leagues to the Tinajas del Tule."

"Eighteen miles," Joshua reflected. "The train can be there before midnight—if it gets there at all."

"But, señor, we cannot keep driving the stock. We must—"

"You can if your scalp is at stake," Joshua said harshly. "Tell Brodie to move on quick."

Pedro began to make his way down the mountainside, sliding a little on the black rock. Joshua saw Callahan standing sidewise behind the cactus, to present a smaller target. Joshua looked up and saw what might have been a center stalk of yucca—except that yucca at that time of the year should have had flowers, if not fruit. He felt short of breath as he brought up the rifle, quietly pointed it at the apparent yucca, and pulled the trigger back to cock it.

Callahan's hand was no longer fluttering. Callahan was not looking in the same direction, but he had brought his rifle to his shoulder.

Joshua watched the yucca stalk grow slowly taller. He let out his breath and took in another, and sighted along the rifle barrel. The head of an Indian appeared over the rock, and in that instant Joshua fired. The Indian, his face gruesomely smashed by the heavy bullet, still had vitality enough to reach for his knife, and then sprawled lifeless over the rock.

For a little while there was no sound anywhere. Up on the mountain there was no sign of life. Then, seeming to materialize out of nowhere, a buzzard circled in the brassy sky far above the dead Apache.

Joshua cocked the rifle again and waited, watching the rocks above. He was fairly well protected on his right side, but up yonder, anywhere to the left, would be trouble, for the mountain was broken and rocky and offered cover. On the right it was open and flat, and no Indian liked that kind of fighting.

Down below, Joshua heard Brodie's subdued voice giving orders to Pedro, and presently Brodie's Mexicans, covered by the wagons and carts, were waiting silently with their flintlocks. The women were not to be seen.

The sun blazed down like a searing iron, and the blood from the dead Apache's smashed head ran down the black rock on which he lay. Most of the rivulets dried up on the hot stone before they reached the ground, but big blue-headed flies appeared, buzzing like bumblebees, and darted erratically about the rock. And still there was no sign of human life on the mountain except for Callahan, who had not moved.

Joshua spent a moment appreciating Callahan's poise, for he had not jumped at all when the rifle sounded behind him, and if he had looked at the dead Indian, it had been by movement of his eyeballs only, for his head had not turned, and his rifle was still in firing position.

Joshua became aware that a hot wind was blowing up from the desert, and he glanced at the sky. Nowhere was there a cloud, and down on the desert even the prickly pear seemed gray and drooping under the increasing heat of the sun.

He heard sounds below, but did not look down. Callahan was sighting along the rifle. From where he was, Joshua could not see the target, but the rifle crashed. Callahan did not move from his position. Another Apache must have found the big chunk of lead too much for even his savage soul.

There were steps below now, and Joshua recognized Brodie's boots. He continued to watch the rocks until Brodie's voice sounded below him. "Indians?"

"So far."

"Any sign of the whites?"

"Not yet."

"Do you think they're here?"

Joshua said, "Of course they're here. The Apaches wouldn't attack us two on their own. We've got no horses—nothing but rifles and pistols."

"Maybe our train is too big for 'em."

"Maybe so. And maybe somebody has paid them to keep Callahan and me pinned down up here while the whites attack the train below."

"Why didn't they wait till you and Callahan got down?"

"They intended to, but we wouldn't let them. Now we've killed two Apaches and the rest of the band are trying to convince White that we're bad medicine. But White doesn't give a damn how many Indians we kill. All he wants is a clear shot at the train."

Brodie stood with his rifle across his arm and watched the rocks. "What next?"

"The logical thing is for us to retreat from the water hole and leave the path wide open. Then White and his men, along with the Indians, can pour down on the train from here. You'll be forced to move whether you're ready to or not, and as soon as most of the hands are busy with the wagons and stock, White will attack. The way he's got it figured, it will be a short fight. They'll kill all the men, give the horses and mules to the Apaches, and drive the oxen back to the Gila crossing to sell to the emigrants, along with the wagons and goods. And he'll also be rid of you and me and Callahan."

Brodie moistened his lips. "And the women?"

Joshua said harshly, "There can be only one answer to that, and you know what it is. No matter who takes them—Indians or whites—the answer is substantially the same."

Brodie turned white around the mouth. "I'll send Pedro on with the train. I'll stay up here with you and Callahan and hold them off."

"No," said Joshua. "They expect us to go back down the mountain and leave the trail clear—but we won't. You go down there and get the train started. Let the women do the driving. Let the men be ready to fight—in any direction. Have you noticed the mountain up ahead?"

"Yes."

"It's quite a ways before there's any place for an ambush, and by that time the trail leads out into the desert. Callahan and I will stay here and keep this trail plugged until you get out of range of the mountain."

Joshua saw Callahan's hand fluttering again, and he looked up to a new spot against the sky. Callahan was covering that one, so Joshua scanned the rest of the horizon before answering. "The Apaches will never make a frontal attack in the desert." His voice was grim. "And by the time we get through with them here, they won't follow you."

"But—"

"It's obvious that White hasn't got enough men of his own to make a frontal attack. If he had, one side or the other would all be dead. So when he loses the Indians he loses the fight."

"Sharp figurin'," said Brodie.

"All right!" Joshua whispered hoarsely. "Get down there and get the train moving!"

"You and Callahan will be alone."

"We're all right. We've got the water hole."

"I'll get the train to Sonoita," Brodie decided. "Then I'll come back and relieve you."

"Don't worry about it." Joshua grinned. "I'll meet you in Hermosillo sometime."

Brodie faced him squarely. "You're takin' a big risk," he said.

Joshua patted the rifle. "We got paid for it."

Brodie shook his head. "I never paid you for making a suicide stand like this."

"It's no suicide stand," said Joshua. "As you can see, we're better than holding our own." He stopped as Callahan's rifle crashed again. "I think he missed him that time, but he's keeping them down."

"I'll stay here and guard the trail," said Brodie.

Joshua turned on him. "Old man, don't be a fool! That's what they want you to do! Get down there and organize your men. Get the train moving! Get away from this mountain!"

Brodie frowned. "You and Callahan—"

"Bill and I are old Indian fighters. We know what we're doing. Now you get the hell out of here."

He turned his back on Brodie, and presently heard the man going down the trail. He heard muffled orders. Then Pedro appeared on the trail below with a small cloth sack. "Señor Brodie has said I should give to you this food," he said.

"Toss it up," said Joshua, "and keep your head down."

Pedro tossed but he forgot to keep out of sight. A rifle cracked up above. It was an Indian's rifle, for the sound was flat and indicated a short charge of powder, but the bullet hit its target, and Pedro, with blood spurting from his jugular vein, pitched forward on his face. For a moment he held his place; then his muscles lost their strength, and his body rolled over and over until it hit the bottom with a dull crunch.

Joshua stayed back in the protection of the overhanging rock. "Maybe that'll start 'em up," he said aloud.

He heard screams from the women, and then the tense silence that meant they had been ordered to keep still. Joshua reached out with his rifle, hooked the front sight in the sack, and pulled it toward him. Another shot came from above and the bullet kicked up splinters of rock that raked Joshua's hands, but he got the sack into the protection of the overhanging cliff. That was the least he could do. A man had died bringing that food; he'd try to use it to advantage.

The screech of dry axles arose from below, and he knew that at last the train was moving.

The fire from above became hotter. Bullets began to clip the cactus that protected Callahan, and Joshua yelled at him, "Come on back, Bill. There's too much lead up there. I'll cover for you."

Callahan looked back to gauge his way, then ran, doubled over. Three shots kicked up rock around him, but Callahan got there without being touched. In the meantime Joshua kept them down by firing at them when he saw them.

"Now," said Callahan as soon as he got his breath, "what do we do?"

"Fight a delaying action."

"How about ammunition?"

"I'm about out—unless Brodie put some in with the grub."

Callahan opened the sack. "Fifty rounds," he said with satisfaction. "You better load up while I watch."

"Don't mind if I do. You can't kill these redskins with rocks."

They stayed close to their cover. The men up on the

mountain, out of sight, must have been displeased over the turn of events, for there was quite a bit of shooting for the next half hour, but Callahan and Joshua answered it only often enough to keep the Apaches from rushing them. The dead one still lay across the rock, and now there were half a dozen buzzards in the sky, gliding, waiting.

The sun was enough to broil a man's brains, but they were lucky to have plenty of water. They ate some dried beef from the sack, and the afternoon went on. Shooting slowed down, but the two men did not relax their vigilance. Heat rose from the desert in visible waves, and the black rocks, where they were not shaded, were too hot to touch.

Callahan began to worry. "I don't like the way they've stuck to us so long."

"I don't either," said Joshua. "Ordinarily they'd have dropped us as soon as the wagons pulled out."

"Of course they've got a dead man up there."

"That wouldn't keep them at it so long. The Apaches have left plenty of bodies in spots like this." He scanned the horizon constantly. The sun now threw the rocks in relief, so that any motion at all could be seen.

"What happens when it gets dark?" asked Callahan.

"I don't know. I never saw an Indian that wanted to fight in the dark, but with White and his outlaws behind them, it's hard to tell what might happen. White wants to get rid of us. He knows we're after him, and he aims to stop us."

They ate some more of the beef. "You think Brodie will come back?" asked Callahan.

"He'll come back, all right," said Joshua, "but he won't make it in time to do us any good."

"What are we goin' to do?"

"We've got water. We can stay here as long as they can."

"And then what?"

Joshua shook his head. "That's a bridge I'll cross later. But we should be able to—"

He never finished that remark, for now it was twilight, and without any signal that the two men could discern, bullets began coming regularly from above, digging furrows in the rocks around them, showering splinters over the water hole.

Callahan nodded. "They're going to risk it."

"I'll believe that when—Callahan, *look out!*"

He pushed the man violently, and Callahan fell back into the water, instinctively holding his rifle up to keep it dry. Joshua flattened against the rock. Bullets coming from their right now were biting at the exposed corner of the overhanging rock. "Stay in there," shouted Joshua. "It's the only place you've got cover."

The sounds of rifles grew closer.

"They've got us pinned down," Joshua said. "White is going to rush us from the right!"

Callahan whirled. A little geyser spouted up from the water hole. Callahan threw himself flat and started shooting across the edge of the spring.

Joshua had drawn in against the rock, but now he saw five men running across the open space—scattered out, bent low. Joshua brought his rifle around to fire. Then he remembered the Apaches at their backs. He jumped across the open space to a position where he could watch both approaches. He reached a rock and slid down. It was almost dark, but he saw the Apaches coming down from above, silently.

He fired, standing, and fired again. Then he dropped down for a moment, not wanting to give the five whites too good a shot at him. He raised up to shoot again, and an Apache was waiting for him. He saw the long barrel pointed at him and saw the yellow flash. He felt a jerk at his scalp, and fought for an instant to retain consciousness. He stood up involuntarily, and another bullet sprayed splinters of rock in his face. The blackness increased. He shook his head. Dimly in his mind he heard the firing of the five attackers and Callahan's steady return. The sound of Callahan's shots changed to a louder boom, and he knew Callahan had emptied the rifle and had switched to the pistol. He felt himself falling backward, and shouted, "Bill!" He was not entirely unconscious, but for a moment he couldn't find his balance, and in that moment he fell backward and began to roll down the rocks.

He hung onto his rifle, and threw up his hands to keep from hitting his head on a rock. He rolled from back to stomach, with his body roughly horizontal. He crashed through a clump of *palo verde* and thumped into a bed of soft sand on his back. The jar knocked the breath out of him for a moment. He heard somebody yell from above, and the shouts of White telling Callahan to surrender. From that he judged that Callahan had driven them back.

He tried to get up but found himself unable to move his legs. He couldn't see the water hole from where he was, but he thought a few shots might scare the Apaches back. He tried to pull back the trigger of the rifle but discovered it was broken off. He remembered the pistol and his hand darted to his hip. The pistol was still there. He jerked it out, held it in the air, and fired it.

CHAPTER TEN

FOR A MOMENT THERE WAS SILENCE ABOVE. THEN HE heard scrambling, and realized it was almost dark. Maybe he had been knocked out for a little while. A body landed beside him. He heard boots grate on sand, and Callahan's guarded voice. "Pickens!"

"Yo!" said Joshua.

"How you comin'?"

"Scalp crease, I think."

"Nothin' else?"

"Not that I know of."

Callahan was breathing hard. "I run 'em back, and the Apaches quit when it got dark. I think we're all right till morning."

"You hit?"

"Not a scratch."

"We've got nowhere to go," said Joshua. "We're in for it."

"Maybe not." Callahan stopped to listen for sounds from above. "They aren't going to come after us in the dark down here, because they don't know where we are. My guess is they'll watch the water hole until the sky lightens in the morning, and then if we don't try to get back to it, they'll go back to the Gila. So about the time the sun comes up, you and me will go back up to the water hole."

"Then what?"

He could sense Callahan's shrug. "Well, we still haven't got our man, but I figger that will take some doin'. Maybe we'd better head out for the next water hole toward Sonoita. We'll have to travel on foot, though. If Brodie left any stock for us, the Apaches have run it off by now."

"Brodie's outfit ought to be at the Tule by now."

"Yeah." Callahan made motions in the dark, and Joshua heard him tearing off the end of a paper cartridge with his teeth. Callahan finished reloading and got up on his feet. "I'll leave the sack here with you. If anybody comes down from the water hole, give 'em hell. Meantime, I'll he scoutin' around on both sides. Don't pay no attention to shots. I'm going to try to make 'em think we're all over the desert so they won't spend too much time lookin' for us tomorrow."

"All right."

Joshua lay there a while. Then he reached the sack and reloaded the six-shooter. The balls were too small for the pistol, but he put them in fairly tightly by using two thicknesses of oiled paper. Then he lay on his back in the sand and listened.

It was very quiet in the desert. Somewhere in the far distance he heard the bray of a mule, and guessed it had come from one of White's animals. He was lying where he had a good view of the pole star, and so could judge the time, and about ten o'clock he heard a cautious movement above him. Using extreme care, he got himself in position to fire the six-shooter in the direction of the water hole.

The sound ceased, but presently it came again, and he knew it was a white man, for an Apache moving anywhere in the dark was like a buzzard in the sky— making no noise and leaving no trail. He braced his right wrist with his left hand and waited. The sound came lower, but still he did not fire. Then the man dropped his caution and scrambled down the rest of the way like a horse rolling in dry salt grass. He hit the

91

bottom and stood up. Joshua did not move. The newcomer took a step, and Joshua, timing his aiming movement with the gritty grind of leather on gravel, drew a careful bead on the center of the dark shadow, rather high, and pulled the trigger.

The explosion sounded loud in his ears, and echoed two or three times. The man balanced for a few seconds, then went limp and dropped almost on himself, falling a little to his right, one arm twisted under him so that his elbow grazed Joshua's face. Joshua pushed him as far away as he could, and then lay waiting.

He didn't know how Callahan would interpret the shot, and he couldn't help him. He lay there for half an hour, listening. Then he heard steps on the sand, and turned his pistol in that direction. When the man was about twenty feet away, a whisper came: "Josh!"

"Yo," answered Josh, relieved.

Callahan stumbled over the body. "So that's what you shot." He felt the man's chest. Dead, too—and messy. Who is he? You musta got him through the lungs."

"I aimed to."

"He's got whiskers, so he's no Apache. One of White's men." Callahan sat down by Joshua's head.

"You sound winded," said Joshua.

"I been halfway around the mountain."

"Find anything?"

"Found the mules. They left a guard with 'em, and I slipped a knife between his ribs and helped myself to a couple. I couldn't tell what they were like in the dark, but they sure won't be any worse than Army horses."

"Where are they now?"

"About a half a mile to the south, tied to a *palo verde*. We can be there in a few minutes, and by daylight we can be at the next water hole."

"It's a good idea," said Joshua. "Why didn't you bring them all the way?"

"They'd hear me up there"—Callahan gestured toward the water hole—"and rush us for sure. That's one thing we don't want—a rush."

"It's good figuring," said Joshua quietly, "but there's one thing wrong with it."

"What's that?"

"That half mile—it might as well be a thousand."

Callahan sounded alarmed. "What d'ye mean? Are you hit in the leg?"

"That fall down the mountain did something to my back. That old bullet aches like sin now, and it must have done something to me, because I can't move my legs."

"You mean—paralyzed?"

"I can't lift them at all. No feeling in them."

"Judas!" said Callahan. "You been holdin' the fort in pretty good shape for a man without legs."

"What else could I do?"

Callahan thought about it a while. "We've got to do something before daylight. They've got the water hole."

"You couldn't bring the mules up here?"

"Nope." Callahan was positive. "Them two shod mules sound like a company of dragoons on this hard desert."

"You could help me."

"I'm scared of that," said Callahan, "but I don't know what else to do."

"You didn't see any sign of Brodie, did you?"

"No. I think he got away clean."

Joshua relaxed, back on his elbows. Then Natalia would be safe.

"I run into some other Indians, though, in a little valley. Don't know what kind they are, but they aren't Apache."

93

"It could be they came from the Gila."

"Don't know what they'd be doing down this far."

"If not," said Joshua, "they must have come up from Sonora."

"No matter," said Callahan. "They ain't doing us any good, and it's worth a man's life to ask help from a strange bunch of Indians down here."

"I heard some are good Indians," said Joshua.

"You heard wrong," Callahan told him. "Injuns are all bad." They were still talking in whispers. "Well, I reckon I better get you up out of that sand. Maybe we can make it to the mules."

He got one arm around Joshua's back, and his shoulder under Joshua's left arm. Joshua held on, and Callahan lifted. Joshua's legs were like dead weights, and they dragged across the hard gravel with a scraping sound that was chillingly loud in the night.

Joshua said, "We'll never make it, Bill. They'll hear this and they'll know one of us is hurt, and they'll be down like an eagle on a young pullet. You better leave me and get away while you can."

"No." Callahan walked heavily under the weight of Joshua's body, but the worst giveaway was the dragging sound of Joshua's legs. It seemed to reverberate from the hard desert surface as from a drumhead. Callahan stopped to rest. "Maybe I *should* of brought up the mules."

Joshua shook his head. "Either we get by with it or we get caught, and there's nothing. Let me down quick!"

"What's the matter?"

"They're coming down from the water hole," Joshua said grimly. "Let me down so I can shoot."

Callahan listened. The men coming down the

94

mountain were whites and they were taking no great pains to hide their movements.

"They heard it," said Joshua. "They know—and they're coming in for the kill."

Callahan flopped on his stomach beside Joshua. "We can make it hot for 'em in the dark."

Joshua reached over. "Let me see your rifle."

"Sure." Callahan let him take it.

"You've got your pistol now?"

"Yeah."

"Then get the hell out of here!" Joshua said harshly. "My rifle's no good. The trigger's broken. Leave your rifle here and I'll cover you."

"You're crazy!" said Callahan.

"I'm using sense. We can't both get away—but one of us can."

"I ain't movin'," said Callahan.

Joshua shoved the muzzle of the rifle in his side. "Get going before I pull the trigger."

Callahan laughed. "You're talkin' through your hat, Pickens. Anyway, I outrank you."

They listened for a moment to the shuffling of boots on rock. Then somebody reached the bottom and stumbled over the dead man's body. There were muffled oaths. Somebody lit a match. "It's Prewett," said White. He kicked the body. "I was hopin' it was one of them Army bastards."

Joshua, sighting along Callahan's rifle, pulled the trigger, and the man holding the match shuddered and threw it into the air with a curse.

White shouted, "Scatter! We got 'em cornered!"

Joshua heard the sounds of their boots as they spread out. As near as he could figure, there were only three of them. If the Apaches had come down the mountain,

Joshua could not hear them. It didn't make much difference. If the Apaches came, you wouldn't hear them anyway—not until you felt a knife between your shoulder blades. But it was better than an even guess that the Apaches were not taking part in this phase of the attack, for no Apache wanted to die at night and have his soul wander through darkness for eternity.

He heard Callahan rolling over and over to change his position, and now he wished he had not taken Callahan's rifle.

The three attackers were spread out and probably surrounding them. Joshua heard Callahan's clothing rub against the gravel, and knew Callahan was moving to face their rear. He kept his head low and watched for a shadow against the stars.

Then the wounded man began to groan. "Water!" he said. "I got to have water!"

There was no answer from the blackness of the desert. Then Joshua heard the movement of rough clothing, and a rock landed some distance away and skidded across a hard patch into soft sand, where its sound ceased abruptly. White's hard voice sounded. "None of them tricks, Callahan."

Callahan fired at the voice. A rifle on Joshua's left blazed at Callahan, and Joshua squirmed around and fired at the blaze, then lay flat.

For a few seconds the desert erupted in flame and thunder. White fired at Joshua, and the bullet went over his head with a dull crack. Callahan fired at White, and the man on the right fired at Callahan. Joshua, now on his elbows again, fired at the man on the right. White and the man on the left fired together, and Callahan fired at White and rolled. Each flash appeared through a cloud of white smoke, and every man was moving but Joshua. He held his fire until he saw flame, but this was shooting in the dark, and nobody was likely to get hit. Bright globes of yellowish-red flame exploded, and bullets ricocheted from the desert and whistled off across the sand.

There was another burst of firing, with all of them still moving but Joshua. He saw that Callahan was working rearward toward the mules, and so held his fire and watched for the best shots possible.

The firing slowed down, and long periods went by without a shot. Joshua sensed the three men were moving slowly after Callahan, and held his own fire because he was a sitting pigeon if they ever spotted him and realized he couldn't move.

The shots were widely spaced now. Each man was getting toward the end of his cylinder, and nobody wanted to be caught with an empty rifle or pistol.

Joshua heard somebody pass him within twenty feet, and after a few minutes he ventured to turn himself slowly so that he faced toward the mules. Callahan now had carried the fight in that direction, and all three of White's men were moving past Joshua.

There was no sound for half an hour. Then abruptly Callahan must have fired. The blaze disclosed him for an instant, on his feet and moving to one side. Then the rifles of all three of the outlaws crashed together.

They were in close, within a hundred yards of Callahan, and Joshua realized that Callahan had fired to find out where they were. Joshua held his own fire, and another half hour went by.

It came again—a shot from Callahan, who was on the move. Three rifles crashed, and Joshua shot at the one on the far left. He heard an anguished cry, "Damn his soul to hell!" and then a cough and the sound of a man falling forward as he ran.

97

After this burst, for a full hour there was no human sound. He heard two coyotes snarl at each other, and guessed they were fighting over the body of the first man. What had happened to the second man, Joshua couldn't guess; the third man very likely was dead, for the bullet had had the sound of a lung shot. That left two: White and one other, and Joshua thought it likely that the two would get their animals and return to the ferry. As far as White knew, the forces were even, and he doubted that White wanted him and Callahan badly enough to look for them in the dark with even numbers.

Nevertheless, he continued to lie still on the open desert. Then a whisper came out of the dark: "Joshua?"

"Yo."

Callahan sat down quietly beside him. "The damned Apaches got the mules," he said. "We'll have to find a hiding place around the mountain until a train comes through. Maybe—"

For the last time the desert exploded with gunpowder and lead; they must have been very close. Callahan fell back over Joshua, and Joshua hesitated to fire because they were both pinned down. Five shots altogether came from less than seventy-five feet away. Then the desert became as unearthly still as it had been violent.

Joshua waited, and after a while Callahan groaned and moved. Joshua tensed himself for shots, but they did not come. Callahan groaned again, and Joshua twisted and got hold of him to ease him to the ground.

The last shot came from a considerable distance, because he saw the flash without ever hearing the explosion. The bullet drove sand into his face like steel needles, and the sudden pain was unbearable. His brain flooded with blackness, and his head dropped upon the gravel of the desert.

CHAPTER ELEVEN

WHEN HE AWOKE IT WAS BRIGHT DAYLIGHT. CALLAHAN was groaning beside him. But they were not on the desert; they were lying under a small, rude shelter thatched with fresh branches of *palo verde* laid on dead cottonwood poles that extended from one big black rock to another, so that in effect they were in a cave of black rock with a thatched roof. The branches of the *palo verde* were not heavily leaved and so the shade was only partial, but it was very welcome, for the sun was directly overhead and the little cup-shaped crater among the rocks was without any breeze.

He looked at Callahan. The man sounded delirious, and obviously he had not brought them in from the desert. Instinctively Joshua felt his head; he still had his scalp, so they had not been found by hostile Indians. Obviously White and his remaining man or men had returned to the Gila crossing, and somebody . . .

He started to get up, but his legs were still dead weights. His mouth and throat were parched and his lips were cracked from the heat. He twisted and pushed himself to a sitting position, and leaned forward to get a look at their surroundings.

In front of the rock on his right, sitting apparently unmindful of the sun, carefully peeling *tunas—prickly-pear* apples—that she took from a reed basket, was an Indian girl. She was young and slim and full-breasted, with bronze skin and very black hair cut straight across her forehead. She wore three garments: a piece of white cotton cloth folded two or three times and wrapped around her hips, and a pair of rawhide sandals very simply made. She sat gracefully erect in the blistering sun, not leaning against the rocks, for obviously they were as hot as stove lids.

Joshua got up on one elbow to see her better. She must have heard the movement, for she turned at once. She had not the shapeless face he associated with older Indian females, but rather an oval outline tending toward a firm squareness. Her skin was clean and fresh, and she was, he thought, not more than fourteen, but she had passed the age of puberty, for from each corner of her mouth were two blue tattooed lines going downward to the edge of her chin. Those indicated the Maricopa tribe, he knew.

She saw his eyes on her, and smiled and nodded slightly. She got up and came and put her hand on his face, and he was astonished to find that her hand was cooler than his skin. But she nodded as if satisfied. She regarded him thoughtfully and asked, "You savvy Spanish?"

"*Si*," he said.

She smiled again. "*Está bien*. You eat"—she looked puzzled for a moment, and he guessed she did not know the Spanish word she wanted to use—"you eat *kal-yap*?"

He frowned, and she extended a shapely arm, two bronze fingers supporting a peeled tuna with a touch so light that she hardly seemed to be holding it. He took it and put it in his mouth. It tasted lemony and sugary all together, but not bad. He swallowed, and she gave him another. "*kal-yap bueno* for you," she said. "You *muy enfermo*." She pointed to his scalp, and he remembered the crease he had got at the water hole. He rubbed the whiskers on his face, and was astonished to find no blood. Apparently she had washed him. His face ached

100

all over where the sand had been driven into it, and he felt lumps where the grains still lay under his skin. He started to get up but his legs were still without feeling and he was unable to control them. His movement brought a knife-sharp pain in his back, and he felt to see if he was bleeding. Then he realized he was naked, and his clothes were in a neat pile about halfway between him and the girl. Apparently he had been examined for other wounds. It occurred to him with a shock that he could be hurt in the legs and not know it, and he examined them.

It did not take him long to find out why he had been undressed. He had a ragged bullet wound through the fleshy part of his right thigh. It wasn't the kind that would cause any trouble unless gangrene set in, but it would hurt and it would bleed until it healed over. The dried blood had been washed off, but a small rivulet of blood trickled slowly from the lower end of the wound.

Callahan groaned again, and Joshua looked at him. Callahan's shirt was off, his shoes and pants still on, and he had a nasty-looking bullet hole in his right side, too low for the lungs and probably too high for the intestines. Joshua pointed to Callahan. "*Cómo está mi amigo?*"

She frowned and shook her head, then shrugged. Apparently Callahan was hard hit but she didn't think he would suffer permanent injury.

She got up from her place, arising with ease. She was a head shorter than Joshua, and not heavy, but well built. "You—" She shook her head negatively. He was not to try to move. She went somewhere out of his sight. Then she returned with a gourd of tepid water, which she gave him to drink.

He drank noisily until she pulled the gourd from his

mouth with strong fingers, and he realized he ought not to drink too fast. The girl sat down, unprotected from the sun, until Joshua finished the water slowly. Then she took the gourd and put her finger on her chest. "Mah-vah," she said slowly.

He nodded. *Usted se llama Mah-vah.* It's a pretty name."

Whether she understood any English or not, she seemed to get the import of his words. The chances were that she did understand a few words of English, for the Maricopas were the last tribe on the Gila before the crossing of the Colorado, and most emigrants were eager to buy supplies by the time they reached the Maricopa villages. Her tribal affiliation also explained why he and Callahan had been brought in from the desert, for the Maricopas were friendly to the whites.

Her knowledge of Spanish was not surprising, for most Indian tribes as far south as the Gila had been more or less in contact with the Spanish for three hundred years.

She got up easily and took the gourd. She went to the left, and in a moment came back with another gourd and some strips of white cloth. She looked at the bleeding wound in his thigh, and frowned slightly. Then she got the other gourd of water and came back to wash away the blood. She got up and looked at him. "You—*revuéiltese,*" she said.

She was asking him to turn over, and he tried, but his legs would not follow. If he could grasp something with his hands, perhaps he could twist himself. He saw Callahan stir and open his eyes. Joshua tried to get a hold on a rock.

Mah-vah watched him trying to turn himself. Then with her strong fingers, being careful not to touch him near the wound, she turned his legs, and set to work to wash the other end of the wound. Then she sprinkled powder from the second gourd, and sprinkled more on a strip of cloth, and finally wrapped the cloth around his leg so that both entrance and exit of the bullet were in contact with the powder. "*Qué es?*" he asked, pointing at the gourd.

Her lips parted wide, and she enunciated distinctly: "*Ic'*."

"*Ic'*," he repeated.

"What the hell is *ic'*?" Callahan growled unexpectedly.

Joshua turned his head to look at him. "Bark from the screwbean root, ground up. Good for wounds, sores, earache—anything."

"Listen," said Callahan. "I can't figure you out yet. Where'd you learn Indian words?"

"I was here in 1846," said Joshua, "and we came in contact with a lot of different tribes—Maricopas included."

"You been everywhere," said Callahan with simulated disgust.

"I been all over the Southwest."

"You was probably born in an Injun tepee."

Joshua twisted a little. "Maybe."

Mah-vah had listened to this discussion with grave interest, probably understanding very little of it, and now she offered a comment. She pointed at Joshua's face and said, "*Rojo,*" then at his chest and said, "*Blanco,*" and laughed, seeming greatly amused.

Joshua grinned. "Yes," he said, "I been out in the sun considerable. That's what makes my face dark and my stomach white."

She glanced at his clothing, and nodded as if she

understood quite well. Then she looked at Callahan and disappeared around the rock.

"Where do you suppose we are?" asked Callahan.

"And who brought us here?" asked Joshua.

"And what do we do next?"

"I can answer that," said Joshua. "We stay right here and hope for the best until we're able to travel. They haven't hurt us so far, so they're not likely to hurt us at all."

Mah-vah came back with more cloth and another gourd of water, which she held out to Callahan. He looked up at her. "You sleep with me, hey?" he asked suddenly. She looked puzzled. Callahan held out some silver coins and made suggestive motions. She looked at him very calmly and threw the water in his face, then turned on her heel and left.

She left them alone for two hours, and for that length of time there was no sound in the small crater-like depression in the hills except for what noises the two men made.

Finally Mah-vah reappeared, carrying a badger by the tail. She sat down and calmly began to skin it. There was a sound of more activity beyond her and out of Joshua's sight, and then the pleasant smell of burning cedar.

"I think we're going to have supper," said Joshua.

Callahan groaned. "You gonna eat that badger?"

"If I get a chance."

An old Indian appeared in the opening between the rocks. He had a very aquiline nose; he was thin and gray-haired, and his eyes looked full of quiet wisdom and sympathy. He observed Callahan's unbandaged wound and spoke sharply to Mah-vah. She answered without looking up, and he nodded slowly, then spoke to her without emotion. She looked up and said something. The old man came in and bent over Callahan and examined the wound. Then he went out, and came back after a while with a basket filled with prickly-pear leaves. He sat down and singed the tiny thorns over the fire. Then he split a leaf, opened it wide, and placed it over Callahan's wound and bound it tightly with a piece of grass rope. Callahan grunted, but the old man stood up, raised his eyebrows understandingly, and said, "*Bueno—ahotk.*"

"You're being told," said Joshua, "to conduct yourself like a big, big boy."

"It looks like everything I do is wrong," said Callahan.

"No. just because it's different it isn't necessarily wrong. That's where a lot of our mistakes come in dealing with the Indians. They don't do what we do, and we assume that's wrong."

"I ain't no prairie-dog lawyer," said Callahan.

"That's interesting, because there aren't any prairie dogs in this part of the country. Where did you learn that expression?"

"Up around Fort Laramie in the forties. Say, listen, do you know this damn' stuff draws like sin?"

"I suppose."

The old man put his finger on his chest. He wore only a breechclout and sandals, and his hair too was cut straight across the forehead and hung down below his shoulders. "Antoine," he said. "Antoine. "B'long *Hah-quah-sie-eel-ish*—Gila."

Joshua thumped his chest. "José. B'long *Pain-gote-sahch*—American."

The old man looked at Callahan. "*Yah-bay-páiesh—es-eélsch?*"

"*Es-eélsch!*" Joshua said emphatically.

Antoine nodded as if well satisfied.

"What's all the talk-talk about?" asked Callahan.

"I just saved your life," said Joshua. "He wanted me to assure him you were not Apache."

"Hell!" said Callahan. "Anybody can take one look at my red hair and know I'm not an Apache."

"In this case it doesn't mean who your parents were—rather which way your stick floats, if you're a beaver trapper."

"Oh. He wants to be sure I'm not a friend of the Apaches."

"That's right."

"I think that cactus is gonna do some good. It's sure pullin'," said Callahan, raising up. "What about you? You *are* in bad shape. You can't move your legs!"

"Not yet."

"Do you think they can fix that?"

"In a couple of weeks, maybe."

Mah-vah came with a reed basket and set it down between them.

"Whatta we got for supper?" asked Callahan.

Joshua tossed him a dark ball the size of his fist. "*Pitáhaya*," he said. "About as soft and sticky as figs, but it tastes like sort of tasteless raspberries, if you follow me."

Callahan looked at the food doubtfully. "Is that the stuff from *saguaro* cactus?"

"I think so."

"What else is on the bill of fare?"

"Here's boiled squash—a piece for you and a piece for me." He took a small, hard loaf of bread out of the basket. "Mesquite-bean flour. It'll put starch in your backbone."

106

Callahan bit gingerly into the *pitáhaya.* He chewed the bite and looked at Joshua. "Wish I had a nice fried rattlesnake."

Joshua grinned. "The Maricopas don't eat snakes."

"If you ask me," said Callahan, "this is a hell of a life."

"Maybe you'd rather be out on the desert."

"NO—but I'm worried about something else."

"What?"

"I don't know what these Injuns are up here in the mountains for, but I do know they aren't goin' to wet-nurse us forever. We won't either one be walkin' for several days yet. What'll we do if they leave us?"

CHAPTER TWELVE

MAH-VAH BROUGHT THEM WATER IN THE GOURD. Joshua did not know how far they were from the spring, but he guessed a considerable distance, for the Maricopas, knowing the Apaches had been on the mountain, were not likely to take any chance of being found by their hereditary enemies.

About sundown three younger men and one woman a little older than Mah-vah came in by a trail over the black rocks. They seemed to carry nothing and had no weapons. They threw themselves on the ground and rested for a while; then the woman, who was about eighteen and had the same good figure and erect posture as Mah-vah but was a little heavier, got up and began to prepare food over a tiny fire that gave off no smoke.

One of the men, a tall, slender fellow with sultry eyes, sat down by Mah-vah and asked her many questions about the two whites. His name was Francisco, and

107

Joshua gathered that he did not at all like the idea of caring for two wounded *Pain-gote-sahch*. Still less, thought Joshua, because he had his eye on Mah-vah and he didn't want any competition. The other woman's name was Le-och, and she seemed to be the wife of the other man, called Mis-ke-tai-ish—a rather scrawny, shy-acting fellow who did not say anything but watched Francisco and Mah-vah with unusual attention.

It was strange, thought Joshua, that he did not watch Le-och, and also strange that she did not look at him, but worked with an air of detachment that seemed to exclude them all from her thoughts. She looked up once when Joshua's eyes were on her, and he was startled at the beauty of her face and the depth of her eyes; it was almost like a hunger in her eyes. Mah-vah, he thought, resembled her very much, but Le-och, being married, had a maturity that was yet to come to Mah-vah.

The fourth Indian was a young man, about twenty, called Tu-naams, of extraordinary physique and good looks. He kept his counsel and studied them all, but especially Francisco and Mah-vah.

Old Antoine came to the shelter between the rocks and held out his hand. "*Oh-oúbe*," he said. "Tobacco. You like?"

Joshua nodded. He didn't often smoke, but he knew this was a mark of esteem, and so he accepted the cornshuck cigarette and the glowing twig to light it. Old Antoine lighted one of his own and squatted down near them. "You feel better?" he asked.

"It is good medicine," said Joshua.

"You can move legs?"

"Tomorrow, maybe."

"You?" Antoine asked Callahan.

"I'll be out of here in a couple of days," said

Callahan. "How come you understand English?"

"I was interpreter for Señor Bartlett. It makes several moons."

"You're a long way from home," Joshua observed. Antoine nodded. "You have come to hunt the *amu*—the mountain sheep?"

"No." The old man sighed. "There are no more sheep, no more antelope. When I was young, there used to be. Not now."

"That is many, many moons," Joshua observed.

"Yes." The old man puffed deliberately at his cigarette. "This has been a dry winter on the *Hah-quah-sie-eel-ish*," he said. "We have come to the Tinajas Altas to see if there will be mescal, so the tribe can come in a couple of moons and harvest it."

"What have you found?"

"There is some mescal, but I do not know if there will be enough to risk an excursion through the land of the *Yah-bay-páiesh*."

"The Apaches are always dangerous."

"More since your people have been coming through our country. The *Yah-bay-páiesh* blame us for allowing them to use our trail, but we are not a warring people. We have fought in the past." He shrugged. "We killed many, many Yumas and Diegueños some years ago when they came to attack us. But we do not live by war, like the Apaches."

The conversation around the small, glowing fire of dried cactus was quite animated, and Antoine got up slowly. "Francisco is not a patient man," he observed. "He wants to marry Mah-vah, but Mah-vah does not want him, and so"—he shrugged again—"what is there to do? You cannot make a girl marry a man she does not want."

"Why doesn't Mah-vah want him?"

The old man watched the group around the fire through eyes that were almost closed. "She says she does not like his eyes. She does not believe he is a man."

Joshua raised his head. "You mean—half man, half woman?"

The old man nodded.

"Are you the father of Mah-vah?"

"Her father is dead, her mother also. Killed by Yumas. I am her father's father, and it is hard for me to tell her what is the right thing, because there are so many years between us. She would listen, because Mah-vah is a good girl, and she would obey what I might tell her, but I am old and I am not sure myself."

"But if Francisco is half woman, why does he want a woman?"

Antoine inhaled deeply on the cigarette. "It is pride, maybe. Mah-vah is much sought after."

Callahan was snoring.

Joshua asked, "Why did you save us?"

Antoine shrugged. "We do not leave wounded people in the sun—unless they are Apaches."

"*Gracias, amigo.*"

Antoine got up. "I will bring you blankets," he said. "It will be cold before morning."

Joshua covered Callahan and drew his own blanket around him. He watched the discussion outside as the glowing embers grew fainter and fainter, and finally the three men and two women got up and disappeared from his sight.

Joshua managed to twist over onto his side, because his back was weary from lying on the rock. Most of the ache had left the area of the bullet, but as yet he could

110

not move his legs. He heard a soft step between the rocks, and raised his head. Mah-vah's proud shoulders were outlined against the stars. "José," she whispered.

"Here."

"I have brought your rifles and pistols."

He went cold. Up to that time he had not realized that all of their weapons had been out of their reach.

"Does that mean you're leaving tomorrow?"

"I do not know." Her gentle hand touched his head. "Francisco wants to go. I do not. Grandfather will stay with me, but Mis-ke-tai-ish is a strange one. Who knows what he will do? Le-och will go with him. And Tu-naams—I do not know, José. Is a great question."

"You will all have to keep together," Joshua observed. "Any smaller group than six would be an open invitation to the Apaches."

"Is so." She said, "Your basket of food and bullets is here too."

"*Gracias*, Mah-vah. Good night."

"*Buenas noches*," José."

He lay awake long after she had disappeared in the darkness. The embers of the fire died out completely, and he pulled the blanket closer about his shoulders, and turned to watch the brilliant stars. A coyote poised on the rim of the bowl in which the Maricopas were camped, and presently raised its head to the stars, singing. When coyotes sang on the hilltops it was all right; it was when they howled in the depths that evil was predicted.

But the coyote's song was small comfort to Joshua. With seventy miles of absolute desert to the nearest refuge—the Maricopa villages on the Gila—it did not look very promising. Mah-vah might have a mind of her own, but still the men would make the decisions. And he did not think Francisco would favor the *Pain-gote-sahch.*

He examined the rifles. One still had a broken trigger and was useless without repair. The other was in firing condition but not loaded. One pistol was empty; the other had one shot left.

He lay there and watched the Dipper revolve, and presently he went to sleep.

Callahan awoke him by yelling in a nightmare, "Shoot the dirty heathen! Shoot him in the belly!"

Joshua put a hand over his mouth, and Callahan came up struggling. Then he stopped abruptly and held a hand to his belly. "Damn!" He whistled. "I hope I don't do that again. I tore the damn' thing apart."

"It will heal," said Joshua. "Listen, Bill. We may be left here on our own. How long before you can walk strong enough to go for help?"

Callahan looked at the high black cliffs around them. The sun wasn't up yet, and the dawn lay cool and mellow over the bowl. "It don't look very good to me, Josh. It'd take a mountain goat in the first place to climb them damn' rocks." He turned to look at Joshua. "And where am I goin' when I get out?"

Joshua shook his head. "I don't know. The Gila is closest—and that's a good jaunt even with a mule to ride, for a man without a hole in his carcass."

"How about you?" asked Callahan.

Joshua raised his wide black eyebrows. "I'm here for a while," he said, "unless an eagle carries me out."

Mah-vah felt his face when she brought food that morning. "Your head very hot." She looked worried. "I get Antoine."

But they were stopped by Francisco, who talked in Maricopa. "There's no sense in helping this *Pain-*

gote-sahch to get well. He will only send more of his kind to cheat us and to give the Apaches rifles to shoot us."

"He is not a man to do harm," said old Antoine.

"All whites do harm. All whites talk lies. They tell Apaches one thing, Yumas something else, Diegueños—who knows?" He spun Antoine by the forearm. "Old man, I will have none of your meddling! I say we leave today, and no more medicine for the *Pain-gote-sahch*. They are both going to die anyway. It is a waste of medicine and food."

The old man straightened. "Francisco—"

"Old man, what is the matter with your granddaughter, that she wants these foreigners to get well?"

Antoine said, "I have many papers from the *Pain-gote-sahch* saying that I am a peaceful man and a friend to those who treat me as such."

Francisco spat on the ground. "Papers from the *Pain-gote-sahch*! What are they worth? They tell you to stay home and raise corn while the Apache is out killing whites and getting many horses and mules."

"We are not a horse-raising people," said Antoine. "And we are not killers."

"Are you then a coward, old man?"

The intensity of Antoine's indignation was like a physical force that radiated from him. "You are like a horned toad," he said. "A sick horned toad. Go back to your dark hates and the black recesses of your small mind, where roost the vampire bats. You are not a good Maricopa. You are not a good Indian. You are not a human being. You are lower than the rattlesnake." He shook his head in grief that he could not express. "You are fit only to harvest the *iciú*." The iciú was a plant

113

used as an abortive, and this was about as low as a man could possibly get.

Joshua knew then that there was something wrong with Francisco, for any normal Indian would have paled at Antoine's words and slunk away. Only an Indian who was abnormal would stand up to these scourging phrases of Antoine. And Francisco did.

"I call for a vote," he said.

"I am the chief," Antoine said with implicit dignity.

But in Francisco he was talking to one who did not feel the psychic force of Indian custom. "You are an old man," Francisco said. "Your arm is withered and you cannot even draw a war bow. Nor have you sons to defend you."

Joshua managed to get the loaded rifle in position to fire without making any noise. He felt Callahan's lightly restraining hand, but he drew a bead on Francisco's forehead. If there was to be violence, there would be a vote from the *Pain-gote-sahch* as well.

Antoine did not back away. "I am staying here," he told Francisco. "Who is staying with me?"

"I am staying," Mah-vah said promptly.

Francisco was scornful. "When do women speak in council?"

"Tu-naams," said Antoine, "do you stay with me?"

Tu-naams hesitated. He looked at Antoine's fierce old eyes and nodded. "I will stay."

"Mis-ke-tai-ish?"

Francisco glared at the man, whose black eyes darted from Francisco to Antoine and back to Francisco and then to Antoine's fierce old face. Finally Mis-ke-tai-ish nodded. "I will stay."

Francisco swelled up like a toad for a moment. He glared at Mis-ke-tai-ish and then at Antoine. Then he turned and strode away, out of Joshua's sight.

Presently there came the smell of bleached-out cactus burning, and Joshua guessed they were low on wood, for dried-out cactus branches burned fast and had to be gathered in much greater quantity than cedar or pine or mesquite.

Antoine came into the shelter, seeming calm and unruffled. "We will take off the bandage," he told Joshua. "I will help you turn over." He looked at Joshua's back. "Does it hurt?"

"No."

"You cannot move the legs yet?"

"No."

"The bullet will have to come out," he said soberly.

Joshua caught his breath. "Can you get it?"

Antoine nodded. "I can get it—but there are medicines I must have. There is in my village an herb doctor who cures anything. He will have the proper medicine to keep the fever from spreading in your bowels after the bullet is taken out. That I must have."

Joshua closed his eyes for a moment. This, then, was Antoine's good-by. "All right," Joshua said finally. "I'll wait. But what about Callahan?"

"His wound is healing but he cannot ride so far. He must stay here with you."

Callahan was silent. Antoine said, "I will leave the cloth away today, or you will have the sickness that turns the flesh black and makes it fall off the bones. Tonight I will put on a new dressing, and we shall ride back to the village. I will see the doctor and get his medicine, and then I will be back in five suns." "*Ahotk?*"

"*Bueno*," Joshua agreed, although he felt it was a death sentence.

As soon as Antoine left, Callahan said, "Well, what do you think of your friend now?"

Joshua pulled the sack over toward him and opened it.

"You know what it means don't you?" asked Callahan.

"I know." Joshua found about two pounds of dried meat in with the cartridges.

"He's getting rid of us. He's not going to fight Francisco for us any more."

"Do you blame him?" asked Joshua.

"Can't say that I do."

Mah-vah came in with the mesquite-bean bread and the rest of the badger meat and two gourds of water. "You eat much," she told Joshua. "You be here five days."

"This is a nice, quiet place," he said without looking at her.

"José!" She was on her knees, holding his face between her hands. "You think I not come back!"

He looked at her. "Sure, you'll come back," he said. "Leave us plenty of water, will you?"

She brought them food again at noon and again late in the afternoon. Then she brought both his and Callahan's canteens. "We found them," she said. "And here are four gourds full of water. It is all we can spare. Be careful with the water. Remember, it must last five days."

He took her soft hand in his hard fingers. "Mah-vah," he said, "I'll miss you. It's worth a meal just to see you come and go."

"I will be back," she said, her eyes large and luminous as she left him.

Antoine returned about two hours before sundown

and put on a fresh dressing. "You are not to take off this cloth or even look under it until I come back. Do you promise?"

"I promise," Joshua said lazily, "but I'm going to look funny running all over hell with that bandage tied around my middle."

"I do not understand."

"It isn't necessary for you to understand. Now run along. I'll leave the bandage on for five days."

"Unless it starts to turn black," said Callahan.

"If it does that," said Antoine, "you might as well save the trouble."

CHAPTER THIRTEEN

HE LAY THERE DURING THE LONG HOT DAYS, TURNING every few hours, twisting his body until his useless legs flopped over with his torso. Callahan got up the third day and walked around the little bowl in which they steamed like ants at the bottom of a pan. Callahan's wound appeared to be well on the way to healing, with a thick scab over it, but Joshua urged him to stay quiet as long as they had food, for undue exertion might open it again and start the bleeding.

Callahan wanted to examine Joshua's wound, but Joshua would not let him. The crease on his scalp was healing, and there was no pain in his back, and he said he would not touch that bandage for five days. "Old Antoine might have put a hex on it." He grinned up at Callahan. "If there's anything strange going on under that bandage, I don't want to know it."

Three days passed, then four. They had nothing to eat the fifth day. Antoine, wisely enough, had known they could live a long time without food but not very long without water, and much longer without water if they had no food. And so the food was gone, and the water would be gone at the end of the fifth day. They were both gaunt and whiskered, and Callahan, exercising in the small area of the bowl, was growing more confident. "In the morning," he said, "I'll go look for the spring."

"That's as good a bet as any," Joshua agreed, eying four black vultures that circled and glided endlessly far above the mountain.

Toward sundown Callahan sat down in the shelter and took his last sip of water. "You don't figure on seein' Antoine now do you?"

"Hard to say," said Joshua. "Hard to say." He lay with his arms spread out. His fever had gone down, but he had no strength left.

"One more night," said Callahan. "Maybe they figured I'd be able to get out of here in five days."

"If you do get out," Joshua said, "you'd better light out for help."

"What do you think I am—a damn' deserter?"

"You can't climb in and out of this thing every day with water."

"D'you think I'm an invalid like you? I've got two legs that I can move."

Joshua shut up. He still couldn't move his legs at all.

They watched the sky darken and the stars come out. The coyotes did not come to the rim that evening, and finally Joshua fell asleep, wondering what the end would be. His feet looked all right, and showed no signs of turning black, but he couldn't move them.

He awoke about midnight, and snatched the pistol. There had been a strange sound, and he stared into the dark and searched his subconscious memory for the

118

sound. Then he heard it again: a whispered "José!"

He put down the pistol and dropped his head on his arms and began to laugh weakly. Callahan woke up and shook him. "Hey, Josh! You goin' crazy?"

But Joshua raised his head and said into the darkness, "Mah-vah!" and she came gliding into the shelter, followed by Antoine.

He seized her hand with both of his and held it for a long time. Then finally he heard what she was saying: "We bring water, José."

Callahan said, "I'll help you get it down him."

Joshua was vaguely aware that his leathery mouth was wet, and then he swallowed, and finally he was able to put his lips to the gourd and drink. "Not too much," said Mah-vah, with her hand at his back. "Not too much. You'll be sick."

He forced himself to drink sparingly, and finally fell asleep with Mah-vah's hand on his head.

Then once more it was morning, and Mah-vah was building a fire of cedar, and they ate mesquite-meal bread until their stomachs were tight, and old Antoine made cigarettes for them while Mah-vah went after more water. When she returned, it was nearly time for the sun to top the rim of the bowl, and Antoine said, "I have talked to the herb doctor and I have told him what is your trouble, and he has told me what to do and he has given me some medicine to keep away the fever." He showed a small deerskin pouch. "But we must first see the evil place."

"I haven't moved the cloth," said Joshua.

"All right. You turn your stomach."

Callahan helped him turn over. Antoine removed the bandage carefully, so that if it stuck it would not hurt, but strangely enough, it did not stick. He lifted the

119

bandage, and Joshua heard Callahan suck in his breath. "Christopher! Maggots!"

Joshua forced himself to close his eyes and remain still. Maggots! His head went down, the left side of his face flat against the black rock, and he tried with his shrunken fingers to get a grip on something besides the smooth rock.

"It is good," old Antoine was saying. "We left off the cloth one day, and the flies were sure to get in and lay eggs if they had not done so before, and now the worms have eaten away all the rotten meat, and there is only clean meat left, and all we have to do is take out the worms and get the bullet out, and then in a few days you can walk, and we will take you back to our village to get well."

Joshua raised his head. "You mean you *wanted* worms in there?"

"That is why I warned you not to take off the cloth."

"Ain't it—Won't he die from them things?" asked Callahan.

Antoine shook his head. "This has been used by my tribe for many generations."

Joshua looked up and saw Mah-vah standing there, straight and strong, and by her eyes he knew the old man was telling the truth, and now from sheer weakness he let his head drop again on the rock.

"I have bring," said Antoine, "a jar of mescal. The herb doctor has said you are to drink it before I take out the bullet."

Joshua took a sip and blinked. "It tastes fine going down," he told Callahan, "but it hits the bottom of your stomach with a jolt."

"If there's any left," said Callahan, "I'll find out for myself."

"You are to drink it all, José—but slow, not fast, or you may have the sickness of the stomach."

It began to feel warm in his stomach, and then a glow spread through him, numbing his lips and the ends of his fingers, and he handed the empty jar to Callahan with one swallow left in it.

"You feel sleepy now, hey?" asked Antoine.

"Sure, I—sure—sure . . ." His head wagged from side to side. He knew Callahan got up and sat on his legs. He saw Antoine produce a knife with a long, thin blade, and he reached for Mah-vah's hands. They were cool and soft against his own, and he raised his head once and shook it and tried to keep it up but couldn't. His face fell straight into the rock, but Mah-vah's hand was there to catch it. Antoine straddled him, facing his feet. He felt the first dig of the knife. It ran through his body like a rivulet of molten steel, and he arched his back against the pain. Antoine dug again, and besides the unbearable shooting pains a sudden terrible ache grew in the small of his back. Dimly he knew that Antoine had a finger in the wound. He felt Antoine brush away the blood with the cloth, and then, when Antoine used the knife again, he passed out . . .

Antoine was wiping his knife blade when Joshua opened his eyes. His head was cradled in Mah-vah's lap, and Antoine, seeing his eyes open, said proudly, "I got him! First time!" He held out a flattened bullet as big around as a half-dollar.

"You got all that out of my back?" asked Joshua faintly.

Callahan was brushing sweat from his forehead. "You got any more of that medicine?" he asked. "I sure need a drink."

Antoine nodded gravely. "We have bring enough for three times."

"Three times!" Joshua felt sick. He thought he was going to vomit, but Mah-vah had a wet cloth on his throat, and he got control of himself.

"We fix good now," said Antoine. He opened the deerskin pouch. "You turn over now so blood run out, hey?"

Joshua turned over, with Callahan's help, and then rolled back again. Antoine examined the wound, shook the powder into it thoroughly, and bound a clean cloth over it. "You rest," he said. "Tomorrow you try legs."

"What did you put on the sore?" asked Joshua.

"Wild gourd. It kills the worms and makes you well. You don't worry now."

At noon Mah-vah brought water and mesquite-meal cakes, dried *saguaro* fruit, and boiled squash.

Callahan ate sitting up, with only a slight favoring of his side. Antoine would not allow him to climb out of the bowl yet. "Is not good," he said. "You get well. We wait."

Joshua split one of the mesquite cakes and pressed the sweetish gob of a *saguaro* fruit between the halves. "You two came here alone?" he asked Mah-vah.

Her eyes widened in innocence. "We know this country," she said. "Our people hunted here many, many years."

"How about the Apaches?"

"We were careful."

"Why didn't Francisco come back with you?"

"Francisco?" She tossed her head. "He is no man."

Joshua thought about that. "Why are you so sure?"

"He too much puts arms around Mis-ke-tai-ish."

"For a young'un," said Callahan, "she's pretty well edjicated."

Joshua nodded. He turned back to Mah-vah. "What of Le-och?"

122

"What can Le-och do? If Mis-ke-tai-ish like Francisco more better, Le-och cannot hope to have sons."

"Le-och looks to me like an armful," Callahan observed, and then began to turn red in the face.

Mah-vah said, "She wants to be a wife, but Mis-ke-tai-ish"—she made a face—"he is no *hudha-va*."

That meant husband, but in the fullest sense—a partner, a man who would work and love and share interests and responsibilities.

Joshua sensed something deeper. "How do you know so much about Le-och?" he asked.

"She is my sister," said Mah-vah.

Callahan nodded wisely. "And she ain't happy in her tepee."

Mah-vah looked sad and turned away.

Joshua thought it over and said to Callahan late in the afternoon, "Francisco didn't like us and he probably knows that White was trying to get us. Do you suppose he'd go to White and tell him where we are?"

Callahan considered. "He might, at that."

"And we're like quail in a barrel. Do you think you could get out of here now?"

"With a little help."

"I think you'd better do it."

Callahan looked indignant. "I got nowhere to go and a long time to get there. Let's wait and see how your legs get along."

"It will be months before I can get out of here. The sides are so steep that none of you can carry me. A good strong man might take me on his back, but you'd split yourself wide open if you tried anything like that, and Antoine's too old."

"And Mah-vah's a woman," said Callahan. "Which is

123

nice, you got to admit, but it don't help us out of this mountain."

"There's one thing in our favor," said Joshua. "If Francisco does decide to tell White where we are, it won't be right away. He'll have to brood about it for a while to justify himself in his own mind. The Indians don't do things like that without a lot of preliminaries."

"Lucky for us," said Callahan, and seemed to dismiss the idea.

But Joshua did not feel so easy. Francisco was a troublemaker; that was implicit in his face, in his contentious manner of talking. As Joshua considered it, he thought it would be only a matter of days before Francisco would go down to the Colorado and relay the information to White that two *Pain-gote-sahch* were somewhere in the mountain of the Tinajas Altas, unable to move—and Francisco knew exactly where they were. The rest depended on White.

Joshua went to sleep that night with the reassuring knowledge that Mah-vah and Antoine were asleep just outside of the shelter, and it was hard to decide which presence gave him more comfort.

He awoke after midnight with sharp pains shooting through the soles of his feet, and his first thought was that Antoine, in digging for the bullet, had cut something he should not have cut, but then he realized the pains were like those felt in a foot that was waking up after it had "gone to sleep," and he waited for a few minutes to see what would happen. The pains died away, and he went to sleep again. It was daylight when he awoke, and Mah-vah was climbing the wall on the opposite side of the bowl, probably going after water. He watched her going up the steep trail—it was almost vertical in many places—sure-footed, easy, graceful.

She turned at the top and looked back. Joshua, in the dimness of his shelter, waved at her, and saw her shade her eyes. Then she disappeared.

In half an hour she was back, with canteens and gourds full of water. She brought a gourd to him, smiling when she saw his eyes on her.

"Your work starts early," he said.

She sat down by him. " 'Work'? I do not understand."

"Work is—well, something you have to do."

"But nobody has to do anything."

If Callahan had been awake he would have said, "You ain't never been in the Army," but Joshua let it pass.

"*Nixnix*," Mah-vah said in her soft voice.

Joshua turned his eyes. Outside a hummingbird was hovering in the cactus, its wings moving so fast they were a blur in the morning light. And over on the other side he heard the song of a mockingbird. He listened to it and formed his lips to whistle an answer. Then he felt something tickle the bottom of his foot, and he looked around. Mah-vah was on her knees, brushing the sole of his foot with a feathery branch of *palo verde*. She saw his head turn, and smiled. "You feel foot," she said happily.

For a moment he did not understand. Then he took a tremendous breath and grinned at her.

"You get well now," she said.

He drew her down with his arms and hugged her. She was solid as a rock and yet yielding too. He could feel her aliveness under his fingertips. He turned her mouth to his and kissed her. She blushed furiously and jumped up.

"Wait a minute! Come back!" he pleaded.

She shook her head. "Not now. You use legs soon. You find me then, if you want."

CHAPTER FOURTEEN

BUT RECOVERY, HE FOUND, WOULD NOT BE SUDDEN OR even fast. That first day he could move his toes a little, and the next day he could turn his feet at the ankles. Three days after that he was able to get to his knees, but there was no strength in his legs. The inactivity, or, more likely, the paralysis, had left his leg muscles so ineffective that he was only one stage above helplessness.

"It'll be weeks before you can walk," said Callahan, watching his clumsy movements. "You ain't got the strength, somehow."

"I can't stay here that long," said Joshua.

"You can't grow wings, neither. Look, Josh. You're being fed reg'lar and you got a beautiful Maricopa girl to talk to. Damned if I wouldn't like to talk to her."

Joshua shook his head. "I've been in this crater so long I feel like a prisoner. And I keep thinking about White, and wondering what will happen if he comes after me."

"You got any reason to think he's comin'?"

"Francisco has had time to make up his mind, and I think to be on the safe side we ought to expect White any time within the next few days."

"You got the rifle loaded?"

"Yes."

"Keep it close, then. I'm going out with the pistol to look for a deer."

"I didn't know you'd been up the trail yet—all the way."

"I was up yesterday. You was asleep. And this morning Antoine said he saw deer tracks at the water hole."

"Don't go any farther than you can come back."

"Don't worry about me." Callahan slapped him on the shoulder.

He was back by noon, carrying a deer ham. Antoine carried another. Joshua had heard no shot, so the spring must be some distance away. Mah-vah built up a bigger fire, and they broiled deer steaks that night, with Joshua sitting by the fire, his back against a rock, his legs out straight. Mah-vah cut up the second ham in thin strips, which she hung near the fire on an improvised rack of green boughs and twigs, for otherwise the meat would spoil in a few hours.

Ordinarily the blazing direct heat of the sun would have made him hunt cover, but today, with his stomach full of meat and his legs beginning to tingle all over with signs of returning life, the sun felt good, and Joshua went to sleep sitting up while Antoine smoked a pipe and Callahan, lying in the shade, studied Mah-vah.

Joshua awoke after a while. Callahan was climbing the far wall; Antoine was nodding; Mah-vah was weaving a basket of willow withes. The sun had moved somewhat and Joshua guessed he had been asleep for an hour. He tried to move his legs, without success, but the effort awoke Antoine, and he watched Joshua's awkward body-bending without change of expression.

"When can I walk?" asked Joshua.

"You walk soon," said Antoine.

"Soon" to the Indian mind was always a relative term; it might mean within the next moment or within the next century.

"You in a hurry?" asked Antoine.

Joshua, starting to answer, saw Mah-vah's eyes on him for an instant, and they made him uncomfortable.

"I need to get back to the gold fields," he said finally.

127

"Gold—yellow iron? You want yellow iron?"

"Yes."

"What you need to buy?"

Joshua considered. "Well, I could buy a ranch, or a farm, or go into business."

"So you can have more yellow iron, hey?"

Joshua frowned. Why was he so intent on finding gold, anyway? It was hard to say, but this was the sort of thing that had inflamed his imagination ever since the days when he had served as an apprentice wagonmaker at twenty-five cents a week after he had been taken from the Comanches. He'd worked years to pay off what they said was his ransom debt, and then he'd seen a man come along with one nugget of gold worth more than all his years of work, and he had made up his mind in a few imagination-filled moments. Since then he had come a long way to carry it out, and he did not intend to be stopped now.

Mah-vah looked at him, got up and went to the shelter, and came back with his black felt hat. He nodded thanks and put the hat on, and Mah-vah went on with her weaving. Antoine got up after a while and climbed the trail out of the crater. Callahan was still gone.

Joshua said to Mah-vah, "Why have you no husband?"

She glanced at him, her eyes unfathomable. "There has been no man whom I wanted to take for husband."

"A girl your age is usually married."

"A girl of my tribe is not forced to marry if she does not want to."

He picked up a half-burned twig and turned it in his hands. "You need a man to plant grain and harvest it.

"You have a husband for me, *tal vez?*"

128

"No," he said thoughtfully. "I was just finding out."

Old Antoine appeared suddenly up at the rim and came down the trail very fast. "There is a wagon train coming from Sonoita, José! From the east! Many wagons, much dust!"

Joshua looked at him sharply. "Do you know who it is?"

"No. We have seen only the signs in the air. I do not know if you wish it, José, but if you would like to go back to the ocean, we will carry you out of the mountains and take you to them."

It did not take long for Joshua to work out the answer. Legless, he would be unable to defend himself from White; and any crossing of the Colorado River in the vicinity of the Gila junction would draw White's attention, and would mean only that he had made it easier for White to find him. And not only would Joshua Pickens himself draw White's wrath, but it was possible that White would exact vengeance from the entire party. Joshua shook his head; that would not do. And there was yet another consideration: Joshua had no wish to return to San Diego until he could take White with him, for alone he would have to face the wrath of Major Heintzelman and the dirt floor of a military jail— perhaps even a term of several years at some penitentiary like the one in Georgia.

No, there was no point in trying to go back to San Diego now.

"It will be as you say," said Antoine.

"My care here has been of the best," said Joshua. "It grieves me that I am a burden to you."

Antoine shrugged lightly. "I have sworn to be a friend to the *Pain-gote-sahch*. So it says in the writing, as I have told you."

129

"Yes, of course. But—"

Antoine waved away his protest. "Then we shall continue to take care of you."

Joshua was studying the old man. You look worried about something, Antoine."

The old Maricopa's face was bland. "I do not worry, José. That is for the *Pain-gote-sahch*. They worry much, and shorten their lives."

"Nevertheless, there's something on your mind."

Antoine looked back at him and said calmly, "I am wondering how many days before you can walk."

Callahan appeared on the rim then and made his way slowly to the bottom. "They're bound to be Spaniards," he said to Joshua. "Anything you want me to tell 'em?"

"Ask about the Brodie train," said Joshua. "Find out about Natalia. See if she's safe."

"Sure, I'll do that."

"When will they pass by here?"

"About sunset—three or four hours."

"That means they'll go on tonight as far as possible."

"Depends," said Callahan. "If they're Spanish, they may stay over tomorrow and rest up for a fresh start tomorrow night."

"Anyway, find out what you can about Natalia."

"That I'll do," said Callahan.

After they ate, Callahan and Antoine got up. Callahan took the canteens. "I'll see what I can find out," he told Joshua.

Antoine got the gourds and prepared to follow him. "I will look to the animals," he said.

Later, Mah-vah came to sit by the cactus. "José," she said in her curiously musical voice, "you have asked about Natalia. Is she your *huadha-va?*"

"No," he said. "I have no wife."

"You like her?"

"Yes."

"Very much?"

Joshua parried. "I don't know, really. I haven't seen much of her."

But Mah-vah persisted. "You think to marry her one time?"

"I doubt it," he said honestly. "We are of two different nations."

"You *Pain-gote-sahch*—she Española?"

He nodded.

"But you and I—different tribes. You could not marry me, then?"

"Well, it's different from that. Her father, you see, has many, many horses—big house."

"Her father is like Apache, he demand many horses for Natalia?"

"In essence," he said, "that's about it."

"And," she said cheerfully, "you have no horses."

He trusted himself to look straight into her eyes. He could have sworn she was triumphant. "No," he said finally, "I have no horses, no mules, no nothing."

"Then," she said, "you cannot have Natalia for your wife."

"That's about it."

She nodded as if to herself, and got two gourds and began to climb the trail.

He called to her. "Antoine and Callahan are bringing water."

She turned—proud, dusky, beautiful in the twilight. Her black hair moved as she answered. "I go to see this girl who is worth so many horses that you would act like a sick beaver because you cannot have her."

He tried to get up, then swore because his legs would

131

not function. "Natalia isn't coming with that outfit," he told her.

"Is no difference. There will be another. I will see."

He was alone for a long time. Then, when it was almost dark, all three of them returned. Callahan threw down a small armful of cedar by the fire. "Them Spaniards come from Guaymas, headin' for the gold fields."

"Gold fields!"

Callahan looked up at him. "It don't mean anything to you. You ain't in no shape to shovel gravel, even if you wasn't in the Army."

Joshua stared at him. "That's my private business," he said. "I've come a long way to reach the gold fields."

Callahan looked at him squarely. "You're foolin' yourself more than anybody."

"Meaning what?"

"Nobody gets rich out of them gold fields. One out of hundreds finds gold, and chances are that he gets killed or robbed before he cashes it in. If he doesn't, he loses it gamblin' or gets his pockets picked by fancy girls. You ever see anybody that brought gold back home with him?"

Joshua stared at him until he no longer felt argumentative. "Did you hear anything about Natalia?"

"They passed at Magdalena on the way to Hermosillo. The old man had a brush with Apaches but run 'em off—no scalps lost on either side."

"I'm glad they're all safe," said Joshua.

"And they say he's told several parties to look out for you and me. But with us salted away up here in this crater, how could anyone find us?"

Joshua nodded. Brodie's outfit would be in Hermosillo by this time, all hands safe.

"Furthermore," Callahan went on, "he has told 'em all to tell us he's organizing a bigger party and he's comin' back to straighten out this ferry business at the Gila. They're to tell White if we're not alive he'll take it out of his hide."

"That's thoughtful, at least," said Joshua. "And about the most he could do under the circumstances, I guess."

"And," said Callahan gleefully, "I talked 'em out of some cornmeal." He held up a cloth sack with about two quarts of meal in it. "Tomorrow we're havin' white man's bread."

There was silence for a moment. Mah-vah looked at the ground, and Antoine said sadly, "You not like Indian bread."

"Well, I—" Callahan floundered. He looked wildly at Joshua, who refused to help, then at Mah-vah. "It ain't because it's Indian. I just ain't used to it. I need a change."

And Mah-vah, with her always astonishing perspicacity, immediately mired him deeper. "You *Pain-gote-sahch*, yes?"

"Sure. I'm American."

"You like 'Merican ways?" She nodded vigorously.

"Yeah, but—?"

Then you like one woman only—all time—no change. Yes?"

Callahan scowled. "Josh, you ain't doin' much for me," he said.

Joshua grinned. "I'll eat the corn bread if you've had a change of heart."

They had corn bread that night, baked in the ashes of the tiny fire, with the fragrant cedar wood filling the crater, and the red glow of the ashes reflecting from their faces—Callahan's reddish, the others' dusky bronze.

"I never knew you could make corn bread," Callahan told Mah-vah.

"We raise corn," said old Antoine, "but this year there is little rain, and the *Pain-gote-sahch* emigrants have reached our country hungry and have begged us for meal at any price." He shrugged eloquently. "We do not care about the price, but we do not like to see children hungry, and so we have sold all our cornmeal."

Callahan began to apologize profusely. "Look here, I'm sorry. I didn't mean anything. Well, after all—"

Mah-vah said, "Eat your bread, Cal'han."

Long after dark a great horned owl hooted up above the rim of the crater, and Antoine drifted away from the fire. Mah-vah went to her sleeping place on the other side of the big rocks that formed Joshua's shelter— rather quietly, he thought.

Callahan reached in his pocket. "I begged two cigars likewise." He held one out to Joshua, who shook his head.

"I forgot you don't smoke," said Callahan. "I'll save this one. No, by gosh, I'll give it to Antoine. Say, where'd the old fellow go, anyway? Ain't that him climbin' the trail?"

"Looks like it."

Callahan held a glowing coal between two green twigs and lighted the cigar. He got it puffing to his satisfaction, and lay back against the rock. "This ain't such a bad life at all. If we didn't have so many things to do—What *are* we goin' to do about White?"

"There's only one answer to that."

"Well, me, I got sixteen years in the Army at stake, and a pretty little Mexican girl named Juana, but you ain't got nothin'."

"I've got my own conscience to satisfy. I turned loose a man who may be a murderer—for six hundred dollars."

134

Callahan stared at him. "You mean you turned White loose deliberately?"

"Yes."

"And why six hundred dollars?"

"I borrowed six hundred from the banker back home. I lost the whole thing in the gold fields, and I wanted to pay him back. It was an honest debt."

Callahan blew a cloud of smoke into the night sky. "It looks like you got quite a program ahead of you. We got to hide out until we're both well. I figure we can stay that long with the Maricopas."

"I don't think it's going to be over a couple of weeks," said Joshua.

"Maybe." Callahan sounded doubtful. "Then we got to take White and haul him back to San Diego. If we turn him in, I figure we can talk the Major into lettin' us off with maybe sixty days in jail. How to put our hands on White—that's the question."

"I figure," said Joshua, "we'll get to Glanton and make a deal with him when White isn't around. We'll tell him straight out we're soldiers and we let a man go and we're running from the Army for it. But won't say who we let go."

"That's mighty close to the truth," said Callahan.

"Then we'll watch for White, and when he comes back from one of his trips—"

He stopped suddenly. Old Antoine had somehow materialized out of the darkness and stood now by the dying fire in his sandals and breechclout, and by his side stood Tu-naams, similarly dressed but magnificently muscled.

"José," said Antoine softly, "I have news."

Joshua stared at the two Indians. "All right."

"I have told Tu-naams to watch Francisco, and if

135

Francisco goes to the ferry to talk with White, then Tu-naams must come here at once, I have told him."

Callahan stood up. "You mean Francisco decided to tell White we was here?"

"Why else would Francisco talk to him?"

Joshua looked at Tu-naams. "You're sure?"

The Indian broke into rapid Maricopa, with many gutturals and peculiar breaks. Antoine interpreted. "He saw Francisco leave one morning, and after a while he trailed him to the river. Francisco had a horse hidden there, and Tu-naams was forced to run hard all day, all night to keep up with him."

"And Francisco didn't know this?"

"No. Francisco went to the ferry and hid in the willows until White came across. Then he talked to White, and White gave him yellow iron."

"When was this?"

"Two days ago. Tu-naams took a mule from a train of Spaniards and came here at once to tell you of this."

"That means we can look for White about tomorrow morning," said Callahan. "He wouldn't waste many hours if he had a chance to catch us like this."

"We must leave at once," said Antoine.

Joshua looked down at his useless legs. "Yes," he said. "I think you'd better."

Callahan crumpled his cigar in his big hand. "What the hell are you talkin' about?"

"I can't climb that trail," said Joshua, "and you're barely able to climb it yourself. Antoine is too old. Maybe we can set up a trap. Leave me plenty of ammunition and—"

Antoine's gray hair was ghostly in the reflection from the ashes. "We leave tonight," he said imperiously.

136

CHAPTER FIFTEEN

JOSHUA NODDED. "YOU'RE RIGHT, OF COURSE. There's no time to waste. When you get back to San Diego, Cal—"

Tu-naams bounded across the fire, turned his back to Joshua, and squatted, balancing on his toes and fingers.

"You hold," said Antoine.

Joshua frowned. "He can't carry me up that trail. I'm a dead weight."

"Tu-naams very strong," said Mah-vah's soft voice. "You hold."

Joshua looked at her. She seemed fresh, as if she had been sleeping. *"Mesahatiz-aye-dotz-a-hot'k,"* he said. "This girl has lovely eyes."

Mah-vah blushed but did not move. "You hold," she said.

Joshua put his arms around Tu-naams' neck, and the Maricopa picked up Joshua's legs and wrapped them around his waist, then arose lightly, easily.

Joshua shook his head. "Maybe he can do it," he told Callahan. "They were making men when he was born."

Mah-vah and Antoine were busy gathering up food, gourds, canteens, rifles, pistols, and ammunition. Tu-naams went to the trail and started up it with easy strides. Joshua leaned forward to help him balance the weight. A hundred and sixty pounds or so was a lot on a man's back on a trail that was almost straight up and down. But Tu-naams didn't hesitate. He pushed himself up with his legs, pulled on roots and projecting rocks with his arms, and in a moment they were in complete blackness, seemingly suspended between the sky and the earth. One slip, thought Joshua, and it would all be

137

over. But Tu-naams made no slip. They arose out of the dark depths of the crater into a world of fantastically shaped rocks of great size, of cactus, and of things that whirred or fluttered or scraped in the night. Tu-naams turned south and moved steadily, seeming to follow a known trail, though Joshua could see no marks to indicate it. Finally he stopped under a gnarled cedar tree and carefully let Joshua down.

Joshua squeezed his shoulder. *"Gracias, amigo,"* he said. The other three came up suddenly out of the darkness. "We have your mules in the next valley," said Antoine, "with our own."

"It doesn't seem possible," said Joshua, remembering the almost vertical climb.

"Don't it?" asked Callahan. "How do you think you got down there in the first place?"

Joshua stared at him. "I hadn't thought," he admitted.

"You didn't have no wings that day," Callahan reminded him.

"But the real question is still to come," said Joshua. "Will I be able to ride?"

"You can have my mule," said Callahan. "That's the singlefootin'est mule ever crossed the desert. Mighty like ridin' in a boat."

"Get me in the saddle," said Joshua.

They tied a rawhide rope just above each of his knees and fastened that to the nearest girth ring, so that if he lost his balance he would not fall out of control. He got a hand on the saddlehorn and picked up the reins.

Antoine led out. "We must be quiet," he warned them. "Is dangerous, for *Yah-bay-páiesh* may be watching the Spanish camp." Caution was always necessary in Apache Country.

Occasionally they stopped, and Tu-naams

138

disappeared silently in the dark on foot, to show up as silently half an hour later and motion them on. Within two hours they were out of the mountains and headed east on the open desert.

"If Apaches watch the camp," said Antoine, "they will be in the mountains."

They walked the animals for an hour, then Antoine said, "Can you go faster, José?"

"I think so."

He slapped the mule into its singlefoot gait, and for a while he thought he would not be able to do it, but the ropes and the saddlehorn helped him to keep his seat, and he learned to relax and maintain his balance, and by that time they stopped to give the animals a breather.

"From here we go north," said Antoine. "There is no water, no spring between here and the *Hah-quah-sie-eel-ish*."

"How far is it," asked Joshua, "to the Gila?"

"Maybe forty miles," said Antoine.

Joshua was trying to gauge his own strength against the distance. Forty miles seemed like an eternity, but he had to make it somehow. Too many had risked a great deal for him.

They turned north and followed the pole star. On their right occasionally were ragged black outlines of low mountains, but the land over which they traveled was hard gravel with a few creosote bushes and sometimes a spidery ocotillo, reaching into the sky like a giant tarantula on its back.

In the morning they saw the first visible evidence of Glanton's tactics at the ferry. Tu-naams saw it first—a black dot on the desert, hard to make out. They stopped for a breather. To the west, beyond the strange-looking black dot, were other low hills—sandy, barren, sterile.

They gathered into a small knot. "It looks like a horse or a mule," said Callahan, "but I'm not sure."

They waited, for the strange object was coming toward them, and finally they heard an agonized cry: *"Agua, por Diós! Agua!"*

Joshua was a little sick when he saw what one day and night on the desert could do to a human being. A small Spanish mule was led by a Mexican woman. Two men were hanging across the saddle, both unconscious. Their mouths were open, their lips dry, their tongues hanging loose. The woman stumbled across the desert, almost blind from the glare of the sun on the white surface, gasping at every step. Her black hair was around her shoulders; her once-white shirt-waist was half torn off, probably from her efforts at putting the men on the mule and keeping them there, and her lips were white from the heat and the sun. *"Agua!"* she whispered. *"Por favor, denos aqua!"*

Callahan and Tu-naams ran to her with canteens. Callahan sprinkled a few drops on her lips and mouth.

Tu-naams wet the mule's muzzle with his hand, while Antoine and Mah-vah untied the two Mexican men and laid them in the shade of the mule. Then they moistened their foreheads and wrists, and finally put a few drops of water in the blackened mouths.

One of the men stirred and muttered, *"Hijo de cabrón!* Son of a goat!"

The girl was not over eighteen, and had been strong and beautiful, with great lustrous eyes, but now she was pitifully drawn by the desert heat and the lack of water. She paid no attention to the first man, but fell on her knees by the side of the second, begging him to speak to her, threatening destruction if he did not.

"The desert is a hard place," Callahan observed.

Joshua nodded.

Finally the second man moved one arm, and the girl fell on him and implored him to speak to her. Callahan pulled her back. "You ain't helpin', lady," he said.

They worked over the man, and finally he rolled his eyes and saw the girl and whispered, "Lupe!" in a cracked voice.

"Pánfilo!" she cried, and would have thrown herself on him again but for Callahan. "They killed him!" she cried. "They wanted to kill us all!"

The first man sat up. He was heavier, and his face was pockmarked. "My Margarita!" he moaned. "What has happened to my Margarita?"

Now the woman had Pánfilo's head in her lap and was soothing him and rocking him back and forth. Callahan kept dribbling a few drops of water into his mouth, and presently some recognition seemed to come to his eyes, and he sat up, supported by the girl.

"What happened back there?" asked Callahan.

"We came to the ferry two days ago," Pánfilo said in a weak voice. "We have been in the gold fields and we found some gold, but the Chileños and the Chinese came also, and the North Americans—and these last have been very angry at all the others of us who found gold, for they say it is their gold and we have no right to it. They have find a North American dead, and they say his gold is gone, and they say we have stolen it, and they take the gold and give us one hour to leave. So we have the one mule, and we decide to go back to Chihuahua, but we have no money for boats. They tell us the women can pay our way for us, but we are not *alcahuetes*, señor. We are not pimps. We work a little in the fields with our mule and we reach Warner's rancho, and they tell us we must not try to cross the desert, but

141

we have said we are going to do so, for Margarita is now *embarasada* and she wants her child to be born in Chihuahua, so the Señor Warner gives us food and gourds for water and a little money, and he tells us to stay away from the ferry." He stopped for a moment, out of breath. "But we have a bad time on the desert. We cannot find water in the wells, and we are almost dead when we reach the river. We have three dollars and we offer this to Glanton, but he laughs at us and says this will not pay for one of us, and he says if the women will stay with his men for a week he will take us all across the river. But we decide to swim, holding to the mule's tail. Some Indians are going to come for us with a canoe, but Glanton's men threaten to shoot them if they do. And Glanton's men are waiting for us at the other side, and they make us give them the three dollars, because they say we owe them that for crossing the river, because the river belongs to them. Then we have nothing to buy food, and they take us to the desert and say this is the way to come, and get the hell out of there and never come back. And the Indians watch but they dare not help. And we start out, but somewhere we lose the road because we cannot see the bones of cattle and horses for a little while, and last night Margarita dies, and we leave her, and then I know nothing more until I find myself here."

Callahan looked grim. "What's your name?" he asked the other man with the pockmarked face.

"I am Jesús."

"Did you see all this?"

The man nodded. "*Sí, señor.*"

"Did he tell it right?"

"*Sí*, it is as he said."

Joshua asked, "Did you bury Margarita?"

"No, señor. We have no shovel, nothing."

"Tu-naams," said Joshua, "can you follow their backtrail and look for the woman? She might be alive."

Tu-naams nodded soberly and looked at the sun. "I will look, but she will not be alive now."

"Make sure," said Joshua.

Tu-naams mounted his mule and rode out.

"Now," said Callahan, "the three of you better come with us."

"Are you going to Chihuahua?" asked Lupe.

"Nope, we're goin' to the Gila, but you're lost—bad lost—and you can't find your way from here, because the wind covers up the tracks in a few hours. But you can go up to the Gila and make a few dollars helping the emigrants, and someday you can go south down to Quitobaquito and join up with a Spanish train. You were damn' fools to cross the desert—only four of you—anyway."

"We have not expect men so bad as Glanton."

Callahan took a deep breath. "We'll take care of Glanton. That seems to be our special job on earth. But you was crazy to cross the desert in the first place with only four of you—and not a rifle in the bunch!"

"We have our knives, señor."

Callahan shook his head. "You come with us. Stay with the Indians a while on the Gila and then do what you want—but don't start out by yourselves through Apache country. Savvy?"

"*Sí* señor, we understand,"

Callahan and Joshua and Antoine had a conference. "We're goin' to be slowed down some," said Callahan, "and it's hotter'n boilin' oil."

"We've got six animals and eight persons to ride," said Joshua.

143

"Five animals and seven to ride," said Callahan. "*You* can't even stand up. Well, I figger we can take our turns walkin' except for you."

"We can walk," said Antoine, and Mah-vah nodded.

"I never felt so useless," said Joshua.

"Your time will come," Callahan said, "when we get to the ferry."

They started north again to the Gila. It was very hot, and the wind over the desert was a smothering wind that drew the moisture out of their bodies, and Joshua could almost see their flesh shrink as the tissue lost water.

They went slowly, and about noon Tu-naams caught up with them. "She is dead," he said. He looked up and made a circle with his hand. "*Ce.*"

"Buzzards?" Callahan asked in a low voice.

Joshua nodded.

They stopped for three hours. The animals lay on the hot sand and heaved. The humans sat with their backs to the sun and tried not to think about water. Mah-vah picked some *tunas* with a small wooden implement shaped like a clothespin. She peeled them and gave them half a dozen each, and they were cooling and refreshing.

In midafternoon they went on. The two Mexicans were in bad shape, and old Antoine was faltering, though he wouldn't admit it. Callahan had lost twenty pounds, but he and Mah-vah and even Lupe seemed to go along as strongly as if they were traveling on the grassy plains around San Diego.

Near midnight they dropped into a grassy flat, and Antoine said fervently, "We have beaten the desert again!"

The animals stopped to snip grass, and within a few miles they came to the bed of the Gila. There wasn't much water in it, and Tu-naams said that a few miles to the west it disappeared entirely into the sand, but here there was water and it was better than milk and honey. They plunged their faces and their arms in it, and the animals drank all they were allowed, and fought at being pulled away. When all were refreshed, they set off up the valley. In two more suns, Antoine said, they would reach the village, and there they could rest, for they would be among friends.

It was hard traveling in the sandy bottom of the river, and almost impossible in the overflow bottomland immediately next to it, for this was full of dead trees and grown up with willows and mesquite and brush, so the small train moved out a few miles and traveled on flats, where there was sparse bunch grass for the animals. On one of these flats they came across two burned wagons, with nothing left but the wagon irons and a scattering of wind-blown ashes.

Antoine went far around these, muttering, "*Yah-bay-páiesh.*"

Joshua and Callahan rode closer and looked for bones, but found none. Perhaps the humans had survived the attack and had escaped alive, leaving their wagons and goods to the Apaches. It was not an easy road, the trail to gold.

Joshua was able by that time to put his feet in the crude Indian stirrups, and that helped to maintain his balance, and all of them, with plenty of water, were able to keep up a good pace.

The Gila followed a tortuous course, and the narrow bottomland ran mostly on the south side of the river. The Pimas and the Maricopas lived together almost as a single tribe, their villages starting 150 miles above the junction of the Gila and the

Colorado. The Maricopas, formerly a Yuma tribe, had a nominal chief, but there were not many Maricopas left, and the real chief of the villages on the Gila was a Pima Indian, Cola Azul.

They followed the emigrant trail, plainly marked and in places heavily rutted by the wagon wheels. Under a cottonwood tree near the trail was a fresh mound of earth, while above it, nailed to the tree, was a thin board from a cracker box, with words laboriously written in pencil: "Henry James Alcester. Native of Georgia. Hanged by vote of the company Dec. 28, 1850."

Joshua frowned when he read that. Callahan read it too, and scratched his sandy beard.

"It don't say what for," he noted.

"No. I guess there wasn't room on the board. The fellow had to write kind of small there at the last, anyway."

Callahan shook his head and put his hat on. "Some people sure want to get to California," he observed, and demanded of Joshua, "What's out there that's so much better than what they had back home?"

"I could answer that with another question: What did they have back home that was worth hanging onto?"

"Most of 'em had folks back home."

Joshua put on his hat and turned the mule. "It seems to be the nature of Americans to want to move to different parts of the country. It's something born in people, I guess."

Callahan was puzzled. "You mean people figger this land is ours and we got a duty to settle it?"

"Thunder, no," said Joshua. "People want to move, that's all. Those who want to move can do it. Those who don't want to can stay home."

"What I'm gettin' at," Callahan said doggedly, "is

what's the special good of all these people goin' to California?"

"Why should there be any? What's the good in their staying home, as far as that goes?"

Callahan said, "You're pretty smart, but you still think you can make a killin' in the gold fields."

Joshua looked at a cactus wren's nest built in the angle between a *pitáhaya* trunk and a big branch. "That's what I came out here for," he said stubbornly.

They stopped to let the animals browse on cane grass and young cottonwoods, and Callahan got off the mule to let Tu-naams ride, for it was his turn. But Tu-naams shook his head.

"We soon be in Sacatón, our village," said Antoine. "Tu-naams say he can walk, let Mah-vah ride."

Later they rode down a gentle slope that looked, in the twilight, like some strange, enchanted stage where the *pitáhayas* rose like columns of an age-old temple long since abandoned to destruction. A few scattered salt bushes softened the ground, and the shadows of the *pitáhayas* were lost among them.

Mah-vah rode alongside Joshua. "Sacatón is beyond the next hill," she said.

He looked at her. Her eyes were shining, and he smiled. "You'll be glad to get home, won't you?"

"It is always good to get home," she said.

At the top of the rise they stopped. Down below them was Sacatón, a tiny village of brush-and-mud huts and a network of canals and rock fences. Down along the river, eating cane grass and willows, were horses and a few cattle. Up on the hills beyond Sacatón were more horses, and on the top of the hill opposite were two guards, one of whom immediately saw them and called in a singing voice that echoed across the hills. Antoine took up the call and sent it back, and suddenly the huts, which had seemed lifeless, began to give forth motion. Men in breechclouts and women in cloth or blanket skirts came from under the suspended blankets that served as doors, followed by children of all ages—the smaller boys naked, all the girls wearing skirts.

Antoine led them down the slope, and they were met at the edge of the area of *acequias* by all the inhabitants. Antoine led the way past the many probing black eyes, past Francisco with his sullen face, standing next to Mis-ke-tai-ish, and Le-och next to him. All the Maricopas watched in silence. They scrutinized the three Spaniards, but especially Callahan and Joshua Pickens.

Joshua didn't like it. There was something in the air and he didn't know what it was. Perhaps it was Francisco's disappointment at seeing the two North Americans turn up alive after he had told White where they were. It was easy to see that when White returned from the Tinajas Altas without having found the men, he would have little use for Francisco. Perhaps he had promised Francisco plenty of tobacco or red calico with which to woo the lady he chose. Now it was quite clear from the unpleasantness on Francisco's face that these thoughts were in his mind. Joshua resolved to keep an eye on him if possible.

Antoine stopped the little cavalcade in the midst of the watching Indians and said simply, "These are my friends."

Mis-ke-tai-ish said hesitantly, "We have not enough for ourselves to eat, Antoine. How can we feed these?"

Antoine said, "These are my friends. My stores of food are for them." He looked at Mis-ke-tai-ish, then at Francisco. "You do not look hungry to me. Perhaps the

Pain-gote-sahch at the ferry have more food than is here."

The huts, Joshua saw now, were large in area but very low. A grown person would not be able to stand erect in them. Antoine stopped before a blanket-covered doorway and motioned to Joshua to get down.

Callahan helped him inside. It was dark but it was cool, and it had a clean smell about it. Antoine spread a bearskin in a corner. "This is your home," he said to Joshua. "You stay here as long as you want."

Joshua sat down, rubbing his legs, and Antoine said to Callahan, "You come with me—next house."

They left, and the blanket was lifted again and Mah-vah came in. He could not mistake her. "I take care of you," she said. "You sleep now?"

"Pretty soon. Where are you going to be?"

"I will be here. This is my house."

He thought about that. She lifted the blanket and sat in the doorway for a while, casually greeting those who passed. Then she dropped the blanket, came inside, and went to a blanket across the floor from him.

He watched this with some concern, and finally said, "Are you staying in here?"

"This my house."

"The people will say you are a bad girl, for you are not married to me."

She shrugged gracefully in the dimness. "You cannot chase me. That is plain. So all will know that nothing happens to me unless I want it so."

"But—"

"If I want it, that is my business."

"But the people—"

"They not talk until you walk. You see. Go to sleep now."

149

CHAPTER SIXTEEN

THE NEXT MORNING SHE WAS GONE WHEN HE AWOKE, and he heard the sounds of a busy place. Callahan came in and helped him sit on a piece of log before the hut. He watched Indian men digging at ditches with small, awkward implements, which, however, seemed to be efficient enough to turn the loose earth.

"Big farms, ain't they?" said Callahan.

Each plot was very small, and fenced with crooked sticks of mesquite. Up on the slope, beyond the reach of irrigation, was wheat, now a foot high. In the little enclosed plots, however, were seedlings of watermelons, pumpkins, muskmelons, beans, corn, and squash, and these seemed to be receiving most of the farmers' attention.

"Ain't those things little cotton plants?" asked Callahan.

"Yes, they raise cotton."

"By jiggers," said Callahan, "I just about changed my mind about Indians. These fellers are pretty industrious."

"Well, they won't do much in the middle of the day, because it will be maybe a hundred and ten degrees, but that's only sensible. And they're about as nice-looking Indians as you'll find."

The smells of cooking began to work on Joshua's appetite, and, with Callahan's help, he found Mah-vah busy in a sort of outdoor kitchen made of brush. She smiled at them and told Callahan, "You have corn bread now."

"I ain't that fussy," said Callahan.

"You no like mesquite bread. I save for us." She

pointed to the roof of the kitchen, where piles of mesquite pods were drying. "We have plenty," she said, "until the wheat harvest."

Tu-naams was out with Antoine, directing the scanty flow of water in the ditches around a tiny field of corn. Mis-ke-tai-ish and Francisco were up on the slope pulling weeds out of the wheat, while Le-och was preparing breakfast in her own kitchen, a short distance from Mah-vah. Callahan watched Le-och.

Joshua sat near the doorway that day in the hot sun. The heat didn't bother him as long as there was water to drink.

Three men, headed by Francisco, set out early to cross the river with bows and arrows, obviously hunting. At the hut next to Mah-vah's, Le-och sat outside weaving a willow basket to carry burdens on her shoulder. Beyond her, an older woman was shaping with her hands a large vessel of clay, which she would carry on her head to transport water; these vessels held as much as six gallons each and were balanced with the help of a special pad that fitted over the scalp.

Mah-vah took a crooked mesquite root and went to help Antoine and Tu-naams till the tiny fields. But she was back before noon, and before the village was burdened by the full heat of the day she climbed a short ladder made of driftwood and rawhide lashings and brought down a basket filled with hard ears of corn.

"You will have your corn bread today," she told him.

Joshua promptly disclaimed any notion that he did not like the Maricopa food, but she brushed it aside.

"You like corn," she said. "I make."

This was the hardest work of all. In the shade of the hut was a large block of lava with the center hollowed out a little. She rubbed the ears of corn against one

151

another and scraped off the kernels into the stone *metate*. Then she got on her knees with a stone pestle and spent an hour grinding the kernels into meal.

Joshua shook his head. "It's too hard work. It's easier to fix frijoles or squash."

She shrugged eloquently. "You will have them, too. And if I did not do this I might have too little to do."

Callahan came up from the river with two straight pieces of dead cottonwood. "They're light but strong," he told Joshua. "You can use 'em for canes until you get back on your feet."

"Thanks." Joshua tried them out. One had a bend that served as a handle. "I'll be able to move around a little with these."

"I got a big scheme," said Callahan. "The river bottom down there is full of blue quail, and I'm going to load my rifle with gravel and bring back a mess of them. Ever eat quail?"

"Sometimes."

"Sweeter'n bear meat." Callahan licked his lips. "We'll have quail for supper tonight." He got his rifle and walked toward the river. Le-och was down there gathering wood. When she came by presently on the way to her hut, her face was pleasantly flushed and her eyes had an absent look in them.

Late in the afternoon the heat relented a little, and Joshua sat before Mah-vah's house and watched the activity of the entire valley spread out before him. Already he was putting on weight, and in spite of the heat he had never felt better. His wounds were healed or healing, and under Antoine's ministrations there were no more dull aches in his back or his leg. The crease in his scalp was scabbed over, and now the quiet industry in the village seemed soothing also to his mind. For a little while the problem of White and the ferry was not quite so pressing as it had been, although he well knew that he would never be completely safe even in Sacatón as long as Francisco was around.

Occasionally he got a glimpse of Indian boys, bronze-skinned, black-haired, silent, hunting game in the river bottom with bow and arrow—it was difficult to know whether for sport or for food. Downstream he heard the boom of Callahan's rifle, and wondered if he was having any luck; it was not like Callahan to waste powder.

Antoine, little and old and wrinkled, came in early, for he was tired, and lay on a blanket alongside Joshua.

"Where are the Spaniards?" Joshua asked him while Antoine rolled a cigarette.

Antoine's seamed brown face was placid and relaxed. "They have gone up the river to look for a cottonwood log big enough to make a *carreta* so they can finish their journey to Chihuahua."

"They can't pull one of those things with a mule."

"I have agreed to trade them an ox for their mule, and give them food besides. They have many relatives in Chihuahua." He shook his head. "I do not know, José. That man Jesús is a hard one to understand."

"Why?"

"He grieves too much over his Margarita."

"It is a natural grief."

Antoine inhaled a couple of times, "Yes, true, but it is over and done with. His grieving cannot bring her back."

"It will take time."

"So. How much time?" Antoine shrugged. "Many moons, perhaps?" He looked at the distant mountains, where the blue haze was turning to purple. "Is not good

153

to grieve too long. Maricopas do not do that. We burn the dead one's body and go on with the work of living day by day."

"That's one trouble," Joshua pointed out. "They couldn't even bury her. They had to leave her body on the desert."

"The buzzards will take care of it."

"True," said Joshua, "but these people are of different beliefs. They have been taught they must be buried by a priest. To them it is a sad thing to leave a loved one's body on the desert for scavengers."

"It is a thing that happens," said Antoine. "This is a wild, savage country. A man lives and travels in it at his own risk." He shook his old head.

The steady crunch and grind of the *metate* now came also from Le-och's kitchen place. Then Callahan came up from the river with his rifle over his shoulder. He was grinning as he strode up the trail of hard-packed clay between the little fields. "There'll be something different for supper tonight," he said, "with three dozen blue quail."

"It worked, then?"

"Like a charm. Only I had to go far enough away to keep from disturbing game where the kids was hunting."

He sat down, and Antoine and Joshua helped him skin the birds, saving the breasts only. Mah-vah came to see what they were doing, and nodded without comment as Callahan showed her what they had. She went back to her corn-grinding, and Callahan looked over at Le-och, a hundred feet away, and said, "Maybe I shoulda got a few more for her."

Antoine shook his head. "No. This bird is taboo to women."

154

"You mean they can't eat it?" asked Callahan incredulously.

"That is so."

"Why?"

"I don't know. It is tradition."

"Like wanting to take the bones of your loved ones home for burial," Joshua said quickly. "With the Spaniards that is tradition too."

Antoine looked up at him, and finally nodded.

Francisco and Mis-ke-tai-ish and others now were driving cattle and horses in to water from the southern slope. At the same time a horse and rider came at a hard gallop over the ridge to the east, and Antoine got up at once. "It is the horse of Kámal Tkak," he said, "son of Mah-vah's brother."

The Maricopas throughout the village gradually stopped their various activities and stood silently to watch the boy on a pinto horse. He reached the edge of the irrigated land and slowed to a trot. He was riding, Joshua noticed, without bridle or saddle of any kind, but he guided the horse along the pathways and stopped it in front of Antoine and slid off.

"Uncle," he said, "there comes a great train of wagons—many *Pain-gote-sahch.*"

"How far?" asked Antoine, getting up.

"A little way."

"Will they get here tonight?"

"Yes. They are three hills over. They will be here at sundown."

Antoine put his hand on the pinto's neck. "You have done well, son. How many wagons?"

"Twenty-two," he said excitedly. "Many horses, many mules, hundreds of cattle, thousands of *Pain-gote-sahch.*"

Antoine shook his head. "No, not thousands. Many, perhaps, but not thousands. Go round up the villagers. Pass the word there will be trading." He looked at Joshua. "I hope these *Pain-gote-sahch are good men.*"

"Why do you say that?" asked Joshua.

"It is a long trail the *Pain-gote-sahch* follow to Maricopa land. Very dry, not very much to eat, sometimes no wood, no grass. I do not know where all these *Pain-gote-sahch* come from, but it is a long way off—farther than San Diego."

"Yes," said Joshua gravely, "it is a long way."

"Some *Pain-gote-sahch* have been treated bad by other Indians. Some have been frightened by the *Yah-bay-páiesh.*"

"The Apaches," murmured Joshua.

Antoine nodded vigorously. "They have little patience when they reach Sacatón. They want this, that. Corn first always, but we have little corn left. They want to buy with money, and money is no good for us. We want cloth, axes, shovels. If they are bad, they swear at us and threaten trouble. I hope they are good *Pain-gote-sahch.*"

Antoine went inside. The Maricopas of the village, aroused by young Kámal Tkak's exciting news, began to move. Some got on top of their dwellings and took corn and beans out of the shallow, cylindrical-shaped containers. Others went into their odd-shaped granaries, made like half a shell on edge, without any protection from the elements in front, and took wheat and dried *pitáhaya* fruit and small *otlas* of *pitáhaha* molasses and *pinole,* which was a mixture of dried corn and wheat, and small amounts of the precious cornmeal, and salt. A number of the Maricopas went down to the river and appeared to dig in the sand with their crude Mexican

156

shovels, and when Joshua asked Mah-vah what they were doing, she said they were digging watermelons—that melons, buried in the sand, kept well until January. It was now much too late, but the *Pain-gote-sahch* would be angry if they could not trade for something.

"But if the melons are old and dried up, they will be angry and accuse you of trying to cheat them."

"They not have to buy," she said with her usual unanswerable simplicity.

The Maricopas began streaming toward the ridge, where already deep ruts marked the Maricopa Trail of the emigrants. But Antoine remained seated.

"Why aren't you going?" asked Joshua.

Antoine shook his head. "I am chief. This is my village. If the *Pain-gote-sahch* chief wants to see me, let him come. If not, let him go."

Mah-vah was over talking to Le-och now. Lupe and the two Mexican men were clustered in front of their hut the only empty one in the village, Joshua had learned. Callahan came from somewhere and sat on the other side of Antoine, opposite Joshua. They waited.

CHAPTER SEVENTEEN

IN THE LAST RED RAYS OF SUNLIGHT THE GREAT wagons topped the ridge, their gray canvas tops moving jerkily as the oxen took their slow, implacable steps. When a wheel met a stone or a root, the canvas seemed to hang for a moment as the axle turned on the kingpin; then it would lurch up and over, down and back, and every wagon in the long train would repeat this series of movements at every obstacle, so that it was a sort of shimmering ecstasy that started at the front and passed the length of the train to the end, almost as if it had been alive.

Riding ahead of the first wagon was a big man with a heavy black beard. This would be a "good man," Joshua saw, because he was riding to leeward to keep from throwing up dust in the faces of those in the other wagons, which were throwing up enough dust of their own.

As they came over the ridge, their sounds came with them: the creaking of dry wood as the wagons swayed, the wailing of the oxbows as the cattle settled into the yokes on a hard pull, the jangling of chains, the crying of a small baby, the song of its mother trying to sing the dust out of its eyes. At the end of a long day under the desert sun there was no cursing and no loud talk.

"These will be good men," Joshua said to Antoine.

Old Antoine nodded doubtfully.

The big man with the black beard held his horse back and met the Maricopas with their products for sale. He talked to them a moment and then left them, coming through the village, riding his horse at a walk, careful to stay in the path so as not to trample the crops.

Even old Antoine was relieved. "This one is good," he agreed.

Yes, and he observed the proprieties even in Indian country. He came to see the chief. He rode up before Antoine, and his red-rimmed eyes were quick to take in Joshua and Callahan, but he said nothing to them.

"You Antoine?" he said.

Antoine nodded. "Yes."

"Have a cee-gar?"

"*Gracias.*"

The big man raked a sulphur match across the seat of his trousers. He held the light for Antoine and then for himself. "I'm General Patterson, from Tennessee," he announced. "Party of a hundred and twelve, bound for Californy. You savvy English?" he asked suddenly.

Antoine nodded. "I savvy 'nough."

"We come a long way," said Patterson, "and a rough way. Them damned Apaches didn't let us sleep for two weeks."

"Apaches very bad Indians," said Antoine.

"Your people look different."

"You general." Antoine seemed satisfied "Sit down, General."

"I'd as soon stand, if it's all the same to you. I been ridin' all day and my rear end is mighty numb."

"All right," said Antoine.

"I met your people over there on the slope, Chief. I was hopin' you'd have some corn for us."

Antoine shook his head. "Corn very scarce." He motioned toward the tiny fields. "It will not be ripe for two moons yet—and there have been many *Pain-gote-sahch.*"

Patterson frowned, puzzled by the word. Then he nodded. "Americans," he said. "You certain you haven't got any more corn?"

"Not enough to feed your whole train. Maybe for two dozen oxen." He shook his head.

"That won't do us any good," said Patterson. He glanced at Mah-vah, who was standing at the corner of the hut, then at Joshua and Callahan, and his lips moved as he speculated. "We figured on going around your village this evening, chief, and camping on the river down below. All right with you?"

"Good," said Antoine. "Is good."

"Grass down there?"

"No." Antoine shook his head. "Grass eaten by

159

emigrants. You go two-three mile, plenty grass, plenty good mesquite for horses."

"All right. It may be a little dark when we get there, but we'll make it. Understand this is the last village before we hit the Colorado."

"Yes."

"How far is that?"

Antoine turned to Joshua.

"About a hundred and sixty miles," said Joshua. "West a ways you'll find the Gila takes a big bend south. You can save time by cutting across and keeping to the northwest of the hills. Follow the foothills until you hit the river again. It's a fairly long trip without water, but not too long."

Patterson's sharp eyes looked him over. "Mind if I ask who you are?"

Joshua considered it for a moment. "No, I don't mind. I'm Joshua Pickens."

Patterson asked, "You a squaw man?"

"Not so far. Would it matter if I were?"

Patterson's quick eyes darted over him. "No, I reckon not. You want me to forget I seen you?"

"I'd just as soon you would."

"I don't know what your game is, mister, but if you tell me straight on the road, I'll forget about seeing you here."

"Another thing," said Joshua. "The river peters out before it reaches the Colorado."

"You mean it goes dry?"

"Yes."

"Hell's fire! They told me the Gila never went dry. That's why we came this way."

"It doesn't matter what they told you. It's been a dry year, and this is a dry time of year, and unless it rains you'll find yourself hard pushed for water."

"I'll keep my canteens and kegs full, then."

Joshua nodded.

"Well . . ." Patterson offered to shake hands.

Joshua started to get up until he found out he couldn't. He offered his hand sitting down.

"I'm damned!" said Patterson.

"This man's Callahan," said Joshua. "Bill Callahan."

Patterson looked at the ragged green rifleman's pants. "Out of the Army, eh? You fellows here on a mission?"

Joshua said, "It would be better to forget us."

"All right." He turned back to Antoine, shook hands, and started to stride away, then wheeled abruptly and came back. "You two," he said to Joshua and Callahan, "look like decent citizens to me. Have a cigar."

Each took one and thanked him.

"Them ain't Mexican cigars, either," he said. "That's genuine Virginia tobaccy."

He turned and walked back toward the wagons, and Joshua felt the jar of his bootsteps on the ground.

Antoine said thoughtfully, "He will not take anything by force, but he will get what he wants."

Again the big man checked himself and returned. "I been hearing some nasty things about this ferry on the Colorado. Know anything about it?"

"What did you hear?" asked Joshua.

"Heard they're holding up emigrants for four dollars a head for people and stock, and twenty-five for a wagon."

"It might be," said Joshua.

"That's robbery!" said Patterson.

"It's a lot of money," admitted Joshua.

"What if a man hasn't got it?"

Joshua looked at the three Mexicans, who watched silently. He looked back at Patterson. "It doesn't seem to make much difference to Glanton," he said.

Patterson, chewing his cigar, muttered to himself. Finally he said angrily, "That would hold us up for about eighteen hundred dollars."

"You can raft across the river—if he'll let you."

"What do you mean, let me?" Patterson demanded.

Joshua looked up at him. "General, Glanton owns the ferry and claims the exclusive right to transport people and cargoes across the river."

"The hell he does!" the General said angrily. "It looks to me like it's time somebody did something about this."

"Such as yourself, General?"

Patterson glared at him. "Maybe!" he snapped, and turned on his heel and strode away.

"He has not much patience with men like Glanton," Antoine observed.

Presently Antoine's people began to come back across the slope, their products gone; in their place were blankets, red and white cloth, knives, and one or two tin pans. Patterson's train got under way and moved on slowly and ponderously.

Joshua, watching the Maricopas return, noted that Mis-ke-tai-ish and Francisco were not among them.

Callahan helped Joshua into the hut, and later Mahvah sat beside him for a moment. "You have no more fever, José," she said, feeling his forehead.

"Not from that bullet," he said.

"You go to the *Xá kwitas* pretty soon?"

"When my legs get well."

"I do not think you are going to help Gal-lanton."

"Maybe—maybe not."

162

She sounded troubled. "He's very bad man. I know that."

"It was one of his men gave me that bullet in the back. What happened to that bullet, anyhow?"

"You did not save it?" she asked.

"I forgot about it," he said.

"You are very careless man." She touched his face and got up and went outside.

He made himself comfortable on the bearskin that was his bed. The sounds of the wagon train died away, and the sounds of the night took over. A mule brayed up on the slope, and oxen grunted as they lay down heavily. A song came from the Mexicans' hut—a rather lonesome song. The woman started it, and the two men joined in, and for a little while their soprano and tenor voices sounded clear under the stars, and then a coyote yapped, and there were the sounds of axes from Patterson's wagon train on the river below, for sounds at that time of night carried far and clearly. Then suddenly, from outside of the hut, came the notes of a flute. It was a rather monotonous tune, played over and over. There were only four notes as far as Joshua could discern, but it was plaintive and rather pretty.

Antoine came in for a moment to see if he needed anything, and Joshua gave him the cigar he had received from Patterson.

"What's the music for?" he asked Antoine.

"That is Tu-maans, courting Mah-vah."

"Where is Mah-vah?"

"She is down by the river, watching the boys wrestle in the dark."

"With Le-och?"

Antoine hesitated. "No, not with Le-och."

Joshua considered. He didn't know how the

163

Maricopas would take it if Callahan made eyes at Le-och, but he figured it was only a question of time until he would find out.

The music of the flute kept up for hours. Mah-vah came in quietly, and Joshua did not speak or move. Before long she breathed evenly in sleep, but the flute continued until after midnight.

The next day two smaller trains came by, and while Antoine was across the river with Tu-naams investigating the mescal possibilities, Joshua tried his legs with the aid of the two canes. Pánfilo came back from one of the wagon trains waving a crude auger. "We have an axe too," he told his companions. "We can build a *carreta!*"

Lupe hugged him, glad because he was glad, while Jesús watched them sadly.

Mah-vah had been down at the river washing her hair, and she came back brushing it out, heavy and glossy in its shining blackness. He waited until she was seated on the ground before the hut, still brushing her hair with a comb made of yucca leaves, and then awkwardly he used the canes to get to his feet and took a step toward her.

She saw the motion and looked up. Her eyes widened, and she put her hand over her mouth. Then, as he stood there and grinned, she hugged him around the knees, and he almost fell. He balanced himself by putting his hand on top of her head, and was amazed at the softness of her hair.

All that afternoon he worked hard at learning to move his legs. Far too many things were developing for him to be unable to walk.

Callahan looked pleased the next morning; Le-och was not to be seen.

The three Mexicans came by Mah-vah's hut and spoke to Joshua with evident pleasure. "We have found a cottonwood log," said Pánfilo, "and we are going to make a *carreta."*

"I hope you don't try that trip through Apache country alone."

"We don't know," said Jesús sadly.

"It's a long way to Quitobaquito," Joshua reminded them.

"We will remember," Lupe promised gaily.

"Mind if I come down and watch you after a while?" asked Joshua.

"No, señor, you are always welcome. We shall be just above the second bend."

Joshua nodded. He looked himself over. He was ragged but he had managed to stay fairly clean, and he was putting on weight and gaining strength.

He got Tu-naams to bring his mule and help him on it, and set off through the tiny fields. But loud voices caused him to turn around. Mis-ke-tai-ish was having an argument with Le-och; he was doing most of the talking, though Joshua could not make out what he was saying. The angry tenor of his voice was plain enough, however, and also the fact that, whatever he was saying, Le-och was unresponsive—perhaps even, Joshua thought, adamant. He turned the mule and followed the path.

He heard the ringing of the ax before he saw the Mexicans. They had found a huge old cottonwood log, brought down from above in floodtime, and lodged in a backwater probably years before any of them had been born. Considering the dry air of the desert and the resistance of cottonwood to rot, the log *might* have been before the conquistadores. Nevertheless, Pánfilo and the lugubrious Jesús were hacking away at it. They were

165

whittling their pieces out of the tree with one ill-made Mexican ax and one good, well-balanced Pennsylvania ax.

Lupe had spread a blanket under a willow tree, where she smoked corn-shuck cigarettes and offered comments and suggestions almost ceaselessly. None of these were heeded or perhaps even listened to, but the birdlike trill of her voice and the twitter of her laugh made the entire work very pleasant. She wore shoes but no stockings; she had no hat, but her black hair was as glossy as Mahvah's in the sun or in the shade; her red skirt was washed and clean, and her shirtwaist, loosely fitting and low cut so that her full, beautifully shaped breasts were not hampered as to movement and not restricted as to display, was freshly washed and creamy white.

They gave Joshua a hand from the saddle, and he sat on the blanket with Lupe and watched the leisurely operations of the men. You could not say they worked clumsily, but of a certainty they did not feel any hurry to finish the job. It seemed to Joshua that they did everything the hardest possible way, and when he suggested that a cross-cut saw would produce solid sections of the tree for wheels, he was met with blank stares from all and a protest from Pánfilo: "But, señor, this is the way to build a *carreta*. We have seen our grandfathers do it."

During the next three days, pondering his various problems, he watched the entire process of building the *carreta,* and came to know the Mexicans well. In fact, on the second day he helped them—somewhat awkwardly, for his physical balance still was erratic, but nevertheless enough to win their confidence and friendship.

He gave considerable thought to his position. His immobilization had slowed down the restlessness that

166

had impelled him to the gold fields and brought him after White. Now he had lived with the Maricopas and watched the Mexicans and he wondered if what he had been restlessly seeking would be better than the simple life.

Mah-vah liked him a great deal, and it seemed apparent that if he should say the word, she would be his wife. He liked her, too. She was clean and lovely and made to be loved; she was intelligent and sympathetic and kind. The question was: Would he be satisfied to stay in Sacatón and live the Maricopa life? The other possibility was to go somewhere and take her with him, but that was a poor choice. She was an Indian and would always be recognized as an Indian, and so subjected to a lifetime of snubs and even distrust and suspicion if he ever tried to settle among whites, for most whites had no understanding of differences among Indians and no tolerance for any of them.

It was indeed a problem, further complicated by the depth of his own feelings. He was at least a little in love with Mah-vah, and he owed it to her to take a stand. Tu-naams was courting her in spite of what the village must be thinking and saying, and that was a tremendous gesture of loyalty on Tu-naams' part, and made Joshua feel very warm toward him. So he owed it also to Tu-naams to make his position clear. And Antoine as well, for Antoine was the chief and had been in the party that had rescued the two Americans, and he was likewise Mah-vah's grandfather.

Joshua shook his head. Life could be very complicated even in an Indian village.

He thought again of Natalia Brodie, as he had done a thousand times in the last two weeks. He had fallen in

167

love with her and would have married her had her father allowed it. She was as desirable and as lovable as Mahvah, but was she truly endowed with other feminine attributes that kept her in his memory, or had he perhaps constructed those in his imagination?

It was a perplexing problem, and he shook his head as he tried to find an answer.

Lupe, stroking Pánfilo's hair as his head lay in her lap, asked, quickly, "You are dizzy, señor? Perhaps it is the heat."

He smiled at her and then laughed without sound. "I'm dizzy, Lupe, but not from heat."

"*El estómago?*"

"No, not the stomach." He tapped his head. "The *cabeza.*"

That day, in spite of the distraction of Lupe, the Mexicans cut a rectangular block of wood from the log, and Lupe and Joshua helped them to cut and burn a hole through the middle for the axletree; the burning was done with a digging iron, which they heated in a fire and then held against the wood until its heat was drawn and it sank in no farther, while smoke curled up in thin streams and filled the air with the smell of burning wood.

They ascertained that the log was solid, and set about cutting four semicircles from it for the wheels. That evening they seemed well satisfied, and they sang as they walked back to the village, while Jesús pretended to play an imaginary guitar.

Joshua too was well pleased. His diet had been changed, for he had eaten freely of the Mexicans' beans, which they had traded from the last emigrant train, and none of the Maricopas' *pitáhaya* or mesquite flour. And yet he was not only glad to see Mah-vah that evening, but reluctant to let her out of his sight.

"What did you do today?" he asked.

She was spinning thread from a ball of cotton. "Just as you see," she said, and added, "and thought if you were happy, and if you were well, and if you were fed."

He laughed and lay down awkwardly beside her, raising himself on his elbow to watch her spin.

That evening Tu-naams reported that two small wagon trains were camped upstream and would pass the village the next day.

CHAPTER EIGHTEEN

THE NEXT MORNING THE FIRST WAGON TRAIN FOLLOWED the road around the village. The wagons stopped—there were only four—and the Maricopas went to meet them with their offerings of *pitáhaya* and molasses and boiled squash and dried pumpkin. But this time the emigrants were not trading, and a Maricopa soon returned and reported that they had no goods for trading, not even yellow iron, but they had a sick child and the mother wanted somebody to cure it.

"They have their own medicine men," said Antoine.

"She says the child is going to die, and asks that you send the doctor who cures anything."

Antoine considered. "I will take Panhop," he said. "He has been our best doctor for many generations. It was Panhop," he told Joshua, "who gave me the powder that kept you from getting the fever in your bowels."

Joshua went along. The leader of the train was a tall, gaunt, black-whiskered man. His wife was plain and hollow-eyed, wearing a sunbonnet that pretty well concealed her mouse-colored hair. The man spoke with a Missouri twang. "We come through Apache country," he said, "and they attacked us one morning 'bout a week ago."

Joshua counted six children of stair-step heights ranged around the man, and all were the image of their mother. Then he noticed the mother held a baby in her arms.

"Baby was born in Comanche country," said the man, seeing Joshua's stare. "We come out from Fort Smith. Left early to get ahead of the rush, so's we'd have a choice at a good piece of land." He looked hopefully at Joshua. "They say it's free for the taking—out in Californy."

"I guess maybe it is," said Joshua. "There's enough for all."

Three men from the other wagons now came up and stood alongside of the leader, all gaunt, silent, grimly determined.

"You have a sick one?" asked Antoine.

"Yes, in the wagon there. The confounded Apaches— we got four of 'em," he said, resting one forearm across the muzzle of his rifle, "but my boy Hez got an arrow in his chest. It weren't all the way through, so we couldn't pull it on, and when we tried to pull it out the way it went in, the head come off. It's still in him."

Antoine translated to Panhop, and the seamed old face was emotionless; only the eyes showed that he understood. Antoine finished explaining, and Panhop broke into rapid Maricopa. Then Antoine said to the man, "He will look at your child."

"Well, now—one thing here, Chief." The man seemed hesitant but determined to stand his ground. "We don't want none of this here heathen hocus-pocus.

170

We're God-fearin' Christians and we don't believe in Injun medicine men. No disrespect, you understand, but we are standin' by our principles."

Antoine stopped Panhop and looked puzzled. "We do not know your ways, señor. We understand Apache warheads, but we do not understand what you have said."

Joshua spoke up. "What denomination are you, mister?"

"Desciples of the Sacred Martyr."

"You've been doctoring your own child?"

"We done everything we could for Hez, and we prayed steady."

"And it hasn't helped."

"He hain't eatin', and he's runnin' a tol'able fever— but we hain't havin' no heathen witch doctor. We're agreed on that." He looked around at the men behind him, and they all nodded solemnly. He looked at his wife, who dropped her sad, hallow eyes for a moment to the baby at her bosom, and then looked up. "Yes," she said, "we're agreed."

Joshua now became aware of a whimpering from within the wagon, and he said to the man, "Mister, your child needs help bad, and this man here might be able to give it to him. But he has to do it his own way. You got to let him take care of the child and have faith."

"We got plenty of faith," said the man. "We got faith in the Lord. And we're agreed—no hocus-pocus."

Joshua listened to the whimpering, and frowned in the sun, his fingers tightening on his canes. "I don't think there'll be any hocus-pocus, mister, but if you're askin' a man to treat your child, you sure can't tell him how to treat it. If you knew how, you could do it yourself."

"Nope," the man said defiantly. "We're agreed."

171

Joshua turned to Antoine and talked to him haltingly in Maricopa. "This man is fanatic, as you can see. He will not trust your doctor."

"The child is near death," said Panhop.

Joshua nodded gravely. "Yes. But the man is not willing for you to treat him the way you wish."

Panhop said, "Ask him where the arrow went in."

The man pointed to a spot below and the left of his breastbone. Panhop shook his head and said to Joshua, "It would be deep. I could get it out, but the child might bleed to death."

"You took the bullet out of my back," Joshua said to Antoine.

"You are a man," said Antoine. "I could give you mescal to drink until you were numb, and you were still a man and you knew it had to be done. But this one is difficult. If the arrowhead were in his own body it would be easier, but it is in the child's body, and the father will not want us to give it mescal and he will blame us if the child dies."

Joshua heard the whimpering, and compressed his lips. But he hardened himself because there was nothing else to do. He had seen these fanatics before. He said to Panhop, "Can you give him some of the medicine you sent for me?"

Panhop nodded gravely. He took a buckskin pouch from around his neck and handed it to Joshua. Joshua gave it to the man. "Dress it with this. It won't bring out the arrowhead, but it may help the infection."

The man glared at the pouch; he slapped it out of Joshua's hand, and his eyes blazed. "I said none of your heathen hocus-pocus. We'll have none of it. We're agreed!"

Joshua picked up the pouch and left reluctantly. He

would hear that whimpering all night in his sleep. He and Antoine and Panhop watched the wagons get under way, dry wood creaking, canvas lurching.

Panhop shook his head slowly. "Apache arrowhead no good. Apaches use hoop iron. Steel all right; steel not hurt you, but hoop iron make poison, much poison."

"You mean it was too late to do the child any good?"

Panhop nodded. "He has not long to live."

"If you got it out?"

"I do not think so. The poison is already in his blood. Apache arrowhead must be taken out quickly."

"Then," said Joshua, "it's probably best for the Maricopas that he wouldn't let you touch the child. This way you can't be blamed if the child dies."

"That is true," said Antoine. "Also true that these people will say we refused to help them."

"I know." Joshua sighed. "But perhaps nobody will listen, for these are very hard people to understand, and many know that."

"The *Pain-gote-sahch* are very confusing," said Antoine. "Some bad, some good, some crazy in the head."

"That is no different from Maricopas," said Joshua. "Some Maricopas are different too." He saw that Antoine was puzzled, and said, "Francisco."

Antoine bit his lip and said no more.

Joshua sent Kámal Tkak for his mule, and rode up to where the Mexicans were working at their *carreta*. They had finished cutting out the semicircular pieces of the wheels, and, using the auger, had pinned two of them together by laying a rectangular piece across them and driving in long wooden pegs. The wheel was considerably out of round, but this didn't seem to bother the Mexicans, for they were working on the second wheel while Lupe lay on the blanket under the willow tree and smoked.

Joshua helped Pánfilo and Jesús a little. They carved out the axletree in the afternoon, and started on a second one, for they would have to have at least one spare. But most of the time Joshua was occupied in exercising his legs and getting their use back.

That evening Callahan and Le-och walked up the slope together. Francisco and Mis-ke-tai-ish were, as usual, not in evidence. Mah-vah spent a long time brushing her black hair, and then set about weaving a willow basket.

Antoine said to Joshua, "That is going to be trouble—Cal'han and Mis-ke-tai-ish."

"Mis-ke-tai-ish had better be around more than he has been."

"All the others know it. Mis-ke-tai-ish will have to recognize it soon."

"Well," said Joshua, "there isn't much I can do. Callahan probably won't listen to reason, for Le-och has smiled at him."

"It is not my business," said Antoine, "except as it affects the peace of the village."

"Does that apply to me too?" asked Joshua.

Antoine smoked a while in silence. "That is another question," he said at least.

Again that night Tu-naams played his flute outside of Mah-vah's house.

Early the next morning Joshua was up and trying his legs. He walked down to the river and brought back a cedar bucket filled with water for Mah-vah's cooking, and watched her surreptitiously during the preparation and eating of breakfast, and went away thinking that he had to decide soon.

He rode across the river and into the hills that day, and when he was out of sight of the camp he tied the mule to a *palo verde* and left his canes on the ground and forced himself to take steps. They were lurching movements that left him flat on his face after a dozen steps, but he stayed with it all day. At noon he ate a lunch of *pinole* mixed with water from his canteen, and after the heat of the day resumed his practice, so that by evening he was convinced that his legs had strength; all they lacked was direction, and they would have that before long.

He rode by the Mexicans' camp. They had carved out a tongue and rough-hewn some planks for the bed, and Jesús was boring holes around the edge of the bed while Pánfilo was wrapping the entire cart with strips of rawhide from a beef that Antoine had had butchered the night before. Lupe was down on the riverbank gathering driftwood sticks to fit into the holes in the bed. Altogether the *carreta* looked about as clumsy as Joshua could imagine any vehicle to be, but Jesús said proudly, "She's a fine *carreta*, no?"

"For a *carreta*, she's fine," Joshua agreed.

Jesús caressed the rough planks with his hand. "We'll go a long way with this fine *carreta*," he said.

They left about noon the next day. They had hitched the single ox to the tongue in a curious fashion: A straight limb of cottonwood was fastened to the bull's horns with rawhide, and more rawhide ran from the center of the piece to the end of the tongue, which extended along his left side. Joshua noted how the rawhide wrapped around the wagon bed and stakes the day before had already dried and shrunken, holding the entire thing together more tightly than nails would have done. The *carreta* was a good vehicle for this place. If it rained, the rawhide would stretch and come loose—but of course the chance of rain was very slight.

Joshua watched them turn the ox and set out, but he saw they were going toward the west. "That's not the way to Quitobaquito," he said.

"No señor," said Jesús. "You have told us not to go that way. Besides, we have a sad duty to perform."

Joshua nodded. They wanted to bury Margarita. If they kept away from the ferry, it would be safer—if two men and a woman with a *carreta* could possibly be called safe is this country. The Apaches were not quite so active to the west, and there was the chance of falling in with a large train for the journey to Tinajas Altos and Sonoita.

That evening Callahan was smoking a cigarette with Antoine when Mis-ke-tai-ish strode up, backed by Francisco. Mis-ke-tai-ish looked confused and a little bewildered, Francisco sullen and spiteful, and Joshua, sensing trouble, guessed that Francisco had put Mis-ke-tai-ish up to this. Francisco was, as Joshua had thought once before, a troublemaker; that was his nature. Perhaps unable to be happy himself, he didn't want anybody else to be happy. And unfortunately Mis-ke-tai-ish was good material for Francisco to work on, for while Mis-ke-tai-ish was undoubtedly masculine physically, still in mind he was unsure and easily swayed.

Mis-ke-tai-ish stopped before Callahan and said, "You take my wife!"

Callahan smashed out his cigarette in the dirt. "You left her runnin' loose," he said, "without even a halter." He got to his feet; he was a big man. "You put a mare in with a gelding," he said, "and the gelding teases her but he doesn't satisfy her, and then what? You can put a

176

stinkin' jackass in with her, and she'll go to him because she's been aroused but she ain't been covered. But let me tell you somethin', Injun." Callahan suddenly looked as big as a giant and fully as dangerous. "You didn't leave her with no jackass this time. You left her, and I took her, and if she's willin' I'll keep her." His voice rang out through the village, and Joshua was proud of him.

"She cannot be your wife," said Mis-ke-tai-ish. "She is my wife."

Callahan said bluntly, "She can't be. You ain't takin' care of her."

Francisco, seeing Mis-ke-tai-ish at a loss as to what to do next, stepped in. "I agree with my friend Mis-ke-tai-ish," he said. "You have taken his wife. He does not like."

Callahan turned ugly when he looked at Francisco. "I know your game," he said, "and if you was a white man I'd turn you out with the buzzards where you belong."

Francisco hesitated, and Callahan pressed the advantage. "Now get the hell out while my patience is in control!"

Suddenly Francisco had a knife in his hand. He moved toward Callahan, circling. Mis-ke-tai-ish too produced a knife. He didn't seem very enthusiastic about it, but he pointed the blade toward Callahan.

These were odds that suited Callahan perfectly. He took one look at Francisco and snorted. He backed a little to keep the hut at his rear. Then he reached into his boot and flicked out his own knife, and waited while the two stalked him.

Francisco, eyes narrow, lunged. Callahan stepped aside, and Francisco crashed into the wall of Antoine's hut. Callahan waited until he was halfway up; then he kicked the knife out of Francisco's hand. He turned to Mis-ke-tai-ish, whose eyes were wide at this turn of affairs. But Mis-ke-tai-ish, astonishingly enough, as Joshua might have anticipated, suddenly finding himself alone with the antagonist, found a courage he had not known he possessed. He began to circle Callahan, and Callahan, thoroughly aroused, began to move warily.

Mis-ke-tai-ish thrust and Callahan stepped aside. But Mis-ke-tai-ish was not entirely a novice; he had seen that move with Francisco, and now, when Callahan moved aside, he stepped into Mis-ke-tai-ish's knife blade. It went through the muscle just above his elbow, and for an instant Callahan stood as if petrified. Then he let out a roar. He jerked his arm away from Mis-ke-tai-ish hard enough to pull the knife blade out of Mis-ke-tai-ish's hand. Then he spun back. He pulled the knife out of his arm and threw it away over his shoulder. Then he held his knife before him, blade up, and advanced on the paralyzed Indian.

But Antoine stopped him. "Cal'han, you can't do this!"

"He came at me with a knife," said Callahan. "He's got it coming!"

But Antoine refused to be pushed aside. "If you do this, Cal'han, you can't marry his widow!"

Callahan stared at him. "Why the hell not?"

"It is law."

"Law!"

"He's right," said Joshua, anxious to avoid any more violence. "You can't kill the man and marry his widow."

Callahan glared at him. He didn't like it, but finally he put the knife in his boot. "If I ever catch you two skunks cuttin' my sign again," he warned, "I'll cut your

178

liver out and feed it to the birds." He was talking mostly to Mis-ke-tai-ish, and this was understandable to Joshua, because it was Mis-ke-tai-ish's wife who was being fought over.

Mis-ke-tai-ish backed away, and Francisco turned to leave, but Antoine stopped them.

"Come back," he said. "I have words to say to you." Antoine looked at the faces around him in the twilight. Most of the village was there now, standing in silence around Antoine's hut: Tu-naams, Kámal Tkak, Panhop with his headband, and most of the women and children and other men of Sacatón. And, Joshua thought, there were two strangers—men he had not seen before.

Antoine looked at them all slowly and without apparent emotion. Then he looked at Francisco and Mis-ke-tai-ish "I have been in the next village," he said, "Buen Llano, talking to the head chief of the Pimas, Antonio Soule."

There was tense silence, for only something very important would send Antoine to see the head chief of the Pimas, because Antoine, as chief of the Maricopas, was supreme in his own village.

"It has been called to my attention," said Antoine, "that you two—Francisco and Mis-ke-tai-ish—have been friendly as no two men should be friendly. I have seen signs of this with my own eyes, and I have seen the signs of discontent in the eyes of Le-och, but there has been nothing I could do. So when the *Pain-gote-sahch* Cal'han saw how it was with Le-och and offered her comfort, there still was nothing I could do, for it was the husband's place. But graver things were happening." He looked into the night, avoiding all eyes. "Francisco and Mis-ke-tai-ish were going off by themselves to secluded spots and acting like neither men nor women. This was

179

seen by a Pima and was reported to me and to Antonio Soule. I have talked to him about it, and he has agreed with me, but I did not want to take such steps. Now it cannot be avoided. Le-och's honor has been broadcast to the four winds, and by her own husband, and so it is not fair that he should escape untouched. Come here, both."

Francisco approached slowly, sullenly. Mis-ke-tai-ish seemed bewildered.

"Kneel!" commanded Antoine.

They knelt.

"For unnatural acts," Antoine said, "I sentence you to banishment in the desert."

Murmurs of astonishment went up.

"You will carry no weapons," said Antoine. "This is insisted on by Antonio Soule, and I have agreed with him. No weapons, no food. One gourd of water each."

Francisco arose, white in the face but still defiant. "Very well," he said. "We shall leave at daybreak tomorrow morning, and we shall go to the north."

Antoine said calmly, "You will leave at once, and you will go to the south."

There was the sound of breath being sucked in on all sides. This was a harsh punishment indeed, for to the south was waterless desert, and it was Apache land the moment they got over the first ridge. These two men had no chance whatever of escaping alive from their exile. The best they could hope for was a quick death. And yet Joshua could see from Antoine's unmoved judgment that in the minds of the Maricopas this was a fitting punishment for two like Francisco and Mis-ke-tai-ish.

"Kámal Tkak!" said Antoine.

The boy came forward.

"Get two gourds of water."

A moment later he handed them to Antoine. Antoine handed one to Francisco and the other to Mis-ke-tai-ish. "Go forever," he said.

Francisco turned, still sullen. There was no way out, and he knew it. An Indian would not commit suicide unless he was completely insane; nor could he force those around him to kill him by refusing to do what was ordered. No matter how rebellious a man he was, the psychic power of the tribal decision was too powerful for him to disobey.

Mis-ke-tai-ish looked dumbly at the gourd of water. He took it and then said to Antoine, "I want to see Le-och."

Antoine shook his head. "You have no right."

"She is my wife!" cried Mis-ke-tai-ish.

"No." Antoine was unrelenting. "You are not a husband to anybody. You are a wife to Francisco. Go with him!"

Mis-ke-tai-ish stared at him, and Joshua felt sorry for the man, for he saw that only now was Mis-ke-tai-ish beginning to understand what was happening. Suddenly Mis-ke-tai-ish straightened up. He threw the gourd from him.

It shattered on the hard-baked clay, and the water flowed over the ground, spreading in a dark, irregular pattern.

Gasps went up. This was the next thing to suicide. A man starting at night might trot all night and the next day, and with everything in his favor and with enough water to last him through the day, he might possibly reach water; but without the gourd it was impossible. Mis-ke-tai-ish straightened and looked at them all. Then he stepped after Francisco, his face turned to the south.

CHAPTER NINETEEN

ANTOINE SAT FOR A LONG TIME WITH HIS HEAD BOWED, and Joshua kept silence. Mah-vah was bandaging Callahan's arm, and Le-och was still in her own hut. Darkness came, and the sound of Tu-naams' flute floated up through the village. Callahan looked at Antoine questioningly, and Antoine nodded. Then Callahan went up toward Le-och's hut, called to her, and went inside.

After a time Callahan emerged from the darkness, with Le-och at his side, and stood before Antoine.

"Chief," he said, "she is not married now, is she?"

"No," said Antoine, "she has no husband."

"Then I'm going to marry her," said Callahan.

Antoine did not seem astonished. He looked at Le-och. "You want this?" he asked.

She had a soft light in her eyes that never had been there before. "Yes, I want Cal'han," she said.

"All right," Antoine said simply. "You are married. Cal'han, you know what Maricopa husband has to do?"

"I know," said Callahan, his big chest filling.

Antoine nodded.

Callahan took Le-och in his arms and kissed her. Obviously it was not the first time for them, but nobody seemed concerned. They were husband and wife now, and their actions were their own business.

Joshua got up and shook Callahan's hand. "Congratulations," he said.

"Thanks."

Mah-vah hugged her sister, and then everybody gathered around with something to say.

Joshua did not trust himself to look at Mah-vah. He

walked back up the path with them, and when Callahan turned toward Le-och's hut, Joshua said, "I'll take your place with Antoine tonight."

Mah-vah heard, but she did not look at him. Tu-naams' flute was still playing . . .

Joshua was up early the next morning. He went down to the river, walking without any canes at all. He wasn't very steady, but with care he managed. He bathed, and then lay on the sand, letting the sun warm his legs, and thinking over the decision he had to make.

Callahan came down after a while, and Joshua grinned. "You got a good wife," he said, "and you've forgotten Juana."

"I got a feeling for Le-och I never had for Juana."

"That's understandable. Juana never would let you get close enough."

Callahan grinned. "Never mind the whys. It works. That's all I know."

"Well, I hope you have all kinds of luck. You've got it coming, Callahan. You may have a problem on your hands when you take Le-och to San Diego, but maybe you can lick it."

"I'll tackle that one when it comes along."

Joshua nodded and began to put on his clothes. "A happy married man is hard to beat, they say."

"Marry Mah-vah," said Callahan, "and find out."

Joshua frowned. "I'm trying to decide." He had turned toward the east, staring hard at the distant hill. "Isn't that a mule train coming over the ridge?"

"Yeah. Looks like it."

"We haven't seen a mule train go by here before. Only wagons."

Callahan squinted. "What does that mean to you? Greasers?"

183

"Mexicans, yes. But why up here on the Gila?"

"Might be worth finding out."

Callahan helped him up. The mule train had stopped. There were about twenty mules laden with pack saddles, and eight or ten *arrieros* or Mexican drivers, all swaggeringly dressed, and they were trying to barter for corn. As usual, Antoine's people had little to offer. Joshua got one of his canes and went with Callahan to the road.

"Where's the *jefe?*" Joshua asked the first Mexican.

The Mexican pointed. "Enrique," he said.

Joshua went up to Enrique, a big fellow, unusually tall for a Mexican, with two pistols in his belt.

"*De dónde es usted?*" asked Joshua. "Where are you from?"

"Durango," said Enrique. "*Y usted?*"

"San Diego."

"You're a long way from home," said Enrique. "Have a *puro?*"

Joshua took one, and so did Callahan. Callahan lit his, but Joshua saved his for Antoine. "You're a long way from home too," he said.

"We're going to the gold fields."

"There's been a lot of trouble in the gold fields."

"We're not afraid of trouble," said Enrique. "We've beaten off the worst robbers in Mexico."

"Tell me this: You came from Durango—why didn't you go from Nogales on through Sonoita to the crossing?"

"We were told there had been trouble with outlaws and Indians. And besides," he added, "it's said there's no water, that the wells are dry all the way to the Colorado. So we came up to Tucson and followed the Santa Cruz River to the Gila. They said it's a better way to go."

184

"You hear anything about a man named Brodie, from Hermosillo?"

"Brodie?" Enrique smiled broadly. "He was at Nogales with thirty men, well armed. They're going to capture the ferry at the Colorado."

"Were there any women with them?" asked Joshua.

"Hmm." Enrique raised his eyebrows. "Some women, yes—and Brodie's daughter, a very fine lady."

"And they're all going to the Colorado?"

"That's what they said."

"Why didn't they come this way with you?"

"Brodie's a man with a strong mind. He said he was going by Sonoita and to hell with the wells. That's the way he's going."

Joshua laughed at Enrique's expressiveness. "We won't keep you," he said. "Watch out for the river down below. It may disappear in the sand."

"We will. Thanks."

Joshua turned, almost losing his balance, and faced Mah-vah, who was lovely even in the harsh and brilliant glare of the sun. "I'm sorry," he said. "I almost knocked you over."

"It is not need for you to be sorry," she said. "I will walk with you to the village."

That was strange, coming from her. But in a moment he understood it. "The daughter of Brodie," she said. "She is the one?"

"What do you mean?"

She looked at him straight. "She is the one you have been thinking of—not me?"

He said, "Let's stop in the shade."

They reached a huge *saguaro*, and she helped him to sit down. He waited for a few moments and then he looked into her eyes. "I have much to tell you," he said.

185

"I have been thinking about this for many days."

Her face did not change.

"You have done much for me, Mah-vah," he began. "I was wounded and unconscious and you picked me up from the desert and carried me to a safe place—"

"That was Tu-naams," she said quickly.

"I know. I count all of you. But you yourself had much to do with my recovery. You took care of me and washed my wounds and brought me water and food. You sat by me and gave me freely of your calmness and your strength, and those were the two greatest things. And the touch of your hands was like cold water to a man in the desert, and your voice was like a mockingbird's, and I became a little in love with you, Mah-vah."

She continued to look into his eyes. "Yes, José," she said softly.

"And perhaps you fell a little in love with me, Mah-vah."

"Yes," said Mah-vah, "I became in love with you, José. You were a man. With a bullet in your back that kept you from walking, you did not complain, but waited only for the time when you would be up again. And the touch of your hands was always warm and tender, like a caress." Her eyes were misty. "I was very much in love with you, José."

He looked away, very uncomfortable. The heat waves rose up from around the creosote bushes, and occasionally their unpleasant smell drifted to his nostrils. "It is always that a man falls in love with the woman who takes care of him when he is sick," said Joshua. "And besides, you were beautiful and kind and very much a woman."

"You did not find me unpleasant to be near?"

186

"By no means," he assured her. "Truly it was the other way. It was hard to keep my hands from you."

"But I expected you to put your hands on me," she said.

"I couldn't do that, for I did not know where my heart was. I might leave and never come back."

"That was to be expected also, for you are *Pain-gote-sahch.*"

He swallowed and frowned. "And if I had put my hands on you?"

"I would not have minded," she said frankly, "because you were a straight man, and our children would have been straight also."

"You mean you would have come to me?"

"Whatever you wanted, José. I trusted you."

He stared at her. " Mah-vah, you have been possessed by many men, haven't you?"

She drew herself up indignantly. "No man has ever put his hands on me," she said proudly. "If I had been yours, I would have been all yours."

He rubbed his chin and tried to think. She wasn't making it easy for him. "I have given this a great deal of consideration in recent days and nights as my strength returned," he commenced.

"I have known that," she said, "and I have waited for you to speak."

He had meant to say that he did not love her enough to marry her, but for a moment, as he looked at her, his courage deserted him. "Mah-vah," he finally blurted, "I have stayed out here to tell you that I cannot marry you."

She watched him steadily. Only one corner of her mouth quivered a little. Finally she said, "You are going to the Red Water?"

187

"The Colorado? Yes. There is a job to do there."

"And you are not coming back?"

He faced her squarely. "No, Mah-vah, I am not coming back."

Her lips tightened a little and she looked away. A cactus wren flew overhead with a bit of dead grass in its beak, and found a perch on a branch of the *saguaro*. She said at last, "Tell me this, José: Is it that you are ashamed of me for being an Indian?"

"No," he said truthfully. "I would never be ashamed of you anywhere, Mah-vah."

"That is good," she said. "Is it then that you are in love with another woman? The Brodie's daughter, perhaps."

He watched the last mule disappear over the ridge. It was a hard thing to answer. "I think so," he said softly.

"And you will marry her?"

"I do not know. Her father may forbid it."

"In Sacatón," she observed, "parents do not tell a girl what man she can marry."

He drew a deep breath. "I know. Customs are different."

"And still she is in your mind and in your memory. It was she you thought of during those long nights when you were unable to move your legs."

"No," he said. "That is the confusing part. During those nights I thought only of you. I waited for your soft step and longed for the velvet touch of your fingers."

"And now you are almost well," she observed, "and you are thinking of her. What is she called, José?"

"Natalia."

"Natalia," she repeated. "Natalia."

"It has not been pleasant to tell you this, for I owe you a great deal, Mah-vah." He felt miserable.

But strangely enough, her eyes were shining. "It is

188

better you be truthful. I would be hurt very much if you would not marry me because I am Indian, but I am not hurt except a little because you love another woman more. That is something you cannot help."

Yes, he supposed it was. The truth was that if he had loved her as much as he did Natalia, he would have married her and would have stayed there in Sacatón, and she had said it herself—the bare fact was that he didn't love Mah-vah enough. But he was astonished at her reaction. He had thought this would be the most cruel thing he could say. "I hope you will forgive me," he said.

She did not answer, and he reached for his cane and began to work his way to his feet. She jumped up and gave him a hand, and the touch of her fingers made him unsure of himself. But she had accepted his verdict.

"Tu-naams will make a good husband," she said. "He is young and he can see no woman but me. And I am very fond of him, José." She helped him stand and looked up into his eyes. "But always in a little corner of my heart I shall be in love with you, José. It will not interfere with Tu-naams, for I shall be very much in love with him and shall bear him many strong and beautiful children. But I shall never forget that those children might have had gray eyes, José."

He started back unsteadily. She had damn' near made him cry.

CHAPTER TWENTY

HE TALKED TO CALLAHAN THAT AFTERNOON. "BRODIE is going to the ferry to fight for possession, and Natalia is with him. I've got to get there. Maybe I can help save some casualties on Brodie's side."

189

"You trying to make an impression on Brodie?"

"No, I'm hoping to save what might be a massacre. If Glanton's men start in on those Mexican vaqueros, I doubt that Brodie will come out of it alive."

"And then what happens to Natalia?"

Joshua nodded. "That's about it."

"When are you leaving?"

"In the morning."

Callahan looked skeptical. "Do you think you can negotiate it with those legs?"

"They're getting stronger every day. They'll be all right by the time I reach the Colorado."

"Well," said Callahan, "I better go tell Le-och."

"Tell her what?"

"Tell her I'll be gone for a couple of weeks."

"You're not going," said Joshua.

"The hell I'm not! Who do you think is going to whip Glanton and White? Not you," he said scornfully, "with them legs."

"I didn't invite you to go along."

"You forgot," Callahan said. "I'm a squaw man now, but I'm still in the Army, and I've got a job to do. Do you think I want my great-grandchildren to find out, someday their grandfather was a deserter from the U.S. Army?"

"I don't think you ought to leave Le-och so soon."

"Don't worry," said Callahan. "I'll be back. Le-och will bring me back if I have to ride backward all the way."

"You can't come back dead," Joshua told him.

"Don't count on it," said Callahan. "When do we start?"

"At daylight."

"I'll be ready."

Joshua sent Ka'mal Tkak to find his and Callahan's mules, while he saw that the canteens still held water and filled them and put in the corks. He hung them outside of Antoine's hut.

Another train of nine wagons of Mormons came by, and they kept their distance. Joshua heard the men had more than one wife, but the women in that train stayed in hiding. What small trading was done was performed by the men, gaunt, bewhiskered men with belligerent eyes but fair manners, and Joshua guessed the belligerence was more for defense than for anything else. Perhaps they had had to defend themselves; it seemed likely.

Mah-vah prepared supper—a fat beaver tail and two rabbits with a generous portion of corn bread made of meal that she had ground that afternoon on her knees, and molasses made from the *pitáhaya*. They sat around on the ground near the kitchen, and ate much and talked little.

"You're a very good cook, Mah-vah," Joshua told her, and she blushed as she never had done over anything else.

Antoine rolled a cigarette and said to Joshua, "You better smoke with me tonight."

Joshua said, "Of course," and he sat on the ground with his back against the wall of Antoine's hut while Antoine sat on the stump, and they smoked and watched the glaring sunlight soften, and heard the night sounds take over, and presently, from somewhere, Tu-naams' flute began to sound its four notes.

Antoine said, "She would have made you a good wife, José."

"I am sure she would." Joshua held the cigarette in his fingers, careful to hold the shuck wrapper so it

191

would not come apart. "And I am certain she will also make Tu-naams a good wife."

"I do not know that it will be Tu-naams that she will choose. She may look for somebody more like you."

"She is young, and so is Tu-naams."

"A young man is not always best for a young girl," Antoine said wisely. "It would seem so, but it is not always true."

"That may be true at first," said Joshua, "but later, when the man gets old but the woman is still young, the difference in age is more important."

"I am an old man," said Antoine, "and have observed many girls and many men, and I do not think that any man who *is* a man would ever get old with either Mah-vah or Le-och."

Joshua got up, stepping on his cigarette. "Do you think the weather will be good tomorrow?"

Antoine sighed. "It will be hot and dry and dusty, and the sun will be blazing, but in another month the snow water from the mountains will be in the river, and we may have floods. At least the lowlands will be filled with water, and when it goes down it will leave a layer of rich dirt that will grow corn or squash or melons or cotton or pumpkins or whatever we may plant. And so the world changes but little. It looks like much to the young ones, for they see only from year to year, but to us who observe from one generation to the next it is apparent that one year cancels out the next, and so all are pretty much the same."

"That is to say, the average is the same."

"Yes."

"Would you still say that if the Americans crowded you out of your land along the Gila?"

For a moment old Antoine studied him. "This may

192

come to pass," he said, "but the average is still the same. It came to pass hundreds of years ago when the Apaches pushed us back from the Red Water altogether. It has always been so because we have been a small tribe, and it was only because the Pimas, who were already here, felt friendly toward us and told us to settle and make our home on the Gila that we have been able to stay here at all. And now we are almost one tribe with the Pimas. We have adopted many of their customs; we understand each other's language, and many words are the same; we intermarry when we wish, and Antonio Soule, who is a Pima, is chief over all. So I say it may be that the *Pain-gote-sahch* will take this land along the Gila, but we shall go somewhere, and perhaps in generations to come we shall end up in some place entirely different, and I am not sure the *Pain-gote-sahch* will exist at all." He was thoughtful for a while, and then sighed. "I think the *Pain-gote-sahch* are strange people."

Joshua saw Callahan go into the hut with Le-och, and the blanket dropped over the doorway behind them. Mah-vah had disappeared. Joshua settled down on his wolfskin in Antoine's hut, and it came to him then that there was a strange silence in the village. For the first time in many nights, Tu-naams' flute stopped playing early.

Joshua thought about it, and for a while he felt sad. He had given up Mah-vah, who probably would have made him happy, for Natalia, whom he did not even know he could have, and of whose capacity to make him happy he knew very little. For a while he felt a loss, and then he consoled himself with the thought that Mah-vah was a great deal younger than he, and, although she had made a very pretty speech that afternoon, telling him that she would always have a little place in her heart for him, still

193

he thought there was little doubt that he would be forgotten as soon as he was out of her sight . . .

He was awake at daylight, hearing the chatter of birds down at the river as they greeted the sun after a night of desert blackness. He got to his feet, pulled on his boots (which were well worn by that time), saw that his knife was in its loop, put his pistol in his belt, and took his rifle in one hand. He threw the tow sack with extra cartridges over his shoulder, and stepped outside. He took the canteens from the stick on which they were suspended and, holding them in one hand, turned around.

He was somewhat astonished to see Mah-vah and Tu-naams watching him.

"We have been talking, down by the river," said Mah-vah.

"We are going to be married," Tu-naams said.

Joshua forced himself to smile. "I know you will be happy," he said to Tu-naams. He didn't dare look at Mah-vah.

But she spoke to him, straightforward as always: "Someday you will come back to visit, José, and see our children?"

"Yes, of course I will visit you."

"And perhaps," she went on, "you will show them the bullet Antoine plucked from your back."

He wondered why she mentioned that, for she knew he had lost it somewhere in the crater. "Perhaps," he said with an attempt to smile.

He turned to go the other way, and faced Antoine.

"José, it would have been a pleasure to see you stay here with us," Antoine said, "but it is easy to know that this could not be, for a man like José is needed by his own people."

Joshua frowned. "You are mistaken. I am not a *jefe*. I have work to do."

But Antoine would not be disillusioned. "You will be a great *jefe*," he said. "We wish you well."

He embraced Joshua, and Joshua hugged him briefly, then set off down the trail. He found the mules under the tree, and looked back up the slope. Mah-vah and Tu-naams and Antoine were still standing there, and he turned and waved. Then he put the saddles on the mules, pulled up the stake ropes, tied the bridle reins of one mule to a saddle ring of the other, and mounted. He struck out away from the village to hit the emigrants' road, for he thought Callahan was still asleep, and he did not want Callahan to go with him. But when he rounded the turn through the giant cactus and faced the west ridge, there stood Callahan and Le-och, each with an arm around the other's waist.

Joshua pulled up and said severely, "I told you I'd call you when I was ready for you."

"Sure." Callahan grinned. "But you forgot."

Joshua said, "I've got a funny feeling about this, Bill. I don't want you to go."

Le-och spoke up. "He should go. He has told me about it, and it is his duty."

"There's more to it." Joshua leaned on the saddlehorn. "Bill, I've got a feeling you won't come back."

"To Le-och?" Callahan snorted.

"What I'm afraid of is that you won't be able to come back."

Le-och nodded. "I think so, maybe."

Joshua stared at her. She had bloomed radiantly with Callahan. "*You* think something will happen to him?"

She nodded.

Joshua turned to Callahan. "You see, she's got the feeling too. Look, Bill, why not stay out this one time? Nobody will know the difference. If I get White, I'll turn him in and say that we both got him."

Callahan was preparing to mount. "You forgot something," he said as he put his foot in the stirrup. "Who's goin' to answer present for me at roll call every morning?"

Joshua shook his head. He rode by Le-och and touched her hand. He saw Callahan reach over to kiss her, and rode on.

They overtook the Mormons that day on the cut-off across the big bend of the Gila. The Mormons toiled on, looking grim and pathetic but thoroughly determined; obviously they had no knowledge of the desert or its burning heat, but they had started with full canteens and water kegs that morning, and, Joshua thought, they probably would get wherever they wanted to get because of their sheer doggedness.

He and Callahan passed them on the lee side, and camped that afternoon on a shrinking slough in the river bed. They watered their animals and got them back from the slough as soon as possible so the water would have time to settle. They followed the wagon tracks half a mile farther and turned in on a flat where the mules could find willow shoots and young cottonwoods from which they could chew the bark, for all the grass had been eaten off close to the ground—evidence of horses' and mules' grazing. What they had fed the oxen he didn't know. The proper way was to let oxen graze first, and put horses and mules on next; that way both animals would get forage. But he doubted that many of the emigrants knew about grazing their animals that way.

As he thought about it, he thought it was a wonder

196

that any of the emigrants got through, as ignorant as they were of the country. It was more than astonishing that people who had never seen a desert in their lives before not only would try to cross this one, but would try to do it their own way.

The Mormons came up late that night, and Joshua and Callahan watched from a distance as they watered their stock. They were low-voiced, sparing of words. In a little while a fire sprang up, and the women cooked in silence. What they cooked he could not tell, but presently the children formed a long line and began to file by with their plates.

"Christopher!" said Callahan. "There must be thousands of 'em!"

Joshua nodded.

They were up the next morning at daybreak again. The Mormons were just breaking camp, and Callahan looked concerned. "With all them kids, I hate to see 'em run out of water."

"Somebody must have told them the river runs dry this time of year."

"Did you?"

"I don't recollect that I did," said Joshua. "They didn't act very friendly."

"They acted scared," said Callahan, "and they probably acted like that everywhere, and they probably think all they have to do is follow the river." Callahan started off afoot. "I'll be back in a little while." He set out across a field of Mexican sunflowers.

Joshua let the mules crop at some salt grass until Callahan got back.

"It was just what I thought," said Callahan. "After they watered the stock this morning they realized the water was too muddy to drink, and so they weren't going to fill their canteens until they got to the next place. But I told 'em there might not be any next place for several days."

"Did they listen?"

"Seemed downright grateful." Callahan went after the mules. "She's a blazer today," he said as he rode back.

A few miles farther on they found the grave of the whimpering child. A piece of wood from the head of a cracker barrel was stuck in the mound of dirt, and on it were the words lettered in pencil: "Here lies *HEZEKIAH EPJOHN*. Age 14. Killed by Apaches Apr. 12, 1850. R.I.P."

Callahan pushed his hat back on his head. "Well, they got him."

Joshua nodded. "The price of going to California," he said.

CHAPTER TWENTY-ONE

THEY HAD PLANNED TO MAKE IT IN FIVE DAYS, BUT water became harder to find. They had to dig in the bed of the river, and even then it wasn't easy and they didn't always strike it, so Joshua suggested they start traveling at night and make it in four days.

"It suits me," said Callahan. "The sooner we get there, the quicker we get it over with."

Joshua looked at him but didn't answer. He wished he could get rid of the feeling he had about Callahan.

They overtook three more trains and then the Mexican pack train. Enrique recognized them at once. "You going to Calfornia?" he asked.

"Later, maybe," said Joshua. "How are your mules holding out?"

Enrique shrugged. "Not bad. They're alive."

"Want to sell a couple of see-gars?" asked Callahan.

"Sure. What you got to trade, hombre?"

"Not much," Callahan admitted ruefully.

"All right. I'll give you credit." He held out two cigars.

"Thanks," said Callahan. "I'll remember this."

They came to the Colorado, traveling on the south side of the Gila, and gave the ferry landing a wide circuit. "Looks to me like they're rounding up some stock down there in the bottom," said Callahan.

Joshua nodded. "Gettin' ready to make a drive, maybe."

They rode down through the willows and mesquite and cottonwoods until they encountered the Yuma camp.

"You want cross?" asked a Yuma, backed by three Indian girls who wore knee-length skirts of bark strips, and nothing from the waist up, like the Maricopas.

"We're just lookin' around," said Josh. "What's your name?"

"Cabello en Pelo, chief of Yumas. You want cross, you ask for Cabello en Pelo."

"I hear hammerin'," said Callahan.

Joshua raised his head. "Sounds like it to me. What is it?" he asked the Yuma.

"Big *jefe* build boat to cross river," said the Yuma.

"Big *jefe!*" Joshua looked at Callahan. "That sounds like General Patterson!"

"It does for a fact." Callahan whomped his mule in the sides with his heels. "Let's go find out."

They found Patterson, big and black-bearded, on a strip of sand superintending some twenty men. They had snaked up some cottonwood logs with the stock,

199

and now were engaged in whipsawing planks out of them, while others were fashioning the framework of a rude flat-bottomed scow, putting the hewn timbers together with rawhide and wooden pegs.

Joshua got down from his mule. "General Patterson," he said, "we see you're busy."

The big man scowled at them. "Where you fellers from? Did you come from Glanton?"

"We were in the Maricopa village when you went by," said Joshua.

The General looked at them more closely. "Sure. You was the man with the bum legs!" He shook hands heartily. "I thought you was squaw men."

Joshua said quickly, "We got business here."

"What kind of business?"

Joshua looked at him. "Private business," he said.

"That's all right. Have a see-gar?"

Callahan took one, and Joshua took one for Callahan.

"I see you decided you could make money by building your own ferry."

"It's like I feared," said Patterson. "Them scoundrels up there wanted to rob us blind—four dollars a man, twenty-five a wagon. I told Glanton he could stick his ferry in his eye and I'd build my own. It'll be the quickest money I ever made—eighteen hundred dollars for six days' work."

Joshua squinted at the hull and saw that it had considerable shape already. "When will it be ready to go?"

"Tomorrow evening, I figger. You fellows want to go acrost?"

"We really came down to get a job of work," said Joshua. "You want to hire a couple of hands?"

Patterson shook his head. "I got all the help I need."

200

He looked up the river. "Glanton's boat is up there a few miles. He should be able to use a couple of hands."

"He's got his own, hasn't he?"

"He's got about fifteen men, all told, but half of them are drunk all the time, and he's got a lot of stock to take care of."

"Where's he get stock?"

"A train comes through and they've got no money. He figures out the price and takes them across, then takes cattle and horses to pay the bill." Patterson growled. "It's murder, what he's doin'!"

"What does he do with the stock?"

"Sells some of it to other emigrants, but mostly he has to drive it to San Diego or Los Angeles."

Joshua looked upstream—east from where they stood, for the Colorado made a big bend right after the Gila joined it. "Maybe we ought to go have a look," he said.

"Now, wait up a minute. Maybe I got a deal for you."

Joshua turned the mule back. "What's that?"

"Look here. I'm gonna have a ferry left over after we get across. I'll sell it to you cheap and you can run it in competition with Glanton. Make him come down in his prices, and you'll make some nice money too."

Joshua shook his head. "We haven't got any money at all."

Patterson scowled. "I don't like to give it to you. I ought to have something for my trouble."

"Maybe you can sell it to some other emigrant."

"The rest of the emigrants haven't got any more sense than my outfit," said Patterson. "Here's a gold mine under their noses, and they all want to go to California."

Joshua squinted at the sun. "Don't blame 'em much," he said.

"Well, hell, I'll give the ferry to the Yumas, then."

Joshua nodded. "Good idea."

Patterson scratched his beard. "I'd be afraid of one thing. The Yumas haven't got no rifles or pistols, and Glanton might take it away from them."

"He'd have no right to do that."

"When you've got rifles and you don't mind killin', you've got the right to whatever you take a mind."

Joshua and Callahan rode back toward the Glanton ferry. From a distance they saw about a hundred horses and mules driven off toward Carrizo Springs. "Profit," said Joshua.

They stayed in the willows along the river and observed Glanton's layout. He had three buildings on a knob of rock that stood about eighty feet above the surface of the desert on the other side of the river, and the rope along which the ferry was operated was anchored in rock on the other side. It lay on the bottom of the river, out of sight, but ran through a winch on the flat-bottomed boat, which was moved either way by two men turning the winch with the rope wound around it two turns. At that moment the boat was on their side of the river, apparently waiting for passengers, while four bearded men sat in its shade and played monte. Four rifles leaned against the end of the boat, which had been drawn up a little on shore.

Callahan said, "I b'lieve I saw White go with the stock."

Joshua looked at the animals, now beginning to file up the trail on the cliff that marked the edge of the overflow land. "I think you're right." He studied the men. "It's White, right enough. Do you know what that means?"

"It might mean a lot of things."

"But especially it means one of us can join up with

Glanton and find out when he's expected back, and then we can light out and meet him."

"Why not go after him now?"

"He's got six men with him. The odds are too heavy."

"They won't be any better when he comes back."

"Sure they will. He'll lose at least a couple of men in town, and all who come back will likely come back drunk. The main thing is, we can't stay out in the desert indefinitely. We've got to get into that camp to find out when he's coming back." He spurred his horse through the underbrush and rode up to the boat. "You fellows workin' for Glanton?"

The four men looked up together but did not move for a moment. Then one, with a long white scar across the bridge of his nose, said, "Who's askin'?"

"Joshua Pickens."

"That don't mean nothin' to me."

Joshua frowned. "This a public ferry?"

The scarred man laughed. "It's a ferry, but it ain't public, not by any manner of means."

"You got any work for us?"

"I've already answered all the questions I'm allowed to answer. Want to talk to Glanton?"

"Yes."

"Cost you four dollars each and ten for each mule."

"We've got no money," said Joshua.

"Swim it, then!"

Joshua considered.

The scar-faced man said, "I'm puttin' two bucks on the next card, Shorty."

Joshua watched the game for a while, but none of the men looked up again. Finally he rode off. When they were out of hearing, Callahan said fiercely, "I'd like to put a bullet through his gristle!"

203

"He's not the one," said Joshua. "Glanton is the one to get if you want to stop this business."

They went back to Patterson. The framework of his boat was beginning to look like something.

"No luck?" asked Patterson.

"They told us to talk to Glanton and wanted to charge twenty-eight dollars to ferry us across."

"The damned outlaws! Listen, I worked up a scheme. You two look like honest fellers—at least, more honest than Glanton's men. Now I been thinkin' and I been talkin' to Cabello en Pelo while you was gone, because I'd like to leave this ferry where it would hurt Glanton's business."

"That's nothing for us," said Joshua. "There are plenty of Yumas to run it."

"That ain't the point," Patterson argued. "There'd have to be a white man on the boat or the emigrants wouldn't pay. They'd abuse the Indians. Let's get the chief over here. Chief!"

Cabello en Pelo, dressed in sandals, breechclout, and straw hat, stalked out of the cottonwoods.

"Chief, you know these two fellers?"

"I see 'em twice," said Cabello en Pelo.

Joshua asked, "Twice?"

"Sure. You come with man Brodie to Sonora. You work hard!" He nodded emphatically.

Patterson was well pleased. "You're all old friends. That makes it easier. Chief, you know I talked to you a little while ago about your taking over the ferry?"

"Yes, I know."

"You promised me you wouldn't charge over a dollar a head. Is that right?"

"I promise," said Cabello en Pelo.

"Now you need white men to run the ferry or the emigrants will cheat you."

Cabello en Pelo nodded vigorously. "They have rifles. We haven't."

"All right. You two fellers run the ferry. The Yumas will do the work, and you'll collect the fares and see that everybody is treated honest—and you keep ten per cent. How's that for a deal?"

"Whoa!" said Joshua. "You're a fast dealer, all right. I didn't even see that last card coming."

"What do you say? You can feed with us until we get across."

Joshua looked at him. Patterson was a man who was used to arranging deals; that was obvious. And from a financial standpoint it was a good deal. The trouble was that he had another objective. "I'll talk it over with my partner," he said.

"All right!" boomed Patterson. "All right. But you won't go wrong—and at least you won't be workin' with scalp-hunters!"

Joshua nodded and led Callahan to the shade of a big mesquite tree. "It's a mighty fair proposition," he told Callahan, "but it doesn't put White in San Diego."

Callahan lit the cigar given him by Enrique. "Tell you what, Josh. This might be my chance."

"Chance for what?"

"Chance to live where Le-och can live with me. We might as well face it," he said. "I reckon you have already—and I did too, only I couldn't give her up." He puffed on the cigar and blew out a thin haze of blue smoke. "I'll never be able to live in San Diego with Le-och."

"It wouldn't be easy."

"But if I stay here, I can make enough money to buy out my enlistment, and I can get my discharge clear. I could live down here and run the ferry, and Le-och

205

could live here with me, and she wouldn't be treated like dirt just because she's an Indian."

Joshua nodded slowly. "Maybe this is it."

"Now I know that ain't gettin' White, and we're both set on gettin' him. But maybe it would be better to have one of us on the inside and the other on the outside. When the time comes, you send me word, and we'll grab him together and hustle him off to San Diego before he knows what's happened."

Joshua considered. "I don't really see anything wrong with that." He stood up, testing his legs. They felt pretty good. "All right, let's do it that way. You stay down here and run the ferry. I'll hire out to Glanton. When I find out about White, I'll let you know."

Callahan said thoughtfully, "I ain't sure you ought to walk into Glanton's place like that."

"There's another reason," said Joshua. "If Brodie attacks, I might be able to help him from the inside—and he'll *need* help to beat that bunch."

They went back to Patterson and told him. He beamed and pounded them on the back and called Cabello en Pelo over to shake hands, and passed out cigars. "Anything," he said, "to beat them dirty scalp-hunters!"

Presently Joshua got Cabello en Pelo to ferry him across in a canoe. He took the firearms with him, and swam the mule behind. "You go upstream," said the chief, "fourteen miles. You find, all right."

"Thanks." Joshua got into the saddle.

"One thing you maybe know," said Cabello en Pelo. "Your friend Brodie camp back yonder three-four mile."

"Brodie!" Joshua stared back across the river.

"He cross desert today. Just arrive."

"You talked to him?"

"I talk. Talk señorita too."

Joshua demanded, "What do you know about the señorita?"

"I watch you look at her time before. You like, eh?"

"Did you tell her I'm here now?"

"I tell her," the chief said. "Eyes big like moon, shine like stars."

Joshua took a deep breath. "Next time you see her, you tell her I'll see her as soon as I can. All right?"

"All right," said Cabello en Pelo.

"And look. Tell Brodie to wait—not to do anything until he hears from me."

Cabello en Pelo nodded solemnly. "I tell him this day, maybe."

Joshua got on his mule and rode east. Suddenly the sun was no longer hot, and the desert was no longer hostile, and he wasn't afraid of John Glanton, for over there, just a little way, was Natalia. And he felt better too because he knew he had made the right decision back at Sacatón.

CHAPTER TWENTY-TWO

HE WAS NEARING THE STOCKADE THAT ENCLOSED THE three buildings at the western terminal of the ferry when he saw Enrique and his mule train on the other side. Enrique was arguing with the scar-faced man but getting nowhere, for the scar-faced man went back to his card game, and presently Enrique's mules were strung out down the shore.

Joshua wasn't sure he liked that. Enrique would join Brodie's party, and between them and Patterson and Cabello en Pelo, who would have done a lot more business if it hadn't been for Glanton, they might decide to do something drastic. On the other hand, maintaining an opposing ferry was equally drastic, for it would force Glanton either to lower his prices or to quit business. In either of those events, how would Glanton take it?

He walked his mule up to the stockade on the hill. The gate was open and he went in. A man was sitting in the shade on the east side of a cabin. He had a homemade table before him, and it was loaded with gold and silver coins that he had been sorting according to denomination, and from the looks of it he had been taking everything—American, Mexican, Spanish, French, and Dutch; they were all legal tender.

On the table were a long telescope and an earthen jug that contained whisky by the smell of it. At each end of the table a man with a rifle lounged against the side of the cabin. These were hard-looking men, unshaved, unwashed, uncombed, their clothes faded from water and sun, their pants greasy where they had wiped their hands during eating. They looked indolent, but Joshua knew the indolence was deceptive. They were Glanton's men, and they were there to kill.

Joshua had almost forgotten the man at the table, but now, impelled by something he could not name, he looked at him. His clothes were like the others', but this man was small and slightly built. He had an ugly whitish red scar that covered the whole side of his face, and against his very brown skin—as brown as Joshua's—the scar was almost shocking. Joshua finally took his eyes from the scar and looked up—into the eyes of John Glanton, the scalp-hunter. His eyes were blue and hard, the eyes of a man who always got what he wanted, no matter what the cost.

The eyes looked at him, held him up, figuratively

208

stuck a pin through him to make him squirm, and then let him go.

"You're Glanton?" asked Joshua.

"What do you want?" he asked harshly.

"I'm looking for a job," said Joshua.

"Doing what?"

"Anything honest."

"We've got nothing honest around here, and you know that."

"How should I know?"

"Because John Glanton is known all over the West, and there's eight thousand dollars on my head in Chihuahua and Texas. I'm no hypocrite. I make all the money I can, any way I can. Who are you?"

"Joshua Pickens."

"Nobody," said the harsh voice.

"He's standin' at attention like he's been in the Army," drawled one of the guards.

"Gunn, maybe you're right. You been in the Army, Pickens?"

"Yes."

"What you doin' now?"

"I deserted."

"From where?"

Joshua took a chance. "Fort Towson," he said.

"And you want work?"

"Yes."

"You was across the river this morning tryin' to get a ride on the ferry. You had a man with you. What happened to him?"

Joshua was startled. Did the man know everything? But he remembered that with a telescope a great deal could be seen across the river. "He got work with Patterson, down at Algodones," he said.

Glanton's jaws tightened a little. "Patterson's building a ferry, I hear."

"It's a boat of some kind."

"He's a fool!" said Glanton in his harsh voice.

Joshua waited a moment, then asked, "Have you got work for me?"

The blue eyes did not waver. "You've got arms and a mule. You can herd stock and work on the ferry when we need it. You're expected to kill Injuns like rattlesnakes. Fifty dollars a month and you buy your own whisky and pay your own funeral expenses."

"Yes."

"And one thing more." Glanton's hard stare impaled him as on the blade of a saber. "No pussyfooting with these goddamn emigrants. If they can't pay, they can swim—and we'll charge 'em for using the river."

"What about Patterson?"

"He had too many men for me." Glanton rubbed the big scar. "But as soon as he's gone, we'll go down there and tear up his ferry. I want no competition!" He pounded the table. "And every Indian I catch on it will be tied hand and foot and thrown in the river!"

Joshua watched him calmly.

"I'll hire you," said Glanton. "I'm short on men."

"Starting when?"

Glanton smiled cynically. "It don't scare you?"

Joshua looked at Glanton and at the two guards and then back at Glanton. "No, it doesn't scare me."

"We need somebody that don't scare. With White and Prewett gone, we're about out of guts."

"I'm ready to start," Joshua said.

The blue eyes sized him up once more. Glanton was not entirely satisfied, but he must have needed help badly.

Joshua nodded. He tossed his gear into one of the cabins but kept his arms. He unsaddled his mule and turned it loose in the bottomlands. Then he went back to the stockade. Glanton was no longer sitting at the table, and the many piles of coins were gone. A fat little man, almost entirely bald, sat at the table now. Around his feet and under the table were four small dogs, and another lay in the middle of the table. The fat little man looked up and said, "You're the new man—Pickens, is it? I'm Dr. Lincoln."

Joshua nodded. He remembered the name; Lincoln was the man Brodie had financed in the first place.

"This one," Dr. Lincoln said, watching the dog on the table, "is named Cerberus. Doesn't look much like the mythical guardian of the Styx, does he?"

Indeed, Cerberus looked like nothing but a fat, lazy dog.

Dr. Lincoln put his finger in the earthenware jug and tipped it a little. Then he held the finger to the dog's nose. The dog's ears pricked up, and he tried to lick the finger. "He's very fond of whisky," said Dr. Lincoln, "especially rye. He doesn't like too much the stuff they have out here, but he'd rather have it than nothing."

Joshua frowned, then backed off and went to find Glanton. The man was asleep on a buffalo robe in the center of the floor of the big cabin, snoring as harshly as he talked. One of the guards answered Joshua's question: "There's nothin' to do right now, but don't worry. There'll be plenty later on. If there isn't any excitement, Glanton will make some."

Joshua, carrying his rifle, went down to the lowland, where the horses and mules were grazing. Casually he made his way to the west, following the river. He had an important item of information to get to Callahan: that Glanton intended to destroy the ferry—for that meant

211

that Glanton would kill anybody on it. It was important that Callahan be warned. Since the Yumas had no firearms, Callahan could leave the ferry itself and hide out where he would be safe, or he could get word to Brodie and Enrique and they could set a trap for Glanton. Either way would be better than leaving Callahan sitting on the boat as an unwitting target.

He stepped up on a shelf of gravel about two feet above the grass, and a shot sounded ahead of him. The bullet plowed a furrow in the ground and threw gravel on his boots. He stopped dead still. There was nobody visible ahead of him. He took one more step ahead, and again a shot sounded, and another bullet plowed up gravel by his other foot. He called, "Who's out there?"

"It don't make no never-mind to you who it is, long as you stay in the grass."

Joshua picked him out now—a fat man with beady eyes, shooting through a mesquite bush. The powder smoke was almost directly in the sun and hard to see.

"I was just looking around," said Joshua.

"You can look in the other direction or I'll blow your head off," said the fat man. "Glanton don't trust you."

Joshua considered that information. "Then why did he hire me?"

"So's he could keep an eye on you. He figgered you come to find out somethin', and he wants to know what it is."

"I can leave when I've got a mind to."

"You sure can—but you might leave dead." His voice rose. "Now get back on the grass!"

Joshua considered again. He could not raise his own rifle before the guard fired—and it looked as if the guard was a good shot. He turned and went back to the lower shelf. It was only half a mile wide at that point, but the grass was long and heavy. He walked slowly upstream, watching the left side for a way out, but the bank grew higher on the left until it was a cliff, and up above was the edge of the desert. Night would be the best time to get away.

He found a place to sit in the shade, and stayed there until another guard passed him, apparently to replace the fat man. For a moment Joshua thought of kidnaping the new man and using him to run past the fat man, but probably the fat man would not hesitate to shoot them both. He got to his feet and walked a few feet out and looked at the stockade. He was only a quarter of a mile away, but he might be able to stay under cover of the cliff.

"Lookin' for something, mister?" asked a new voice, and for an instant he froze. Then he looked up and saw another guard on top of the cliff. "Just wondered about supper," Joshua said.

"You can quit wonderin' and go on up."

Joshua turned and walked toward the stockade. It was clear now that in his determination to trap White he had made a serious blunder.

He ate corn bread and venison in silence, watching with some disgust as Dr. Lincoln fed his pet dogs on the top of the table. Joshua finally took his tin plate to the ground outside of the cabin.

"You don't like the doctor's dogs?" asked the beady-eyed man.

"Not when I'm eating."

"Mighty fussy for a deserter."

Joshua frowned. "Is it anything to you?"

The beady-eyed man shrugged. "Not unless you try to pull out without notice."

"Why can't I quit?" Joshua asked as casually as he could.

213

"People that work for Glanton know too damn' much, and he don't like for them to run around talkin'."

"I don't know anything."

"No matter. Don't try to leave."

Joshua demanded, "You mean I'm a prisoner?"

The beady-eyed man grinned wolfishly. "Why don't you ask Glanton?"

After supper Joshua lay on his back just outside the stockade, where he could see the animals below. He was in a bad position. Glanton was no fool. He was suspicious and was keeping him under watch while he decided what to do with him. There were two ways to play it out: either act innocent and wait for Glanton's suspicions to cool down, or make another try to escape. The latter seemed to be the only sensible course.

He went into the stockade at dark, and busied himself making a place to sleep. There was no candle in the cabin where he had put his gear, and from all appearances its usual occupants must be gone to Los Angeles with White. Joshua pretended to get ready for sleep, and then went out and up to the main cabin. "Got any tobacco?" he asked.

"I'll advance you a pound. Got a pipe?"

"No, I'll roll a cigarette."

"Got a few cigarette papers." Gunn pushed a dog-eared book at Joshua. "Put your mark here."

Joshua signed.

"You can write!" the man said.

"I can write my name," said Joshua.

"Real nice writin'. I wouldn't pick you fer no spy fer the Army."

"I'm *not* a spy for the Army," Joshua said.

The man paid no attention. "Here's your stuff." He

214

handed him a paper sack of cut tobacco and a packet of papers.

Joshua went outside, sat down by the door, and rolled a cigarette. He went back and got a light from a bear-oil lamp on the table, and then went outside and walked leisurely toward the gate of the stockade. He stepped into the opening, and felt something in his back. "Where you goin'?" asked Glanton's harsh voice.

"Out for a look around," said Joshua.

Glanton said, "Get inside and stay inside! I got no idea what your game is, but you're playin' with house money. The next time you try to get out of here you'll be stopped with lead instead of talk."

Joshua went back to his own cabin. Now there was only one alternative: play along with Glanton and get on his good side—and hope he could do that before White got back, for he realized that White's return would mean his immediate execution.

Joshua spent the next day walking around and ascertaining that he had pretty good use of his legs. He tired after half an hour of steady walking along the flat by the river, but that was to be expected. He was sent in toward evening, and found Glanton drinking and cursing, for strung out over the desert to the west, almost at the limit of eyesight, was a tiny line of black dots that undoubtedly were General Patterson's wagons. Glanton studied them through the telescope between drinks, and finally fell on the table, unconscious. The men around him were drinking too, but not to the point where a man could tackle them with any hope of success. Joshua wandered down to the gate and ascertained that an alert guard was there. He went back to his bed. It looked as if he had stuck his head into a bear trap, and he might have to fight his way out.

CHAPTER TWENTY-THREE

TWO TRAINS CAME ACROSS ON THE GLANTON FERRY the next day, and Joshua tried to get close enough to somebody in one of the trains to send word to Callahan, but Glanton's men were all around.

Another train came the next day, and still they watched Joshua as an eagle would watch a young cottontail. He was getting discouraged and a little desperate, but he still had his legs to consider; the longer he could put off a showdown, the better shape he would be in.

On the third day, as he was coming in to eat, Glanton met him.

"Come along with me," Glanton ordered. He was a head shorter than Joshua, but that was not unusual, for Joshua was a tall man. "I don't like your looks," said Glanton. "You've got the color of an Apache, and I don't trust those bastards under any circumstances. But you've got the features of a white man. So come along with me—and remember, Pickens, one false move and you'll die with a bullet in your head or a knife in your heart."

He motioned Joshua to precede him to a small rowboat tied up near the anchor end of the ferry rope. "Get in and row," he said. "There's a train comin'."

Joshua rowed with his back toward the ferry, and consequently did not see the train until the boat was beached and Glanton went up the trail, accompanied by two of the men from the ferry, both carrying rifles. Then Joshua saw the gaunt, fierce-eyed man of the Disciples of the Sacred Martyr, and felt sick for a moment, for this man was like a child in the hands of a man like

216

Glanton. A man who had sold the scalps of unborn babies to the government of Chihuahua would listen to no foolishness from these people.

Joshua cringed at the way Glanton looked at the man, for Glanton was shrewd enough to take the fellow's measure at first glance. "Yeah?" he said harshly.

The gaunt man marched forward. "Keep the mules, Sary," he said, and came to Glanton. "You runnin' the ferry, mister?"

"That's right."

"We would like to negotiate passage."

"No negotiatin'," said Glanton. "You pay the price and we take you across. You got money?"

"Very little."

"Then why are you comin' West?"

"We are on the Lord's work," said the man. It might have rolled out portentously in a church building, but it sounded pretty feeble out there in the desert.

Glanton's eyes were running over the train. "Four wagons, eighteen head of animals. How many people?"

"Twenty-two."

Glanton looked coldly at the man. "I'll make you a special price because you're on the Lord's work."

The man was blind to Glanton's sarcasm. "It will be appreciated, sir."

Glanton's voice was rough and penetrating. "One hundred and eighty dollars for the lot," he said.

The man blinked. "How much?"

"I'll say it once more, and only once more—a hundred and eighty dollars, gold or silver, any legal tender."

The man swallowed hard. "We don't have that much money among us."

"Then swim," said Glanton coldly, and he came back

to the boat. "If they want to trade stock," he told the ferrymen, "allow them fifty for mules, twenty for oxen."

"They have just enough stock to pull the wagons," said Joshua.

Glanton looked at him coldly. The reddish-white scar stood out on his face. "Allow them thirty for a wagon," he told the ferrymen, and got into the rowboat. "Get me across!" he ordered.

Joshua, rowing with his back toward the ferry headquarters, saw the gaunt man go back to the wagons and the men and women conferring, but heard nothing. Then the scar-faced guard, who was on the ferry, shouted at the people, "Move on! Don't clutter up the highway! Move on!" He emphasized this order with a shot from his rifle into the gray canvas of the first wagon. There was a crackling sound as the bullet went through a wagon bow.

Glanton did not look around.

"Come on up to the fort," he said when they landed, "and get fed."

When Joshua went in for dinner; Glanton was using the telescope, and presently swore with harsh ferocity. "Them damn' stinkin' Yumas are runnin' Patterson's ferry." He glared. "I knew we should of busted it up."

"It ain't too late," said the beady-eyed man.

"Get your rifles loaded."

Joshua started for his cabin. It would have to be now. But Glanton barked at him, "Got a knife, Pickens?"

Joshua stopped and turned slowly. "Yes," he said.

"You'll go with us."

Joshua nodded. He put his pistol in his belt, took his rifle in his hand. Both were loaded. He went to the bottomlands with the rest of them to get the animals.

Nine men went across on the ferry and rode down the

east side of the river. Whether by accident or design, they kept Joshua hemmed in front and back, and he began to get nervous. He raised his rifle to pretend a shot at a duck swimming in a backwater, but Glanton stopped him with a pistol in his back. "Don't do it," he said in his grating voice. "The man that gives a warning dies quick."

For a moment Joshua was tempted to whirl and start the fight, but he thought better of it. Algodones was fourteen miles below the ferry, and they still had a good way to go. Surely the Yumas would see Glanton's outfit a long way off, and would warn Callahan.

They rode through a swampy bottomland in thick cover for a while, and then Glanton went ahead with his telescope. After a couple of minutes he came back and faced them. "We're about a mile off. A red-whiskered man is sittin' on the boat smokin' a cigar. He's the one running it for the Yumas, no doubt." He looked at Joshua with those flinty eyes. "Your friend, Pickens."

Joshua whammed his mule in the sides with both heels, and the mule lunged forward. The mule jumped over a drifted log, and at the same time Joshua got out his pistol. But the mule went up to its knees in soft mud, and Joshua went over the mule's head and landed an his stomach in the water. He got up to find seven rifles leveled at him.

"Get out of there," said Glanton.

Joshua got up slowly. His pistol was fouled with mud.

The rifle was too far away to reach. He said to Glanton, "The mule broke a leg. Somebody better shoot it."

"Shoot, hell—and give more warning?" His harsh

voice rose. "The mule got himself in there. Let him get himself out."

They rode on in silence, with Joshua walking ahead of Glanton. They drew near the ferry, and all dismounted. Glanton turned the horses over to one of the men and motioned to Joshua to go ahead. "He knows you. Go up and start talkin' to him. Keep him busy."

Joshua looked at the rifles leveled at him and then at Glanton. "You're a fool," he said, "if you think I'd do that."

"There'll be rifles lined up on your back every minute," Glanton said coldly. "We can get within a hundred yards under cover of the cane, but you'll have to keep him busy while we cross the sand bar."

Joshua looked at him and opened his mouth to shout. Something crashed on the back of his head, and he collapsed in the trail. He remembered squirming and twisting to get away from a possible knife thrust, and his face was in the mud and he almost suffocated. Then he raised his face and shook his head and blew the mud out of his nostrils.

He heard firing, and shouted, "Bill! Bill!" although he realized it probably was too late.

He got up and ran toward the ferry. Callahan was saving his shots. Glanton's men were closing in, but Callahan was not answering their fire. The beach was open sand, and they must have tried to shoot Callahan before they crossed it. Callahan was lying flat on the deck of the ferry, his elbows on the deck, his rifle in his hands.

Joshua approached through the closing semicircle.

Callahan fired, and one of Glanton's men went down, but the other six started running, bent over. Joshua reached the man who was down. Callahan's shot had smashed the man's left shoulder, and blood was spurting out as the heart beat. It wouldn't beat much longer. Joshua seized the man's rifle. The trigger was caught on the man's clothes, and it took a minute to get it untangled. Then he straightened, cocked the rifle, and turned to look.

Glanton's men were already on the ferry. Joshua fired, and a man slumped sidewise and fell into the water. The others were bent low, doing something with their hands, and Joshua raced across the sand. Glanton straightened up and fired at him but missed. Joshua leaped onto the deck.

At that moment they tossed Callahan, tied hand and foot, headfirst into the river.

Joshua shouted. They turned together, and Glanton cried hoarsely, "Kill him!"

They fired together, but Joshua threw his rifle at them and dived headfirst into the water.

He heard shots as if from far away. He swam under the boat until the light told him he was clear of it, and he stayed under as long as he could.

Then he came up as quietly as possible, took a deep breath, and looked for Callahan, who was floating along face down about thirty feet below him. Callahan was twisting all he could but he wasn't having any effect. Joshua took clean strokes and reached Callahan and turned him over so his face was out of the water. He heard Glanton's hoarse shout.

Joshua did not waste time diving. He jacked himself up and then went straight down, feet first, as the first bullet ricocheted from the water two feet away and sprayed the red water of the Colorado in his face. He heard more shots. He stayed under as long as he possibly could, swimming hard. He came up almost under Callahan. He gave him a push, and dived. More shots hit the water around him, but he had only a short way to go when he bumped into the mud bank of the river. He stood up and shook his head. He was behind a willow tree, and he looked for Callahan. Bullets were making little geysers in the water; some of them ricocheted and screamed off downriver. A bullet hit Callahan and rolled his body back on his face. Joshua started to dive after him, but a second and a third bullet hit Callahan, and around Callahan's throat the red water was stained a brighter color. While Joshua watched, horrified, the body rolled again, and Callahan's head flopped loosely. His spine had been broken by a shot through the neck. And still they fired at the body.

Joshua crawled out of the water, sick. It was as he had feared. Callahan would not go back to Le-och.

He heard Glanton's hoarse shout, "Look out for them Injuns!"

He stayed in the willows. Chief Cabello en Pelo was advancing at the head of several hundred Indians from their village, a quarter of a mile away. Joshua saw no rifles, but the Indians, well spread out, were carrying clubs and bows and arrows. Glanton had no compunction over killing Indians, but he would have to hesitate in the face of so many.

Joshua looked through the willows. Two men were sawing at the rope with knives. A third was lighting a fire in the middle of the boat. The Yumas got closer, and Glanton with one other man held them off with rifles while the third man got the fire going, then jumped down and took his place facing the Yumas. Then the two finished cutting the rope, and the boat swung slowly out toward midstream.

Cabello en Pelo shook his fist angrily at Glanton. "General Patterson gave to us that boat. He say we can take emigrants across for one dollar a head."

Glanton snorted. "I say it's going to burn up."

Cabello en Pelo stalked back and forth, but there wasn't much he could do. The Yumas could have overwhelmed the five scalp-hunters, but some of the Yumas would have been killed, and it was Indian nature for each man to visualize himself as the one to be killed. This wasn't their kind of fight, and Glanton knew it.

"You burn our boat!" shouted Cabello en Pelo. "All right, we will take emigrants in canoes, and we will swim the animals."

"Like hell you will!" said Glanton, shaking his head. "This is my river, and nobody else runs a ferry on it."

Pascual, another Yuma chief, said, "We live here a long time."

"That don't count," said Glanton. "You're a bunch of ignorant savages, and you've got nothing to fight with but clubs and bows and arrows. We've got rifles, and we'll shoot you down like dogs."

"We have right to ferry in canoes," Cabello en Pelo insisted.

"No, you ain't," said Glanton, "and what's more, how do you like this? No Indian is gonna cross the river except on my ferry, and you'll pay like anybody else when you do!"

Cabello en Pelo strode to Glanton. "You go too far, scalp-hunter! Indians get mad!"

Glanton laughed. He pushed the muzzle of his rifle into Cabello en Pelo's stomach, and the Yuma froze. Glanton reversed the rifle and swung the butt at the Yuma's head. The Indian ducked, and Glanton kicked him brutally in the crotch before he could straighten up.

Cabello en Pelo grunted as if he had been hit with a Sharps bullet, and doubled up in pain. Glanton cast a look at the boat. It was burning fiercely, with great yellow flames and clouds of black smoke rolling into the clear sky. "The first Indian I catch swimming the river gets a bullet in the head," he warned. "All right, let's go back."

He and his men marched away across the sand. They didn't bother about the one who had been shot and had fallen into the water. They came to the one in the sand, and Glanton looked at him. "Dead," he said, and left the body where it was.

The few men made their retreat, while the Indians gathered around their chief, and Pascual shouted threats.

Joshua stayed where he was. The Yumas began to drift back toward their camp, and Joshua thought it over. The murder of Callahan, he resolved grimly, would not go unavenged. Brodie was not too far away, and there was now a bunch of *arrieros* with him. They should be able to get up a sizable force.

He saw a canoe put out toward Callahan's body, but shook his head sorrowfully. Callahan was long past help.

He heard a giant hissing as the boat planks burned through and the river water rushed into the floating hull. The ferry turned one end up, slowly, ponderously, and then slid under.

Joshua took a deep breath. He still had his knife, and the mule was stuck in the mud with a broken leg. He crossed the sand and entered the brush. He stopped dead still for several minutes and listened, but heard nothing except the distant muttering of the Yumas. He saw, far ahead, several men on horseback, and followed the trail with less caution. He heard the mule braying piteously, and found it where he had left it. At every move to free itself from the mud it was tortured by the pain of the broken leg. Joshua stepped up and cut its throat. Then he stooped to get his rifle out of the mud.

A familiar voice stopped him. "He said you'd be back to see about that mule."

Joshua straightened. The man with the scar across the bridge of his nose was holding a rifle on him. Joshua started to speak, but there was no use, for the man was about to pull the trigger. He thought of running, but his boots were deep in mud. He ducked suddenly to escape the first bullet, and heard the crack of the rifle. He ducked the other way, expecting another one, but heard a splash instead. He looked up. The man had dropped his rifle in the water, and was falling forward with a widening red spot between his eyes at just the place of the scar.

Joshua looked behind him but saw no one. He called out, "Who's there?" but there was no answer.

He got his boots out of the mud and went to the Glanton man. He was dead. Joshua picked up his rifle. It had not been fired. He studied the willows and the mesquite and the cane all around him, but saw no sign except that a flock of red-winged blackbird flew up suddenly about four hundred yards away. He watched but saw nobody. He got his rifle from under the mule's body, and went back to the path. Again he scanned the brush, and called out, "Who's there?" but nobody answered.

He went back down the river to where the canoe had towed Callahan's body in to shore. Callahan had been hit six times, and Joshua, looking down at the body, felt a great hardness come over him.

He went to the camp and borrowed a shovel from the

Indians. The Yumas sent two men to help him. He cut the ropes from Callahan's arms and legs, and they carried the body back from the river to a ridge of sand that Joshua thought would be above the floodwaters. They took turns digging a grave, and Joshua laid Callahan in it. He covered his face with his own shirt, and they shoveled the sand back in and laid rocks on top to keep out the coyotes.

Joshua's legs were getting unsteady. He borrowed a broom-tail horse and rode it bareback toward the Sonoran camp. It was a little after sunset when Enrique and Brodie came out to meet him.

"Pickens!" shouted Brodie. "I'm glad to see you, lad."

They shook hands warmly.

"You and Callahan fought like an army back there at Tinajas Altos, and saved my train. We'd never have got away from there alive any other way."

Joshua slid off the horse and almost fell. Brodie caught him. "You in trouble?" he asked anxiously.

"Just tired."

Brodie sounded anxious. "You must have stopped some lead."

"It was that bullet I got up at Carrizo Springs. They dug it out, and I'm just getting back on my feet."

"Put an arm around my shoulders."

"Let me sit a minute." He looked at Brodie. "They killed Callahan," he said in a low voice.

"I heard that. The Indians told me. I'm sorry, mighty sorry."

"It was Glanton and his men. We've got to wipe them out."

"How about the man White that you two were looking for?"

"Gone to Los Angeles. I'll get him when he returns. But Glanton and his men killed Callahan. We've got to wipe them out," he repeated.

"It suits me fine." Brodie held out a cigar.

"No, thanks," said Joshua. "Smoke one for Callahan."

Brodie struck a match. "I sent a party back from the Tules to look for you, but we never located hide or hair."

"We both stopped some lead and hid out for a while."

Brodie got his cigar going and tossed away the match. "I got Enrique and his men to join up, but I figured I needed one like you to help run things. We were waiting to see what would come of Patterson's ferry."

"Now you know," said Joshua. "And it's time to straighten things out up at the Gila crossing."

"Come on up and have some frijoles. We'll plan what to do next."

They passed a tiny fire, and a Mexican girl cried, "José!"

Joshua waved feebly. Lupe jumped up and hugged him.

He shook hands with Pánfilo and the sad-eyed Jesús. "You came pretty far off your trail, didn't you?" he asked Jesús.

"We have found what we came for, señor."

"You never did tell me what you were coming for."

"They are here, señor." He went to the crude *carreta*, and Joshua followed him. A bundle wrapped in white cloth was in the cart, and he opened one end of it.

"You got her bones?" Joshua asked, finding it hard to believe.

"We have their bones, señor."

Joshua stared, hardly seeing.

"It is important if you have loved them, señor."

227

Brodie said, "They hit our train about the middle of the desert. They were in bad shape, and we persuaded them to come on to the river with us."

"A good thing," said Joshua finally.

He kept his eyes open for Natalia, but didn't see her and didn't ask. Brodie would tell him if he wanted him to see her. They had chile and beans, and sat back to drink coffee. It was almost dark.

"What do you think we can do with Glanton and his men?" asked Brodie, puffing on a cigar.

"I think they'll all get roaring drunk tonight, but I think we'd be better off to lay siege during the day. We can scatter out in the desert and they'll hardly be able to see us. There's no use rushing them, because they'll fight like cornered coyotes, and a lot of men will get hurt."

"Why not cross tonight," asked Brodie, "and get in position to put them under fire in the morning?"

"We'll have to swim, since they burned the other ferry," said Enrique.

Joshua nodded. "That will have to be done at night, for I have no doubt they'll send a couple of riflemen down the river to shoot at the Yumas who try to swim across."

Brodie asked Enrique, "What do you think?"

"I like it better than rushing. I have known this Glanton." He shook his head ominously. "He's a bad hombre."

"Fifty dollars apiece for your men if we capture the ferry," said Brodie.

Enrique brightened. "Very good, señor. Very good."

"And you," said Brodie to Pickens, "what do you want out of this?"

Joshua looked at the fire. "I'll have my own reward," he said.

"I don't doubt it, but let's say a hundred dollars. All right?"

"That's enough for me."

"Let's get at it, then. Draw me a plan of the fort. How far do you make it—about sixteen miles east and north from here?"

"About." Joshua got a twig and drew the fort in the sand, and showed where the gate was and how the main cabin stood higher than the others. "We can throw some men out to the west. There's a little cover in the desert, mostly creosote bush. And we can spray lead on the west end of the ferry from several points on this cliff."

"Are there any washes near the edge of the cliff where a man can take cover?"

Joshua nodded. "When the firing gets under way, I figure the men on the ferry—if there *are* any on it that early—will head back for the fort, and I think half a dozen men hidden in the willows along there can wait until they get out in the stream a way and then throw lead all over them, and they won't have too good a chance to shoot back. But remember one thing: Glanton has a high-powered telescope up there."

They talked it over for an hour, and finally Enrique went to gather up his men, and Brodie gave orders to Salvador, who had replaced Pedro, to take twenty men with rifles. "That will leave fifteen here to protect the camp, which ought to be enough."

"It should be," said Joshua. "The Apaches aren't likely to come this far west."

"We'll need half a dozen men to take the animals back to the river—and be sure every man takes a full canteen. If we're still at it by sundown, we can come in for water and food in relays.

"Remember one thing," said Brodie. "Dr. Lincoln

229

was my partner. He might be a little touched in the head, but I don't think he'd ever have turned the ferry over to Glanton if he hadn't been forced to."

"So you don't want him killed," said Joshua.

Brodie nodded.

"Of course, there's a possibility," said Joshua, "that nobody will be killed. But I doubt it, with these men."

Brodie got up. "We'll meet beyond the first wagon there."

Joshua got up. "I've got two rifles here to be cleaned up," he said.

"Take two of mine. Then the ammunition will be all the same. And by the way—" He was speaking in a low voice.

"Yes?" said Joshua.

"You risked your life to protect Natalia. You're entitled to see her."

"I'd like that," said Joshua.

And without further warning Natalia stood before him, somehow materialized out of the desert night, her olive skin dusky in the glow of the firelight, her eyes large and lustrous, her head averted a little as she waited to see what he would say.

He drew a deep breath. "You are very beautiful, Natalia," he said, hardly trusting his voice. "I'm glad to see you—and perhaps I shall see you again before too long."

She nodded slowly. "I hope so," she said, and then abruptly, she was gone, and he stood there staring into the night for a sight of her. No, he had not chosen wrong.

CHAPTER TWENTY-FOUR

THE MEN GOT ACROSS THE RIVER WITH NO GREAT trouble. This was April 22, and the spring rise was still to come. Enrique rode with eight muleteers; Joshua rode with Brodie and Salvador and nineteen of Brodie's men, most of them dark and pockmarked and fierce-looking with their big sombreros. All told there were thirty-one riflemen, and at the last moment they decided not to divide the force, but to try to cover the ferry from the west side of the river.

There were no Indians along the river where they crossed. "They may be mad at *all* white men," said Joshua, "after the way Glanton treated their chief."

"That wasn't fair," said Brodie vehemently. "Cabello en Pelo and Macedon and Pasqual have been mighty decent Indians for a long time. I used to come through here in the 1830's, and these people always helped me. I never had any trouble with them."

They got across and rode out into the desert to avoid any possible sentinels Glanton might have posted. After three hours of steady riding, Joshua pulled up. "About a mile ahead and a mile to the right," he said. "Is everybody all set?"

They kept their voices low, for sounds carried far over the desert at this low altitude.

"Take your men on about two miles," Joshua told Enrique, "and dismount. Close in. You'll see the fort against the skyline. Get cover at about four hundred yards."

Enrique said dubiously, "It's a long range, four hundred yards."

231

"They can throw lead. You and I and Brodie and maybe a few of the men can really shoot. It doesn't take many who can put a bullet where they're looking."

"I'd like to cut his throat," said Enrique.

"Remember that telescope, and watch your cover. Don't shoot over the bushes. Shoot from one side or the other." Joshua slapped Enrique on the shoulder. "Let's get set."

They rode off. Joshua and Brodie dismounted their own men and turned the horses over to the horse-holders, who started back to the river with them. The men stayed close together, and they all moved northeast. The fort showed up as a black silhouette against the stars, and there were no lights in it. Joshua spread his men and saw that each man had cover. He established contact with Enrique, who said his men were all set.

"When do we start shootin'?" asked Brodie.

"At daylight."

"You thought about them gettin' away on the ferry?"

"There's no chance of that. The ferry's too slow. Anyway, we're not supposed to be here for revenge. We're trying to get your ferry back in your hands."

"I hope I remember that if I get a shot at Glanton."

"It's an hour or so to daylight. Keep your men down on the ground."

Joshua and Brodie had posts commanding the gate in the stockade, and Joshua lay on his back and watched the stars while he waited for the sky to lighten. He wondered who had shot the scar-faced man on the trail. It must have been an Indian—but the Yumas had no rifles.

"Hey!" whispered Brodie. "Something's moving ahead of us!"

232

Joshua rolled over, keeping his head low. Something that looked like a big caterpillar was inching toward the fort. He looked to his left and saw another, and—many of them. He looked to his right and saw a solid mass of movement in the night, all toward the stockade. He crawled over to Brodie. "It looks as if the Yumas are about to beat us to it," he said.

Brodie frowned. "You think we ought to let them?"

Joshua looked up toward the fort. The desert seemed alive with creeping dark forms. "I don't know how we could do it without killing an awful lot of Yumas—so it's a question of which. Why not let the Yumas take care of Glanton? They've suffered enough at his hands—much more than we know, I feel sure."

Brodie sounded worried. "There ought to be a sheriff or somebody to take charge of things."

"There should be, but there isn't. I think we'll have to call it a private fight and let them settle it the best they can."

"There isn't much else to do. I don't want my men to fire on the Yumas."

Joshua made the circuit and passed the word about the Yumas and told the men not to shoot unless further orders came.

"There are hundreds of them," said Brodie in awe. "It looks like the Yumas are about ready to take over the place."

"With a threat by Glanton to shoot the first one who swims the river, what else can they do?"

"I don't like it," said Brodie. "I wanted a crack at that scalp-hunter on my own."

"Let's go up a little closer," said Joshua, "and see what happens."

"Remember to keep your head down."

It had lightened enough by that time to show that the area around the stockade was alive with Indians. They weren't painted like the Plains Indians, and they had no feathers or ceremonial decorations, but they looked deadly as they moved silently over the ground, closing in until they were almost in a solid pack. They carried bows and arrows, war clubs, and big rocks.

Joshua shook his head. "They must be pretty desperate."

"They are," said Brodie. "I been hearing how these coyotes treated the Yumas. A bunch of them would came through the camp at night and pick out the women they wanted and finish the business right out in public, keeping the Yumas back with rifles. That was only one of their dirty tricks."

Joshua said, "In that case they've sure got it coming. Let's circle far enough so we won't get an arrow in our gizzards, and get where we can watch the gate. That's where they'll have to go in."

The desert became rapidly lighter. The scrubby, evil-smelling creosote bush gave it a gray-blue tinge, and a jack rabbit, startled by an Indian, leaped high in sudden, silent fright, and fled in a zig-zag trail across the desert. For a moment nothing else moved. Quail were calling down on the lowlands, and a mule brayed. Joshua and Brodie kept low, and suddenly the sky was filled with soft bright light. A Yuma stood up within fifty yards of the gate and waved his arms.

"Cabello en Pelo," whispered Brodie.

The Indians rose up from the prairie as a solid mass and converged on the gate. So far no vocal sound had been made, and apparently not even Glanton's sentries had stayed sober after the emotional binge of the assault

234

on the Yumas' ferry. In the light of Glanton's contempt for the Indians, that was understandable. Joshua and Brodie moved over to get a more direct view, but stayed low.

It seemed as if the entire yard filled with Indians within a few seconds. Then Cabello en Pelo waved a war club above his head. The Yumas leaped toward the doors of the cabin. The main cabin had windows, and the Indians poured through those openings. Somebody made a sound at last, and Joshua let out a long breath. The Yumas began to yell; it wasn't like the war cry of the Apaches or Comanches, but an indignant howl of savage satisfaction.

Men began to run into the yard, to be met with clubs and arrows. Dr. Lincoln ran out in a nightshirt, and a big Yuma knocked out his brains with a club. His dogs barked and squealed for only a few seconds. One of the drunken men must have reached a rifle, for a shot was fired, but almost immediately the man was catapulted from the main cabin and stopped, staring at the horde of Indians with his mouth open. He brought up his rifle to fire, but it was knocked out of his hands by a swinging war club. He began to curse thickly, and those were the first words said aloud that morning. He staggered back to the doorway and faced them. An arrow landed in his abdomen with an audible *thuck,* and he doubled over for an instant and then tried to straighten up, his face contorted with pain. "Stinkin', dirty—"

He never finished. The Yumas had been abused too long. A dozen arrows suddenly bristled from his body. He fell forward, weirdly suspended on the long shafts of the arrows for a moment until his dying movements toppled him to the ground.

All over the yard Glanton's men were being

pincushioned with arrows and brained with clubs. The Yumas went after them like tigers, and one by one the whites went down under a swarm of red bodies.

Finally John Glanton appeared in the doorway of the main cabin. He swayed a little, and even at a distance his blue eyes were discernible. He started to curse the Indians, and then one, bigger than most, loomed up above him and brought down a huge rock on top of his head.

His skull split like a ripe pumpkin, but the Indian raised the rock and brought it down again before Glanton hit the ground. And then rocks were raised in the air all around him and brought down with all the force of which the Indians were capable.

A shout came from Salvador. "Two have escaped!"

Somehow two of Glanton's men had broken loose. Perhaps they had been sleeping off their drunkenness outside the walls. Now they ran heavily down the slope toward the river. They were almost at the bank before the Indians began to fire arrows at them.

The two men appeared down on the grass flat a moment later, each mounted on a barebacked mule and flogging it downstream. But the Yumas were busy in the stockade, and a thin haze of blue smoke wavered upward into the still air. In a moment there was crackling, and yellow flames appeared. The Yumas threw the bodies back into the cabins, and within five minutes all the cabins were blazing pyres of red and yellow flames and grayish-blue smoke that indicated dried-out cottonwood.

Joshua and Brodie stood there with their rifle butts resting on the ground, and Joshua said, "Maybe we better get out of here."

The roar of the flames and the crackle of the dry wood made it difficult to talk. They went back, called in the men, and started west, to give the Indians a wide berth.

Cabello en Pelo ran out of the stockade and shouted, "José! José!"

"I wouldn't go," said Brodie.

Enrique looked scared, and Joshua didn't have too much confidence, but he said, "Don't worry. I'll see what's up. Maybe he wants us to sign a paper that it was justified."

The chief ran to meet him. His eyes were glowing from the excitement. "We kill eleven!" he said. "Two got away, but we find. We tie up and throw in river— same as Cal'han!"

Joshua nodded, a little overcome to find that part of this night's work had been for Callahan.

"Yumas can swim river now," said the chief. "All us very happy."

Brodie's men met their horse-holders about halfway, and rode the rest of the way into camp. "Two of Glanton's men came to our camp for refuge," said the first horse-holder. "We ran them away with rifles."

"That wasn't very neighborly," said Brodie, taking the bridle reins of his horse.

"They are bad men. We not want."

"Where'd they go?"

"Back to river."

They found the two men when they reached the river. Each had been tied hand and foot and thrown into the Colorado, and each was floating face down. Enrique pulled them out of the water, examined them, gave his men a signal. They picked the bodies up and tossed

237

them back in the river. "They're very dead," said Enrique.

"They'll stink up the river," said Joshua.

"Don't worry. The buzzards will be floating on the bodies within five miles, and there won't be anything left by the time they get to the gulf."

They went to the Mexicans' camp. "There'll be hell to pay in San Diego when they hear about this," said Brodie.

"That's what bothers me," said Joshua. "They'll probably send a bunch of soldiers out here to chase the Yumas, and kill a few, and burn their crops, and then go back to San Diego and be heroes."

"Can't we stop that?"

"No easier than we could have stopped the Yumas this morning. They were crazy mad and this was one time the Indians didn't care how many of them got killed, just so they got vengeance. Indians don't generally fight like that, but these had been pushed too far."

Natalia was standing in the midmorning sun when they rode up. She scanned their faces with anxiety, and finally her glance settled on Joshua. "Nobody was killed?" she asked.

"We weren't in it," Joshua said shortly.

"That's fine. Now you can help Papa run the ferry."

Joshua dismounted. His legs were a little trembly but otherwise he felt fine. "No, Natalia, I'm afraid not." He helped himself to a tin cup, and while he was pouring coffee into it he looked up into her eyes. "There's four more gone to the Pueblo of Los Angeles," he said. "I've got to go after them."

"But this is not right," she said. "You cannot kill these men like—like wolves or bears."

238

He sipped the coffee. "No." He stood up, and his gray eyes were full on her and took in every detail of her red lips, large black eyes, cheeks that reminded him of ripe *tunas*, hair as black as night on the desert. "This isn't for vengeance," he said. "One of these hombres is wanted by the U.S. Army. I'm going to deliver him to San Diego."

CHAPTER TWENTY-FIVE

AT DINNERTIME JOSHUA SAID, "I WISH YOU'D GIVE ONE of the Yumas a couple of cigars to go back to Sacatón and tell Callahan's wife what happened to him."

"I heard he married an Indian," said Brodie.

Joshua nodded. "They were in love."

"I'll talk to Cabello en Pelo." Brodie pulled out a cigar and studied it. "I take it you're going after White now."

"Yes."

"It'll be one against four or more."

Joshua shrugged. "This time I won't be reckless."

Brodie lit his cigar with a burning twig. "I owe you a debt," he began.

"Not me," said Joshua. "You gave me a rifle and pistol and a mule for the job at Tinajas Altas."

Brodie appeared not to hear him. "And I owe Callahan a debt."

Joshua looked curiously at him.

Brodie puffed his cigar harder than usual. "I'm going with you after White," he said.

Joshua cupped a tortilla around his index finger and scooped chile and goat meat out of an *olla*. He was filled with a rapid succession of feelings: astonishment

239

at Brodie's announcement, gratification at the offer, and finally a realization that he had no right to subject Brodie to such danger.

"It's not your fight," he said. "I'm responsible for the fact that he's loose now. If I hadn't had a weak moment, he'd still be in jail—or hanged."

Brodie glanced at him. "We all have weak moments," he said, "but that's neither here nor there. The thing is, you've got to get him, and you can't do it alone."

Joshua recognized the finality in Brodie's voice. After a moment he said, "We'd better do some figuring, then."

"The way it looks to me, White should be comin' back any day now."

"Yes, and three men with him—maybe more."

"We could wait for him at the crossing," said Brodie.

"No. The next train that comes across will carry the word about the massacre, and White would evaporate. He's probably left plenty of money in the Pueblo, and he could head right back up there and then on to Yerba Buena and ship out for China or somewhere. We've got to figure it out better than that."

Brodie got out a cigar. "You still don't smoke?" he asked Joshua.

"No."

"Not for any moral reason, I hope," said Brodie, puffing.

Joshua grinned. "As a matter of fact, it makes me sick at my stomach to smoke cigars."

"Well," Brodie growled, "I'm glad I found one thing wrong with you. I'm scared of a man that's perfect."

"There are other things," Joshua said easily. "Some people think I'm crazy to want to go to the gold fields, for instance."

Brodie looked up sharply. "Not crazy—but you're a damn' fool if you expect to get rich at it."

Joshua thought about it for a moment. Was his enthusiasm any less, or was he just tired? Somehow going to the gold fields didn't seem too important.

"I got an idea about this man White," said Brodie.

"I'm listening," said Joshua.

"You know as well as I do there's only one place to tie onto him, and that's at one of the water holes. But in the meantime you've got to keep him from hearing about the massacre."

"That's right," said Joshua.

"I got an idea. The ferry's mine and I can do what I please with it. I'm going to sink it!"

Joshua stared at him, not quite following the reasoning.

"With the ferry on the bottom of the river, the emigrants can't get across—at least not very fast. I'll talk to Cabello en Pelo and he'll co-operate by refusing to take anybody across for a couple of days. In the meantime my men will be busy raisin' the boat again, and they'll persuade the emigrants to stay hitched and rest up for the trip across the desert. Soon as they hear from us, they'll start moving them."

Joshua nodded decisively. "We'll do that." He got up. "Any extra ammunition? And we'll need a rope."

"Plenty. Salvador!"

"I look for a short, quick fight," said Joshua, "and we should know the answer in a hurry."

Salvador came with ammunition and rope.

"When do you want to start?" asked Brodie.

"With you along, it changes things a little. We can go to Warner's. He knows you and won't pay much attention to me. We can hide out in the hills around

241

Warner's and wait. You can make up a story—say we're looking for gold or something—so we'll have an excuse to go in for supplies. When White comes through, we'll follow him down to Carrizo Springs and then close in."

Brodie's eyes were alight. "You're a good schemer," he said. "You think your legs will stand up?"

"They'd better."

But Joshua wasn't sure they would as he and Brodie got out of the Yuma canoes, pulled their mules out of the water, and let them shake for a minute. He looked across the gray-brown flatness of the desert and knew it was a long way to go.

They rode up on the desert tableland and started for Cooke's Wells. There was no water, and Brodie asked, "How do you feel? We can dig."

Joshua looked toward the forbidding mountains. "We'd better go on to Alamo Mocho," he said.

They stayed at Alamo during the heat of the next day, then moved on to the Big Lagoon. But a high wind came down from the mountains, driving sand and dust before it to fill the wheel ruts made by emigrants' wagons and erase all signs of the trail within an hour. The sand moved along the hard clay floor of the desert with a rustling sound, while the finer particles were driven into their faces with blinding force.

Brodie shouted, "You got your bearings?"

Joshua nodded. He had a bearing on a distant barren mountain ridge, in the very top of which was a V-shaped indentation like the notch in a rifle's rear sight.

They stopped at the Lagoon for water, and during the night the wind died down. They left at daylight for Carrizo Creek, and there was an hour of calm, in which they seemed to be entirely alone in the desert world. All

242

traces of the passage of humans were eliminated, and ahead of them were only small drifts of sand, running into countless thousands as far as they could see.

Then the wind hit them again with greater force than before. Joshua ripped off part of his shirt to tie over the mules' noses, and the two men pulled their hats down hard over their eyes. The dust was high in the air and they could not see the mountains ahead or even the sun. Joshua tried to keep facing into the wind, aware though he was that its direction might change. They came to a slope, and Brodie grabbed his arm and pointed at the ground. It was still gravelly, but some bunch grass grew in scattered clumps.

Joshua nodded. They rode along and then started cutting across the foot of the slope to the north. Presently the wind went down, but the air was filled with dust, and still they could not see. Joshua got down and found a mesquite bush and knew they were on the right track, for mesquite grew only near water.

They turned up the looping trail into the mountains, and hours later sat their mules looking down at the scattered bones of horses and mules and oxen around Carrizo Springs. They watered their animals, and Joshua led the way across to the other side of the springs. The wind, he saw, would cover their tracks in minutes. They found a small, deep ravine where they could talk without shouting.

"Do you suppose we passed him in the storm?" asked Brodie.

"I don't think so. They wouldn't have left the springs in this kind of weather."

"What now, then?"

"We might as well stay here the night."

They unsaddled the mules. There was a little grama

243

grass in the ravine, and they staked out the mules where they would not be seen from below.

The wind went down during the night, and the dust in the mountains settled faster than it did out on the open desert. By morning it was bright and clear, the sun hot and brassy. Joshua said, "We can look for him around ten o'clock if he comes in today. And they'll have to camp here, because the wind has dried up the creek lower down. If he doesn't come this morning, we'll go on to Warner's as we planned."

Brodie watched a road runner walking through the mesquite looking for an unwary rattlesnake. "You thought about the odds?" he asked. "Two against four?"

"Yes. But we've got surprise on our side."

"I hope it's enough."

Brodie was watching the trail toward the mountains. "There's a little haze in the air, away up yonder," he noted. "See how it's forming like a layer? You can't tell where it's coming from, but it isn't a storm."

Joshua studied it. "No, that's from animals—several animals, probably. It may be White." He climbed the side of the ravine and studied the springs. "I think down there is the best place to do it—right at the springs. They'll stop there close to water. I'll hide among the rocks on this side. You go downstream about a quarter of a mile, cross over, and come upstream on the ridge, then down among the mesquite on the other side to where you can command the area around the springs. When I start shooting, cut loose."

"We'll be shootin' toward each other."

"No, we'll both be above the springs, and we'll shoot at an angle downhill."

"All right."

Joshua studied the haze. "They may be closer than we think. You better start now."

Brodie put percussion caps on the nipples of his rifle cylinder, squeezing the caps a little so they wouldn't fall off in rough going. Then he started downhill and soon was out of sight. Joshua noticed that he was kicking up no dust.

Half an hour later he caught sight of Brodie making his way through the mesquite on the other side. The haze of dust was growing thicker above them, and Joshua eased out of the ravine and went quietly downhill. He found a position ten yards from the spring where he was protected on both front and uphill sides by rocks and mesquite, and sat down. He could see the dust cloud without standing up, and he judged they were half an hour away. The wind was light, coming down the valley, but erratic—resting a minute, then blowing in gusts, and sometimes changing direction.

He felt the clatter of iron shoes as the men crossed a rocky shelf, and knew they were riding horses, for mules' hoofs took the hot desert sand better than those of horses, and consequently mules usually were ridden unshod. He crouched, waiting. They came in view half a mile up the trail for a moment. Four of them, all riding horses. They must have got good prices for the mules at Los Angeles. He moved around to look for Brodie, just in time to see a coyote loping off downstream. He studied the mesquite. Finally he saw a waving frond of the lacy-leafed plant, and presently made out a dark form behind it. He signaled with his rifle, briefly. The frond dropped out of sight, and all was very quiet.

White's outfit came into view, unexpectedly close,

the horses' iron shoes crunching in the gravel.

"This is it," White said. "Unsaddle and water. We'll leave here about midafternoon."

The four men—White, Prewett, and two others, all unshaved, hard-looking men—got down and unsaddled. Each carried a rifle and a pistol, and each laid his rifle aside while he unsaddled—two of them standing upright against mesquite bushes, one on the gravel, one across the dry white skull of a horse.

White led his horse to water first, and Joshua waited until the other three were on the way to water. He didn't want those rifles to be too handy. He had his own rifle resting on the rocks, aimed at White, and had just opened his mouth to shout, "Hands up!" when one of his mules brayed up on the hill behind him.

White looked uphill for just a second, and Joshua swore to himself. White's horse was a mare, and any mule, scenting her, would, of course, bray. The give-away factor was the fact that the mule was hidden.

White sensed this too. "Back!" he shouted. He dropped the reins and ran for his rifle. Joshua dropped a shot in front of him, and then ducked low as two pistol shots slapped through the mesquite around him.

A shot sounded from higher up, and the bullet ricocheted and whined off across the valley. Joshua took advantage of this diversion to rise up and look. One man was diving for his rifle. White was fading to his right, to the opposite side of the springs from Joshua. Joshua dropped a shot in the middle of the bones, and then quietly left his ambush, keeping low to take advantage of the cover, and made his way to the right to meet White.

A shot sounded, and a man fell, groaning. Joshua worked his way through the mesquite, still keeping low. He saw White coming his way. They were both low, but White was looking to the left of Joshua.

Joshua lifted his rifle a little and said, "Get 'em up, White!"

White ducked and fired. Joshua dived to one side. He was handicapped here, because this man had to be taken alive.

There was silence in the bushes for a moment, then up on the hillside Brodie sent another shot toward the spring.

Joshua raised his head slowly. He saw the top of White's dirt-colored hat not over six feet away. He shouted, "I got you, White!" and leaped toward him.

White's rifle pointed at him, but Joshua used his own rifle as a club and knocked the weapon out of White's hands. White came at him with a knife, his lips thin as he leaped through the mesquite bush. Joshua had his pistol out of his belt, and he stuck it in White's stomach. He could feel the point of White's knife in his ribs, and he said, "Your knife isn't near my heart, White. Drop it!"

They stood that way for a second or two, and then the pressure of the knife was released. White dropped it slowly and started to raise his hands. Then he rolled away from Joshua's pistol and grabbed it with both hands. Joshua, trying to get his footing, slipped and went down, with White on top him. Joshua rolled, beating at White's face. They rolled over a stone, and Joshua slammed White's head down against it. He felt the grip on the pistol momentarily loosen, and he raised the man's head and slammed it again on the rock.

White went limp, and Joshua slammed his head once more for good measure. He was still lying there, unmoving, when Brodie found him.

"What the hell happened to you?" asked Brodie.

"My legs gave out. I had to rassle with my arms. Only way I could take him alive."

"How do you feel now?"

"I feel fine. I may wobble a little when I walk, but I'll be all right."

Brodie helped him up. Brodie had a bloody forearm where a bullet had cut a furrow, and he had wrapped it with his neckerchief. "I killed one," he said. "The other two lit out on foot. They weren't lookin' for a fight."

They tied White's wrists behind him. By that time he had come to. They took him to the spring, and Brodie said, "Now we got to deliver him to San Diego."

White said earnestly, "Listen, I put eight thousand dollars in the bank at the Pueblo. I'll give it to you. You can split it up."

"There ain't no bank at the Pueblo," said Joshua.

"I left it with Mario Fernandez. He'll deposit it in San Diego. I'll give you an order on it."

Joshua said, "I turned you loose once. Do you think I'd do it again?"

"I'll make it eight thousand apiece. I can get more from Glanton."

"You'll cover a lot of desert if you do," said Brodie. "Glanton's in hell."

White said, "You're lying!"

"We've got nothing to lie about," said Joshua. "If you've got anything in your saddlebags to eat, I'll get it for you. We're starting back in half an hour."

They fed him rather than untie him. Then Joshua tied

a rope to White's ankles, pulled them up behind his back, and tied the rope to his wrists. He left him there on his stomach and went with Brodie to gather up the stock.

"Listen, Brodie. There's no need for both of us to go back to San Diego now."

"You think you can get him there alone?"

"It's my job."

"All right with me," said Brodie. He studied Joshua. "You coming back to the Colorado when you get it settled?"

"I'll be back."

Joshua rode into San Diego at noon two days later. He went to the Army encampment and asked for the officer of the day, who turned out to be a Captain Grush.

"Sir," said Joshua, "Private Pickens reporting under arrest. Also delivering an escaped prisoner."

Captain Grush looked up from his paper work. "Why are you under arrest, Private Pickens?"

"For being absent without leave, sir. I thought I had a chance to recapture the prisoner."

"Very well. Sergeant, put Private Pickens under arrest."

As he had foreseen, they were very lenient with him, because they now had White, who was charged with murder. Joshua also put in a word for Callahan and suggested they complete Callahan's record with the notation "Killed in action."

Major Heintzelman sent for him that evening. The Major was brusque. "Knowing Callahan as I did," he said, "I don't think you've given me the entire story. However, you did bring back the prisoner, and I think you've also made some valuable contacts with the

Maricopas and the Yumas, by which every emigrant along the trail is bound to be affected."

"Yes, sir. I think we have, sir."

"Now, there's bound to be a hue and cry over this massacre, and I'll have to send troops out to the Colorado, and there'll be more trouble. But in the meantime I've got an idea that might make it easier on the Indians and easier on the emigrants."

Joshua kept his eyes straight to the front. "Yes, sir."

"I am promoting you to sergeant, Pickens, and sending you with a detail of four men to the ferry crossing at the Gila. Your special job will be to keep order and see that the emigrants get across the Colorado in safety, with dispatch, and without undue cost."

"Thank you, sir."

"Later, when I send an officer out there, as I shall be forced to do by public pressure, I will advise him that you are on special duty."

"Yes, sir."

"One thing more, Sergeant. In case you think I've lost my head, your papers finally caught up with me while you were gone. You have an excellent record as a lieutenant of volunteers in the Mexican War. That's why I think you might do a good job at this particular assignment."

"I'll try, sir."

Joshua went back to the Colorado, over the mountains, out across the blazing desert of creosote bush and ocotillo. He saw the stockade from far off, sitting up on its eighty-foot-high knob of rock, and his breath came a little faster as he led his men straight across the heat-baked land. He left them sitting their horses for a moment as he went inside the new cabin. He saw Brodie stooped down to the fireplace, getting a light for his cigar. Natalia's glossy black hair was drawn to the back of her neck, and she was making very neat and precise figures with a quill pen in a small notebook bound in leather. Joshua said quietly, "May I arrange passage for myself and four men, señorita?"

Brodie looked up quickly. Natalia straightened, and her arm, poised in the air, seemed to turn to stone for a moment. Then she said, "José!" and dropped the pen and came into his arms.

Brodie said grumpily, "It looks like you got yourself squared with the Army—and then some."

Joshua nodded. Natalia's fragrant hair was in his face.

Brodie said, "It don't look like there's any getting rid of you."

Joshua, his hand on Natalia's shoulder, said, "It can be done, but it isn't easy."

"Well, I thought this over some. I broke into the old prejudicies when I married her mother." He pointed his cigar at Natalia. "Maybe this is the way the two nationalities will get together."

"It's as good a way as any," said Joshua, smiling.

"By the way." Brodie reached into a vest pocket. "I got something for you."

Joshua took it in his hand. It was a bullet, with the forepart mushroomed. He tossed it up and down in his hand. It was heavy. He remembered where he had seen it last: in the crater at Tinajas Altas. He remembered also that Mah-vah had spoken of it twice. He looked at Brodie.

"Where did you get this?" he asked.

"We got it from Lupe, the Mexican girl. She said a

Maricopa girl gave it to her for Natalia. You know anything about it?"

Joshua nodded. "The old Maricopa chief dug it out of my back." He looked at it, and realized it was the symbol of Mah-vah's final and complete acceptance of his decision. She would not grieve for him, and that was good. But she would not quite forget him either—and he would always think of her with great tenderness. Too, there was old Antoine, who had dug the bullet out of his back, and Tu-naams and Le-och and all the rest of the Maricopas. They had treated him like one of themselves. If Antoine had not dug the bullet out of his back, he might not be alive today. To go back further, if he had not stayed behind to protect Natalia, he might have carried the bullet the rest of his life and never have noticed it. Or to go back still further, if he had not had a weak moment in San Diego, he would not have had the bullet in the first place. "I'll keep it," he said, sliding it into his pocket. "It might remind me sometime not to be in a hurry to get rich. I guess that was at the bottom of it." He put an arm on Natalia's firm shoulders. "That was Glanton's trouble, come to think of it." He looked toward the river, fringed with willows and mesquite. "I suppose there will be more like Glanton."

"And more like you and Callahan," said Brodie, adding with a look at Natalia, "though I hope you won't try to throw away your life on a mule again."

Joshua stared at him. "Did you—" He stopped.

"I saw you going back, and I thought maybe you were going to try to lick the whole bunch, so I followed, out of sight, thinking I might help."

Joshua took a deep breath. "Thanks." He looked around uncertainly for a moment. "You never know who holds a debt over you," he observed finally.

"We never live alone," Brodie answered, and turned back to the fireplace.

Joshua looked down at Natalia, and was astonished to see tears in her eyes. "Natalia," he said, "I'm going to ask your father if I may marry you."

She sighed, her lustrous eyes closing slowly. *"Te estoy esperando,"* she said, which meant she was waiting, but the tense of the words indicated she did not expect to wait very long.

We hope that you enjoyed reading this
Sagebrush Large Print Western.
If you would like to read more Sagebrush titles,
ask your librarian or contact the Publishers:

United States and Canada

Thomas T. Beeler, *Publisher*
Post Office Box 659
Hampton Falls, New Hampshire 03844-0659
(800) 818-7574

United Kingdom, Eire, and
the Republic of South Africa

Isis Publishing Ltd
7 Centremead
Osney Mead
Oxford OX2 0ES England
(01865) 250333

Australia and New Zealand

Bolinda Publishing Pty. Ltd.
17 Mohr Street
Tullamarine, 3043, Victoria, Australia
(016103) 9338 0666